SPIDER-MAN 3™

SPIDER-MAN 3™

a novelization by
Peter David

based on the
Motion Picture

screenplay by
Alvin Sargent

screen story by
Sam Raimi & Ivan Raimi

based on the
Marvel Comic Book
by Stan Lee and Steve Ditko

POCKET STAR
New York London Toronto Sydney

An *Original* Publication of POCKET BOOKS

A Pocket Star Book published by
POCKET BOOKS, a division of Simon & Schuster, Inc.
1230 Avenue of the Americas, New York, NY 10020

This book is a work of fiction. Names, characters, places, and incidents are products of the author's imagination or are used fictitiously. Any resemblance to actual events or locales or persons, living or dead, is entirely coincidental.

ISBN-13: 978-1-4165-2721-3
ISBN-10: 1-4165-2721-4

This Pocket Star Books paperback edition April 2007

10 9 8 7 6 5 4 3 2 1

Manufactured in the United States of America

For information regarding special discounts for bulk purchases, please contact Simon & Schuster Special Sales at 1-800-456-6798 or business@simonandschuster.com.

SPIDER-MAN 3™

PETER PARKER DOES NOT believe that old notion that, when one is about to die, one's life flashes before one's eyes. He considers it a sort of "after the fact" add-on. Someone has a near-death experience and, in recalling it, mentally inserts all the highlights of his existence after the fact as a sort of mental counterpoint to life's near termination. Memory, after all, is a tricky thing, possibly the most deceptive aspect of the brain's function.

The main reason Peter has come to be dismissive of the concept is because, in his activities as Spider-Man, he has been near death more times than he can count. More times, in fact, than any reasonable person should have to experience. In all those times, all those close shaves, he has never once seen his life go flashing before his eyes. Not when the Green Goblin had him on the ropes, his uniform tattered and his last dregs of energy seemingly used up. Not when Otto Octavius had him in a stranglehold while Ock's fearsome machine sped on a particle acceleration toward destroying the entire city. Not once, during the myriad encounters with various petty crooks, bank robbers, muggers, and gunmen.

Never. Not even close to it.

This time, however, it's different. At this moment, as Peter thrashes his arms and legs about in midair, a good fifty stories above the cold and unforgiving streets of New York, the recent developments in his life rip through his skull, like a projector unspooling from somewhere deep in his cerebral cortex and projecting a picture on his retinas.

He hears his own voice speaking. It sounds distant, calm, as if he has managed to detach himself completely from his current predicament. He does not currently "see" the night, nor feel the chill of the stiff wind in his bones, but instead "sees" the sun creeping up over the East River. This is a day seen at its beginning, filled with promise and hope, not a day ending in sorrow and death.

What a day! *Peter's chipper voice tells him. Inwardly, soundlessly, he laughs bitterly over the irony of such shortsightedness.* Well, anyway, there's a fresh breeze.

The sun gives way to the spider symbol that typically rests upon his chest. Nevertheless, it is not his symbol, or at least not his chest. He sees a boy, a young boy, clambering up a high tree limb in Central Park. Peter is standing a few feet away, cutting through the park but pausing to take in the amusing sight of a boy pretending to be, not a cowboy or a robber or ninja or pirate, but instead Peter himself. More correctly, Peter's alter ego, for the boy is sporting a crudely stitched facsimile of Peter's costume shirt. It reminds Peter a bit of the makeshift costume he'd first worn when he'd embarked on his short-lived wrestling career.

Then the higher branch abruptly snaps in the boy's hand. Peter senses it just before it happens, and he is already moving to intercept the boy's plunge. He is not the only one, as it turns out, who is keeping an eye on the lad and is in possession of a hyperawareness of danger. The boy falls, and suddenly his mother is there, deftly snagging him before he hits the ground, faster than even Peter could have gotten over there. She rights him and scolds him, No more climbing up there! You're not Spider-Man!

The boy retorts, Am too! *With that defiant declaration, he starts right back toward the tree. The mother lets out a long-suffering sigh of infinite patience, and a smiling Peter turns away, confident the kid's safety is in good hands.*

As he turns, the scenery shifts around him once more, as it is capable of doing since all this is flashing through his mind between beats of his heart. Rather than being landbound, he is soaring above the city. He had been halting and uncertain in his earliest days of web slinging, careening off buildings through mistimed leaps and swings. Now he switches hands deftly, left and right, left and right, arcing through the concrete mazes of Manhattan with an ease that is literally lyrical, since there are no less than three songs about him by various artists in the Billboard *Top 100.*

The city is safe and sound. I guess I've had something to do with that. *It is a modest thought, and a false modesty at that. There is no "guess" about it, especially when one considers that the giant video screen in Times Square has the words "NYC ♥ Spider-Man" rolling across it.*

It is a true out-of-body experience because Peter is not, in fact, in his costume and swinging among the spires in Times Square. Instead, he is watching himself on the giant video screen. The image of Spider-Man web slinging across Manhattan is playing out above the Spidey adoration text, part of a video advertisement that has been purchased by the New York City tourism board. With everything that the city has been through in the past several years, they're anxious to do whatever can be done to reassure visitors to the Big Apple that they can feel safe. And they have chosen Spider-Man to be the symbol of that safety.

Peter stands in Times Square, watching the video, thinking that his uncle Ben would have been proud. Tourists who had been watching the video start to walk away at its conclusion, and Peter calls out, It's going to run again in a couple minutes! *They spare him a puzzled glance and then go on about their business. He supposes they have the right idea. He should be on about his business as well. He slings his backpack over his shoulder, and the world shifts around him once more.*

And I still get to school. Top of my class.

Dr. Curtis Connors is lecturing his students. Peter is listening attentively. Once, not long ago, he would have felt so torn, so conflicted over his double life, that he would have been unable to concentrate on anything his favorite science professor was saying. That's no longer the case because of . . .

(Wait for it. Take your time. Let it all unfold in order. That's how it's done.)

The Hamiltonian shows us that the energy levels are perturbed by the electric field, *Dr. Connors tells them, tapping a complex set of equations and graphs on the board.* From the form of this matrix, we can see . . .

He pauses, looking for the answer. Peter's hand shoots up. Connors points in Peter's general direction, and Peter is about to open his mouth and respond when Connors says, Miss Stacy!

. . . that only the *m*-equals-zero quantum states are affected.

Correct! Good work, Miss Stacy!

Peter looks toward his lab partner, Gwen Stacy. She is a vivacious, attractive blonde, her long hair cascading around her shoulders. Paired off by luck of the draw as partners, they had promptly hit it off. She had recognized his name immediately; it turned out her father was a police captain who had been first on the scene after Uncle Ben had been murdered. He'd told his daughter all about the grief-stricken youth who had been there, cradling his uncle as the old man had passed away, and Gwen admitted she had been moved to tears by the telling of it. Consequently, Peter has found Gwen easy to talk to and a good listener. He almost thinks she'd be a good match for Harry Osborn, but Gwen is in a tangled relationship with some guy, and now isn't the time.

Besides, it's not as if he could set up something with Harry even if Gwen were available.

He sees himself riding his motorbike through the long shadows of the city.

All that's missing is my friendship with Harry. I need to explain to him how his father died. But he won't see me.

He is standing in the reception area of OsCorp, pleading with a sympathetic receptionist to give him ten minutes, make it five, make it one minute, of Harry's time. She just sadly shakes her head. This isn't the first time he's been here, and likely won't be the last. He could simply scale the side of the building, clamber in through Harry's window. What would be the point, though? Harry would just start screaming at him and insist that he leave. He can't force himself on Harry. He can't cram down young Osborn's throat the fact that his father was the demented Green

Goblin and died because of his own machinations rather than anything Peter had done. Harry has to willingly accept him into his office or home. He has to be prepared to listen. Until that time, attempts to get through to him are doomed to failure.

There is no point in pressing the matter or obsessing over it.

Life goes on.

(Does it? For you? For much longer?)

Peter is no longer at OsCorp. Instead he is hurrying down the street, dressed in a sharp gray suit. It is dusk. He passes a pawnshop, then stops and backs up, something in the window having caught his eye.

It is a wedding ring, the gold band glittering in the twilight. It is small and modest, but it would convey the thought and intent quite well. If one did not know by the smile on his face and the spring in his step that Peter Parker was a man in love, his gazing at the ring would certainly have been the tip-off.

Would you believe it? I've finally got the girl of my dreams.

She, of course, is the reason that everything else in his life is working. She provides the light that chases away the darkness that had settled upon his soul the day Ben Parker died. Without her, nothing works. With her, everything in his life runs with the precision of an atomic clock.

He had almost lost her to another man. Through his indecision and inaction, he had nearly allowed her to slip away. But after all the times that he had saved Mary Jane Watson, finally, Mary Jane Watson had saved him. She had shown up in the nick of time, clad in her own unusual costume—not gaudy red and blue, but instead a wedding dress—having fled the church to find Peter and let him know that she would be there for him, always.

And there had been Peter, trapped in endless night, looking into the face of the sun and feeling the warmth.

That was months ago.

Just as Peter's life has straightened itself out, so has Mary Jane's. No longer a struggling actress, she. MJ is now headlining a new musical, Manhattan Memories, *playing at the Broadhurst Theater. All right, technically not headlining: two other actors named Linda Curtis and Solomon Abrams are billed above her. But there she is in the poster, dead center, and Peter could not be more proud, or more in love, or more punctual. Oh, yes, punctual. The memory of when he'd arrived late for her previous production and been kept in the lobby by a supercilious usher was still far too fresh for him. Nowadays he makes certain to arrive a half hour before curtain.*

He moves to his front-row seat and waits. Even though this is all recollection, even though it's all happening in a flash while a demented cackling is filtering dimly through his subconscious, it still feels as if it were taking forever. Finally, finally *the orchestra finishes tuning up and launches into the overture. The music swells and the thick, red velvet curtain parts.*

Manhattan Memories *is intended to be a love letter to the musicals of yore. None of the songs are new: Cole Porter, the Gershwins, many of the famous tunesmiths of times gone past, all represented and with their songs strung together via a new book that is—Peter has to admit—a little flimsy. He'd had the time to make that assessment since he'd been to half a dozen of the show's performances while it was in previews. He'd decided that it didn't matter all that much. After all, who leaves a musical humming the script? It was all about the songs, and in that regard, the show was rock solid.*

Tonight, though, is not a preview. Tonight is opening night. There is an additional charge in the air, an intensity that had not been present at any of the earlier shows. This is the make-or-break, the one that counts. It's as if the entirety of Broadway is somehow spiritually poised, like a lion in the high weeds, waiting to see if the show will join the pride or instead become prey for the jackals (i.e., critics).

There is a collective murmur of approval from the audience as the opening curtain reveals a vista of "stars" hanging in the heavens. But the approval is not merely for the scenery. It is largely for the gorgeous redhead who appears to be standing on air, like an angel gazing down upon earthbound mortals. Unless one is looking carefully, it is impossible to see the wafer-thin platform on which she is situated, or the narrow series of steps that lead down. It's an effective illusion.

She is clad in a long, flowing blue dress, her red hair piled elegantly atop her head. Helen of Troy may have had the face that launched a thousand ships, but Mary Jane's smile alone should be good enough to launch a thousand performances.

Mary Jane starts down the stairs, every foot carefully placed (she'd stumbled on the first day of previews and almost taken a header down them; she'd learned her lesson that night about hurrying). She begins to sing, and although she should really be directing her efforts toward the back of the theater, she cheats and instead gazes directly and lovingly at Peter.

He's not entirely thrilled with the quality of the sound system; it's making MJ's voice sound reedy and thinner than it should be.

That doesn't matter, though. Her mere presence is magical. Certainly everyone will realize that and ignore such minor technical glitches.

Reality and fantasy begin to blend, the barrier between them breaking down. Peter is no longer in his seat. He is floating out of it, reaching toward Mary Jane. She stretches her hands toward him, laughing gaily, and then he is above her.

(This isn't happening. This part never happened.)

Cool air rushes against his face. He can still see the balcony from where he is, and from this vantage point, he notices someone watching him through a pair of opera glasses. The watcher lowers the glasses and glares balefully at Peter.

(All right that part did happen. He was there. And afterward, you and he—)

Peter feels a jolt. The glittering stars are still around him, but the theater is gone. Mary Jane is gone. He is hanging, suspended. One of the stars breaks away, tumbles toward him, and he sees that it's a diamond engagement ring.

Gravity is suddenly making its presence known. It's not happening all at once. More by degrees, like with the coyote in those cartoons. The more he becomes aware of his predicament, the more gravity stakes a claim on him. He tries to defy it. He stretches, strains, the tumbling ring just out of reach, and then he's falling, except not straight down. Instead he's falling sideways, as if something has propelled him, and then he slams into the wall of a building. He does so with such velocity that he's not able to get a grip on it, and he tumbles away from it.

Harry! Harry, wait! *Peter cries, which might well serve as his last words, but they're not. He's said them before, and Harry is turning and glaring at him, the time before and the time right now crashing together. Floating above the then and the now and quite possibly all that is to come is a high-pitched, demented laugh that sounds both familiar and unfamiliar.*

And then consciousness slips away, and Peter's life review ends prematurely as the stars coldly glitter around him like diamonds while he plunges toward his death. . . .

And nothing is as it should be.

I

ARRIVALS AND DEPARTURES

"HARRY! HARRY, WAIT!"

Peter hadn't believed for a moment that Harry Osborn would miss the opening of Mary Jane's show. Despite all that had happened between them, and all that remained unresolved, the bottom line was that Harry still had to feel something for Mary Jane. She had been his first major love, had been too much a part of his life, for him to let such a landmark event pass. Hell, Harry had attended MJ's previous theatrical endeavor four times (a fact that Mary Jane had pointedly made clear to Peter, back when he'd been so unable to manage his time that he'd alienated her by missing performance after performance). Still, Peter hadn't seen Harry in the theater. Now he realized why. Peter had naturally assumed that, considering Harry's wealth, he would have obtained the best seats in the house. Instead, as Peter made his way up the aisle, he spotted Harry coming down the stairs that led to the balcony. Harry had obviously wanted to see without being seen.

Just as Harry reached the bottom of the stairs, some instinct caused him to glance Peter's way. For half a moment they locked eyes, and then Harry pushed his way past several people in front of him. He nearly knocked an old woman off her walker as she was busy extolling the virtues of Cole Porter and wondering loudly why they didn't write tunes like that anymore. When Harry shoved her aside, she surprised Harry, Peter, and the people she was with by snapping out an extremely explicit profanity at him. Harry blinked in surprise and then moved away from her. He was out the door, and Peter found his way blocked by the same elderly people. He looked around desperately, spotted an opening on the upper section of the wall next to them, and prayed no one was watching too closely. With one quick move he jumped six feet in the air, rebounded with his feet off the wall, and landed in front of the slow-moving party. Their heads snapped around in confusion, since Peter had been little more than a blur in the corners of their eyes. By the time they had any real inkling of where he'd been, he was already gone and out the front door of the theater.

Peter got there just in time to see Harry stepping into the backseat of his town car. The chauffeur was standing there, waiting for Harry, holding the door for him.

"Harry! Harry, wait!" Peter called as the chauffeur slammed the door closed. Peter looked at Harry's driver, and to his surprise, something akin to sympathy was there. It underscored for Peter that Harry's staff had to be aware of the slow deterioration of their employer's personality. They must have felt, in their own way, as helpless as Peter. Probably worse, since a number of them had served the Osborns for many years and had known Harry since he was very young.

How many people are you going to hurt, Harry? What's it going to take before you let me in?

Peter brought his face close to the window as the chauffeur headed for the driver's side. The window was tinted, but Peter could still make out Harry on the inside looking out at him. "Don't keep locking me out. You need to hear the truth."

Peter couldn't be sure, but he thought that something in Harry's expression just then seemed to be wavering. It was as if he wanted to hear what Peter had to say but couldn't bring himself to do so. Or perhaps there was even more to it than that.

Then Harry's gaze shifted. It was the strangest thing, but it looked to Peter as if Harry was staring intently at his own reflection. He had no idea why Harry would possibly do that. A change passed over Harry's face then, and whatever curiosity or compassion or consideration might have been in his expression moments earlier was now replaced by distance and harshness. The window rolled down barely half an inch, just enough so that Harry could be sure that his voice would be heard. "Tell it to my father," he said coldly. "Raise him from the dead."

"I'm your friend," Peter said desperately. "Your father was my friend." That might have seemed insane to say, at least on the surface, but as far as Peter was concerned, it was the truth. Norman Osborn had been helpful and supportive to Peter . . . sometimes, it seemed, even more than he was with his own son, an inequity that Harry had appeared to take in stride. That was the person whom Peter thought of as Norman Osborn. Not the crazed, cackling, flying demon into which circumstance and accident had transformed him. The real Norman Osborn, Peter's friend and Harry's dad, died the day the Green Goblin was born. Everything else after that had been the unfolding of a Greek tragedy.

The window slid back up, and seconds later the car pulled away from the curb. Peter could have run after it. For that matter, he could have leaped atop the roof and clung to it. He could have webbed it to the spot, preventing it from moving forward. But what good would any of that have done? Just what Peter would have needed: Harry leaping out of the car and screaming at him that he, Spider-Man, had killed his father. So much for his secret identity.

As he sighed heavily and headed around to the stage door entrance, where the stage manager knew him well and would let him pass with no problem, Peter had to wonder why he even had a secret identity anymore. What in the world had stopped Harry from telling the police, or J. Jonah Jameson, or taking out a billboard? What prevented him, in short, from blabbing Peter's secret to the world?

Three reasons occurred to him.

The first was that, on some level, Harry knew that not all was as it seemed with his father's passing. Perhaps Harry had even figured out that his father was the Green Goblin. If the truth of Peter's identity came out, then sooner or later that truth would lead to the revelation that Norman Osborn was the Goblin. The sins of the father would be laid at the feet of the son. Not only would

Norman's legacy be forever disgraced, but anyone who had suffered damage at the hands of Norman Osborn might turn around and sue his estate. Harry could be wiped out.

Second, Harry would logically be asked how he knew the secret of Spider-Man's identity. What would Harry say to that? "I hired the known criminal Dr. Octopus to assault Spider-Man, kidnap him, and bring him to me so that I could unmask him?" Not only would he then be exposed to even more civil suits from the damage that Doc Ock had done at his behest, but he would also face criminal and felony charges. Harry could bring Peter down, but Harry would go down right alongside him.

Then there was the third, least appealing reason. If Peter's identity became public knowledge, it would be the equivalent of painting a target on his back. He'd never have a moment's rest. Anyone who'd ever hated Spider-Man would come gunning for Peter, and sooner or later, they'd get him. Even Peter Parker had to sleep eventually. He'd be a dead man for certain. Why wouldn't that suit Harry Osborn, who so despised his former friend? The answer was obvious: Harry wanted to save the privilege of killing Peter for himself.

Oh, yeah. That's making me feel a whole lot better.

It required great effort on his part, but Peter was determined to put all such thoughts out of his mind. This was Mary Jane's night, her evening to shine, and he'd be damned if he would drag her down with his depressing musings.

It was a madhouse backstage. The narrow corridors were packed with well-wishers and fans. People were thrusting their *Playbill* programs at whatever cast members they could find, and the actors were reveling in it. Peter noticed some good-looking man clad in a suit also signing an autograph. He wasn't a cast member; Peter assumed he was someone famous. Hard to say for sure who it was. Peter wasn't especially good at identifying actors.

He saw Mary Jane back up and pause in the entrance to her dressing room. She was clearly studying the crowd, looking for (he hoped) him. "MJ!" he called, and immediately she turned and spotted him.

Her face split with a grin. "Peter!" Then, just as quickly, her expression transformed into concern bordering on agitation. As he approached her, he wondered what could be wrong. Had she seen Harry? Were the same worries that Peter had had occurring to MJ as well?

She gripped him by the shoulders and, as if asking a doctor whether the tumor was malignant or not, demanded, "Was I good?"

It was all he could do not to laugh. It was ludicrous that she'd even have to ask. "Good? You were great! You're just . . . how can I say it? You're a . . ."

"You said great," she reminded him as if she were an auctioneer making certain that he was sticking to his previous high bid. He smiled and nodded in reaffirmation, and she pulled him into the dressing room, leaving the door open behind him.

He immediately saw the simple, tasteful assortment of

flowers that he had sent, sitting on a table nearby. But they were dwarfed by another arrangement so ostentatious that it might have looked at home atop the coffin of a dead princess. MJ had to push past them to rest a hand on the flowers that Peter had sent. "I got your flowers, thank you. They're beautiful. And these . . ."

They're from Harry, he thought grimly without even having to be told.

". . . are from Harry," Mary Jane finished. She looked confused, glancing over Peter's shoulder as if she expected Harry to be walking in right behind him. "Was he here tonight?"

"I saw him, but . . ." Peter paused, not wanting to say too much, but not wanting to say so little that it was obvious he was holding back. "He wouldn't talk to me."

Peter tried not to introduce any melancholy into the moment, but there it was anyway. MJ's face fell as she said, "I'm so sorry. What is it with you guys, anyway?"

Well, his father was the Green Goblin, and Harry thinks I killed him, and . . .

"It's complicated," he said with an air of finality, hoping that MJ wouldn't pursue it.

His wish was granted. It wasn't all that surprising: ultimately, Mary Jane was an actress on opening night of her play, and her thoughts weren't going to wander far from the performance for long. "Tell me again, did you really like it?" she asked, all concerns about Harry forgotten. She laughed, although it was a laugh tainted with an edge. "I was so nervous. My knees were shaking."

"Your knees were fine," he assured her.

Clearly she still had doubts. "The applause wasn't very loud."

Peter had noticed the same thing, but he had an answer at the ready that he had even managed to convince himself was completely true. "Yes, it was," he said quickly . . . perhaps too quickly, but she didn't notice. "It's the acoustics. It's about diffusion, which keeps sound waves from grouping." Mary Jane didn't look entirely convinced, so he spoke faster, random technical words spilling over each other in a suicidal rush, like lemmings: "It's all about slap and flutter and nulls and hot spots—"

Mercifully, the celebrity that Peter had spotted earlier drew Mary Jane's attention away from Peter. He was walking past the open door of the dressing room, and he saw that Mary Jane had noticed him.

There was a brief silence, which Peter might have considered uncomfortable if he hadn't been distracted by the hopeful look on MJ's face. The celebrity cleared his throat and said, just a little stiffly, "Congratulations, my dear. You were quite good."

As he walked away, MJ clapped her hands together in delight. "Peter!" she almost squealed. "Do you know who that was?!"

"No." He was looking forward to finally learning for certain.

But Mary Jane was clearly enraptured, lost in her own little world of sudden notoriety. "He won a Tony Award . . . he liked me!"

"I thought that was him," Peter said, as if that settled it.

She grinned so widely that, had New York suffered another blackout, her smile would have illuminated the room.

"I think I'm happy," she announced. "Let's celebrate!"

"Got my bike!"

The traffic out of the city had been formidable, but Peter had deftly maneuvered his motorbike between the lines of traffic that were stacked up in the Lincoln Tunnel. His natural agility helped him keep it steady no matter how hair-raising the maneuvers. Mary Jane clung to his back the entire time, her warmth suffusing him, and she got to burbling about the play. With the helmet over his head, he couldn't hear half of what she was saying, but it didn't matter. All he had to do was nod and say "Yeah!" or "That's great!" or just laugh loudly every so often, and that was sufficient.

Soon the city had been left far behind. He drove them up to the Palisades, to a beautiful section of the woods where his uncle Ben had used to take him when he was very young. It was a terrific place for stargazing, a pastime that was hard to indulge in the city, where the lights made quality viewing difficult. Up in the Palisades, overlooking the Hudson River, the view was unimpeded. Peter thought with amusement that it was almost up to the level of the fake stars that had dotted the Broadway stage where MJ had made her debut. To top it all off, a spectacular meteor shower was underway, dazzling streaks of light zipping within and around the constellations.

The ground was a bit damp, making lying down problematic. Peter was unfazed. He rolled up his sleeves, exposing the spinnerets on his forearms, and in short order had fashioned a web hammock between two large trees. With his bike parked nearby, he and Mary Jane lay in the hammock, swaying gently in the breeze, gazing up rapturously at the array of stars and the meteor shower overhead. He was busy imagining Mary Jane descending from the stars above on an invisible staircase when she spoke with an air of wonderment, "Where do they all come from?"

"Maybe Mars, a hundred million years ago," he replied carelessly. He could have given her a detailed dissertation on the falling space rocks burning up in the atmosphere, and on the big bang and the forces that had created a billion balls of gas, but he didn't think she was really that interested.

Once again, he had sussed her out correctly. "You know what?" she said. "I'd like to sing on the stage for the rest of my life with you in the first row."

"I'll be there." He gestured toward the heavens as if an earthbound stage were simply insufficient to contain her talent. "I'm going to build you a stage on the Milky Way."

She laughed. "Can you swing that high?" she asked teasingly.

"I'm working on it."

Mary Jane paused, and then, her voice dropping low and becoming filled with intense need, she said, "Tell me you love me. I like to hear it. It makes me feel safe."

He turned slightly so that he was looking into her eyes, their faces only a few inches apart. "I will always love you, Mary Jane. I always have."

Their lips came together. "Mmm . . . strawberry," he murmured.

For a second, Peter noticed something flashing high in the sky. Another meteor, this one very close. Shooting stars. Heralds of great changes to come for anyone who witnessed them. Then he put such unscientific thoughts out of his mind and focused his attention instead on the woman he loved.

The shooting star that Peter had observed, speculated about, and then given no further thought to, thudded to earth in a nearby field. A small, smoking crater provided evidence of where precisely it had struck.

Had Peter endeavored to turn his analytical eye upon the aftermath of the space rock's fall, he would have seen something that defied any manner of scientific explanation.

It was a thick, black gooey substance, which oozed from the meteorite's porous surface as if the space rock were a car and the hard landing had caused an oil leak.

To describe the behavior of something from space as "unearthly" would certainly seem, on the face of it, to be belaboring the obvious. Nevertheless, it would have been warranted in the case of the black substance, for it now wasn't merely oozing from the rock. Instead it was as if it was pulling itself—extracting itself—consciously from the meteorite.

The black goo separated from the meteorite entirely and sat there for a moment, an animated puddle getting its bearings. Then it started across the field, propelling itself a few feet, halting as if trying to orient itself and acquire a sense of its surroundings, then undulating forward once more.

Then it reacted to something, some sort of growling noise. Even though it was a newcomer to the planet, it could still differentiate between a sound made in nature and something that was technological. It sped toward the source, eager to see what this world had to offer. It was impossible to determine whether the black goo was some sort of higher species of individual with a refined thought process, or some sort of animalistic thing operating purely on instinct. Either way, the result was the same. Its rapid slither brought it within distance of what appeared to be two biological forms, possibly native to the sphere, perched atop something perhaps designed to transport them. It scrutinized the both of them and was immediately drawn to one over the other: the one on the front of the vehicle. The one who radiated power and energy.

The creature was no more than a few inches in diameter, so it wasn't noticed at all as it slithered up onto Peter Parker's shoe when his foot shoved down on the starter once more. This time the engine caught and the bike rolled forward. The abrupt movement gave the creature a brief moment of disorientation. It clung fiercely to the underside of Peter's shoe and settled in, basking in the power that Peter's molecular structure was generating.

With Mary Jane holding tight, her hair whipping about in the wind, Peter maneuvered the motorbike down onto the road toward New York City, unaware that the city was under alien invasion, and equally unaware that he was the means by which it was happening.

II

FATHERS

WHEN HARRY OSBORN HAD seen the desperate face of Peter Parker peering in through the window of the town car, something about the intensity of his sincerity had almost prompted Harry to listen.

For a moment, he saw Peter not as the enemy who had destroyed his father or the rival who had snatched Mary Jane away from him. Instead he was the whiz kid who had taken a young Harry under his wing and had helped him succeed in high school science classes, an accomplishment that at least half a dozen tutors had sworn to Harry's father was an impossibility. Peter had seen hope when others had declared Harry to be hopeless. Unlike just about everyone else in Harry's life, Peter had been under no obligation to do so. Norman Osborn didn't own him, didn't pay him, couldn't compel him. Peter had just done it out of the goodness of his heart because he thought Harry was a decent guy who could use a friend.

That was the man who was standing there at curbside, begging Harry to listen to him.

What would it hurt? Really? Giving him five minutes to explain his side of the story? Harry was pretty sharp and could usually tell when someone was lying to him. If Peter tried to feed Harry some sort of bull, Harry would know. Harry would—

Don't weaken.

Harry couldn't tell if the voice was sounding in his head or was in the car with him, but the identity of the speaker was unmistakable. Harry was staring at the window, but it was not his own reflection he saw, or even Peter's image through the glass.

Instead it was the face of his father, Norman Osborn, glowering at him.

Don't weaken.

Norman Osborn, who had thought so little of Harry during much of his life, was now counting on Harry to be strong. To remain focused and not lose sight of what had to be done . . . and to whom it had to be done.

Lowering the window slightly, feeling as if an invisible hand were laid upon his throat, Harry said, "Tell it to my father. Raise him from the dead."

He rolled the window back up, ignoring everything else Peter was saying, then leaned forward and rapped on the privacy partition that separated him from the driver. The car rolled away from the curb, leaving a frustrated Peter Parker in its wake.

Good job, Harry. You had me going there. For a minute I thought you were going to listen to my murderer.

Harry said nothing. Instead he put his hands to the side of his head as if battling a migraine.

His father continued speaking to him, whispering into

his ear, inside his brain. He saw Norman's image in the privacy partition.

Harry had spent months wondering if he was going out of his mind. Then, one day, he'd stopped caring. He'd simply accepted this condition as his new status quo. He was to spend the rest of his life being haunted, like Hamlet, urged by the ghost of his father to exact revenge on those who were responsible for his death.

There were two problems with that: First, he didn't know how to go about it. And second, he knew *exactly* how to go about it . . . and was simply daunted by the prospect.

Bernard, the stately family retainer, came to Harry unbidden as the young Osborn sat in his study, staring at the wall. Bernard was carrying a glass of warm milk and said gently, "I thought this might help you sleep, Mr. Osborn. You've been up until all hours lately, and I was becoming concerned."

Harry barely afforded him a glance. "No thanks. Could you go now, please?"

"I thought there might be something el—"

A sudden burst of rage seized Harry. "I'm not a child, all right, Bernard? I don't need your concern! I don't need your damned milk!" With a sweep of his hand, he knocked the glass off the table, sending it clattering to the floor. The milk splattered and the glass shattered.

Harry's immediate impulse was to apologize, to offer to clean it up. But instead he closed his eyes and let his head sag back against the chair. He didn't know how much time passed. All he knew was that, when he opened his eyes once more, Bernard was gone and so were any traces of the mess he'd just made.

Harry began to wonder if Bernard had even been there at all.

Maybe Harry's father wasn't there either.

Hell, perhaps even Harry wasn't really there. That would explain everything, wouldn't it?

The night that he had learned Peter Parker's other identity—the night that he'd discovered his best friend was responsible for the death of his father—Harry had stood upon his balcony and contemplated throwing himself to the street below, rather than live with the unwanted knowledge. His recollection was that he had not done so. But perhaps he had. Perhaps all of this was just a wild fantasy, a last burst of synapses firing before his body struck the sidewalk and his tormented existence was terminated.

Don't think that way, Harry. You have a destiny. You have a job to do.

"Aw, God," moaned Harry, rubbing his temples. He didn't want to see his father's reflection again. Sometimes days would go by during which he'd see and hear nothing untoward, and he'd think that finally—oh, thank God—it was over. Then his father would show up unexpectedly, and it was off to the races once more. He'd never forget the time that Norman had appeared in his mirror one morning while he was shaving. Harry had almost slit his own throat. Perhaps that might have been a blessing.

Harry . . . it's time. Look at me, son.

Slowly, Harry forced his eyes to open. For the life of him, he couldn't have said whether he was dreaming. Norman Osborn was standing in front of him, no longer reflected in a surface but instead as big as life. He might well have strolled through the door and sat down, ready for a chat.

His mouth was moving, but his voice was slightly out of sync, like a badly dubbed film. *I've been waiting for you to be ready. I now believe you are.*

"Ready for what?" Harry whispered.

To avenge me, Norman said with a trace of surprise, as if it were stunningly self-evident. *Against Parker. Against all of them that took me away from you.*

"But . . . Peter is—"

Peter is the sickness, Norman told him heatedly, *and you are the cure for that sickness.* Then his tone shifted, becoming more cajoling, even sympathetic. *Don't you remember, Harry? I'd finally come to appreciate you for the loving, loyal son that you were. It could have been a new chapter in our relationship. But it was cut short by your friend.*

"It was cut short because you were the Goblin," Harry snapped back at him. "You threatened Mary Jane—"

To get to Spider-Man. To get to the man who had declared himself to be my enemy. The Goblin existed only to destroy my enemies . . . your *enemies as well. The ones who would have taken all this*—Norman gestured around the mansion—*away from you. They would have reduced us to poverty because they were jealous of us, Harry. They were jealous and seized with a sick need to destroy us. I was defending myself . . . defending you. No father could have done less. And Spider-Man sided with our enemies, and I died because of him. I died fighting for your future. Are you going to take that lying down?*

"I . . ."

Norman drew closer, his voice more intense, his eyes almost hypnotic. *See him in your mind's eye. That smug bastard. He took your girl. Took your father. Took your peace of mind. He keeps taking and taking, and haven't you had enough? For God's sake,* haven't you had enough?

Harry saw Mary Jane on a field of stars, singing of love . . . singing to Peter right there in the front row. He felt an acid taste in the back of his throat, and a thudding in his head, and a buzzing in his ears.

He had thought he could live with it. He had thought he could keep himself from acting upon this terrible knowledge, because the knowledge of what he would have to become to combat it was almost as terrible. But seeing her tonight . . . seeing him . . . knowing what they were likely off doing now . . . Peter enjoying the life that should have been his . . .

"More than enough," grated Harry.

That's my boy.

Norman Osborn embraced him. He had no substance at all. Harry didn't care. He hugged him as hard as he'd always wished he had in life.

Then Harry rose from his chair, guided by his father. He headed for the entrance to the lair hidden by a full-length mirror that Harry had once shattered, then quickly replaced once he'd realized what was concealed behind there.

He pushed the mirror aside and stepped through.

The equipment beckoned to him, and he would heed the call, for the son could do no less for the father than he, the father, had done for him.

Flint Marko, aka William Marko, aka William Baker, pressed himself flat against the alleyway nearby a row of run-down apartment houses. A police car was cruising by, and although Marko had fairly unremarkable features—light brown hair, a square jaw—the prison garb he was wearing would have been a dead giveaway.

He was having trouble catching his breath and wondered not for the first time if he was having a heart attack. Curiously, the thought of dropping dead in the alleyway wasn't all that disturbing to him. Flint Marko had lived his life in a way that didn't engender much love for his own existence or much care as to whether he lived or died. A guy like Marko knew that when your number was up, there was no use whining about it.

He remembered once, when he was young, seeing a big hourglass in a pawnshop. He had turned it over, watched the steady stream of sand as it filtered to the bottom, then reversed it just before the sand had completely run through. Then he'd watched as it fell through the other way, then again and again, turning it over and over until his mother was done hocking her wedding jewelry and informed her son that it was time to leave. He had found it frustrating because he'd felt as if he were in competition with the sand, and if the sand made it all through to the other side, he was going to lose. Defiantly, he'd laid the hourglass on its side in hopes of thwarting the sand.

The hourglass had rolled off the table and crashed to the ground, spreading sand everywhere. The angry shopkeeper had demanded compensation, taking back just about all the money he'd given to Flint's mother, and young Flint had gotten an earful and a good beating when he got home.

It had been a hard-learned lesson: the sand always wins. Because the sand represents time, and nothing can stop time from passing.

But he'd be damned if he was going to spend any more of his passing time in the custody of New York State, that was for sure.

He was clutching a stack of letters to his chest, held together by a rubber band. The edges of some of the envelopes were battered, and the ink was smeared on a few of them. Closer inspection would have revealed the words DELIVERY REFUSED: RETURN TO SENDER stamped on the front of every single envelope.

Marko hugged the shadows, not wanting to make the slightest move until he was certain the police car was long gone. Once he was satisfied that—for the moment—he was safe, he made his way over to a familiar fire escape. The ladder was above his reach. He glanced around and found a length of frayed, discarded rope nearby amidst the rest of the garbage in the alley. It wasn't much, but it would serve his purposes. He tied the end of the rope around the packet of letters, then tossed the letters upward. He missed the first time, but the second time, the packet swung up and over the lower rung and dropped halfway down again. Marko reached up, now able to grip both ends of the rope, and pulled down as hard as he could. The ladder resisted at first, then gave up and slid noisily down toward him.

The racket caused Marko to step back into the shadows to wait for a reaction from anyone. But there was nothing. No response at all from any of the windows above. He supposed that shouldn't have been a surprise. This was New York, the city where, years ago, several buildings' worth of people had turned away and done nothing—not even call the cops—while a young woman was brutally murdered, screaming for help the entire time. If cries for succor weren't sufficient to get neighbors interested, certainly the creaking of a fire escape ladder wasn't going to prompt any involvement.

He scrambled up the ladder like a monkey on a mission and, moments later, was clambering up the fire escape. He was doing so as quietly as he could; no use tempting fate by counting too heavily on the perceived apathy of New Yorkers.

Marko drew close to a familiar window and briefly considered the possibility that the people supposedly living within had moved. Why not? He'd have no way of knowing. No one ever came to visit him in prison, and with his letters returned, who was to say that they weren't currently residing in New Jersey or Connecticut or Outer Mongolia. Peering into the darkened room, he saw someone asleep in the bed, and for a moment his worst fears were realized. It wasn't Penny. It couldn't be. Penny was much smaller than this child. . . .

But then he recognized the array of medicines upon

her night table, and the snow globe he'd gotten her for her fifth birthday, and his concerns were eased. He even took a moment to appreciate the humor of the situation: that he had been thrown off by the simple fact that Penny had grown. Well, of course—he'd been in jail for eighteen months.

Flint slid open the window and eased himself into the room. He almost tripped over a doll she'd left on the floor. Cautiously he picked it up, praying it wouldn't make any noise, and placed it on a chair. Marko moved like a thief in the night, except he was dropping off rather than taking away.

It was a reckless indulgence, but he leaned down and kissed his sleeping daughter anyway on the top of her brunette head. She didn't stir. A bit more boldly, but still being careful, he eased the stack of letters under her pillow. There. That way Penny would be sure to see them in the morning, provided "other people" didn't stumble over them first.

He paused by the snow globe and picked it up. He recalled when he'd first found it in a curio shop, with its tiny castle surrounded by swirling snow. He remembered imagining Penny's delighted reaction and hadn't been disappointed. She had clapped her hands with glee and thanked her father profusely. Even Emma had smiled, and that wasn't something she did easily in those days . . . and, admittedly, probably even less these days.

Marko made his way carefully out into the living room. His old trunk was there, right where he'd left it. He opened it slowly so as not to cause the hinges to creak.

Just as he'd figured: all his clothes had been stuffed into it. Emma had cleared out his closet and his drawers. He supposed that shouldn't have been too much of a surprise. Perhaps he should have been relieved she hadn't donated them all to Goodwill.

Quickly he doffed the clothes he'd been wearing and pulled on a pair of dark trousers and a black-and-green-striped sweater. He kept the shoes he'd been wearing. Then he moved quickly to the kitchen, desperate to fulfill the craving for food at the pit of his stomach.

He felt like a trapped animal, and every bit the loser that his wife had pronounced him to be. Emma had made it clear that she wanted Flint out of her and Penny's lives. But how could she say that? Didn't she understand what he was capable of doing to help? Some freaking compassion was all he was looking for, some acknowledgment that he was just doing the best he could to help. Doing the best one could had to count for something. Why couldn't she just—

The kitchen light snapped on.

Flint turned and froze, as if the beam of light had lanced through him. The bread was still in his mouth as he found himself staring into the startled face of Emma Marko. Then that expression of surprise faded, replaced by a total lack of surprise, as if she'd expected that—sooner or later—he'd show up at their apartment, desperate and on the run like an idiot.

Being a well-meaning idiot didn't earn him a lot of cred from her these days.

He opened his mouth slightly and allowed the bread

to drop into his open hand. Flint both looked and felt foolish. The weight of their mutual history settled between them like a vast invisible barrier.

Without the slightest indication that she was at all curious how he'd managed to break out—perhaps she'd read about Marko having slipped away when a fight had broken out among fellow convicts during an enforced outing to clean up local highways—or what it was he wanted or hoped to achieve in having come here, Emma brusquely said, "You can't hide here, Flint."

Her hair prematurely graying, her face careworn (both of which Marko blamed himself for), Emma drew her ratty pink bathrobe more tightly around herself, as if that would protect her should he choose to attack her.

Ultimately Flint Marko decided that, despite the dire situation, he need not forsake at least the slightest indication of respect and even—dare he say it?—affection. Pulling together what little charm he had left, Marko forced a smile and asked, "How are ya, Emma?"

She looked as if she wanted to laugh at the question. Obviously she considered it ludicrous. "How's it look how Emma is?" she demanded. She gestured broadly, trying to encompass the entirety of her miserable life. "She's on welfare and got no insurance. And we have this beautiful furniture," she added sarcastically. She shook her head and, in a fairly decent impression of his deep, growling voice, mimicked, " 'How are ya, Emma?' "

She was trying to put him on the defensive. She was lashing out, and he had to keep reminding himself not to react in anger. In truth, she had every reason to be pissed off at him. He'd brought all of this down on them. Granted, he had just been trying to help. In the end, though, what difference did that make? He was still a lousy con on the run, Penny was still sick, and Emma's life was still in the toilet. Intentions didn't mean a damn. Only results mattered.

"I'm just here to see my daughter," he said, forcing himself to keep his voice calm and even.

"You're an escaped convict," she snapped. "The cops are looking for ya. You're not getting near her. You're nothing but a common thief, and you maybe even killed a man."

"No, I—!" Marko could feel his self-control slipping. Emma sensed it and, perhaps worried that she'd pushed him too far, took a defensive step back. He took in a deep breath, let it out, regained control. "It wasn't like that. I had good reason for what I was doing, and that's the truth." He knew it was futile. She didn't care about the truth. She didn't care about him.

"You and the truth sitting in prison having three meals a day," she sneered. Her face was so twisted in fury, it was hard for Marko to believe that she had ever loved him. How was it possible for someone to change that much? "You wanta talk truth? I live in the presence of great truth. That's the truth you left behind." She pointed toward Penny's door. "Right there in that bedroom."

Flint reflexively looked in the direction that Emma was pointing and was startled to see Penny's limpid eyes peering at him from the narrow opening in the doorframe. He could see that she was clutching the packet of letters to her chest. He could see the recognition dawning in her eyes, and the indisputable look of pleasure upon seeing him.

Let Emma scream at me. Let her vent. Let her blame me for everything. Ain't nothing she can say that one smile from Penny can't turn right around.

Emma was still yelling at him, but now Flint was ignoring her. Instead he took a step toward the bedroom. Tossing aside hesitation, Penny threw wide the door and her smile broadened. At first Emma didn't see her, because Marko had stepped into her line of vision as he faced his daughter. Then he knelt down in front of her, like a humble supplicant, and whispered, "Your mother's got me all wrong. I *do* care about you."

Penny's smile was incandescent, and Flint felt her press something small into his palm. He looked down at it and was surprised to see a small locket. He was so taken by the gesture that he actually forgot that Emma was in the room, but was reminded harshly enough when she shrieked in fury and came right at him. She was acting as if he were some sort of monster or child molester or anything but what he truly was: a loving father stealing a few seconds of affection from his daughter.

"You get outta here!" Emma bellowed, and she shoved Flint, hard. Because he was crouched and she was standing over him, she came close to knocking him to the floor. Flint stopped his fall with an outstretched hand and clambered to his feet. Emma aimed a kick at him and missed. Penny looked terrified. The irony was not lost on Marko; here Emma thought she was protecting her daughter and all she was really accomplishing was scaring the crap out of her. "Out of my life, outta my daughter's life! Always hiding, climbing in 'n' out of windows! Look at you, never having the pleasure of knocking on a front door. Now get out!"

For a fleeting moment, he considered punching her in the face, breaking her teeth. At least that would get her to shut up for a short time so he could have a few seconds to think. But it went against the grain, and besides, it would just alarm Penny. Plus Emma would use that as an example for the rest of Penny's life as to why her dad was a bad, evil man.

Then the entire matter of staying became moot when Marko heard the distant sound of a siren. It might not have anything to do with him. Might be a fire or some police activity nearby. On the other hand, it might also be that a neighbor had spotted him and called the cops. He couldn't take the chance.

Quickly he headed for the window. He put one leg over the sill, turned, and said in a final endeavor to gain sympathy, "I'm not a bad guy. I just had bad luck."

Emma displayed about as much compassion as he had expected—none. "There you go," she remarked, as if everything she'd just said was supported by his exit. "Out another window."

"Pray for me!" he called as he exited the apartment.

He stood on the fire escape, out of sight of the apartment's interior. From within, he could hear Emma attempting to console Penny . . . except, curiously, Penny didn't sound at all upset. Emma was the one who sounded as if she needed consoling. There was none of the furious bravado or anger that had been present when she'd been talking to him. Instead she just sounded . . . sad.

He heard Penny say, "I think he was going to cry, Mama."

Perceptive kid. Marko blinked his eyes hard, trying to get the last of the tears out of the way.

"He always cried," Emma told her. That much was true as well. He'd cried when they'd married. When Penny was born. When Penny was diagnosed. When he'd been dragged away to prison. Emma had always been the strong one and had resented the hell out of him for that.

I gotta be strong, he thought grimly. *For Emma. For Penny. Hell, for myself. I've got to get the job done, because nobody else can and nobody else cares. God . . . the things fathers do for their kids.*

With that resolve thundering in his thoughts, Flint Marko slid down the fire escape ladder and vanished into the night.

The small room was alive with the sound of hissing gas. An assortment of Green Goblin masks "looked on" from the wall, watching in mute approval. Their attention, such as it was, was focused on the clear, enclosed chamber at the far end of the room.

Like a poisonous emerald snake, the green gas continued to fill up the chamber. The swirling gas obscured the naked figure within, which was writhing and twisting in torment.

For you, Dad. It's for you . . . I'm doing it for you . . . I never wanted this . . . hurts so much . . . but it's for you, for you, just please, be proud of me, be proud—

Then the agony became too much for Harry Osborn. He thought he was going to die, and right at that moment he would have welcomed death's release.

Just as he reached his breaking point, the gas began to dissipate. It didn't register upon Harry at first that it was over . . . that he had survived. In fact, when the pressure doors whooshed open, it still took him a few minutes to process exactly what had happened.

Even then he didn't immediately step forward. Even though he was alone in his father's lair, Harry felt incredibly suspicious, as if the entire world were lying in wait just outside and preparing to pounce upon him. Then the suspicion started to clear away, to be replaced by a smug, arrogant defiance. *Let them be waiting. Let them all be waiting.* He would be able to dispose of them with absolutely no problem. Nothing could conceivably pose a serious threat to him. Nothing . . .

. . . except the traitorous bastard who had killed his father.

Harry Osborn was going to make sure that that didn't remain a consideration for much longer.

Deep, deep within his brain, in the small piece of gray matter that was watching the proceedings like a hog-tied passenger shoved into the back of an out-of-control bus, Harry shied away in horror over what he had become, and the forces that had compelled him down the same destructive road that his predecessor had trod.

The things kids do for their fathers, he thought grimly,

and then, for no reason, that suddenly struck him as funny.

He started to laugh, a maniacal cackle that continued loud and long and out of control.

And soon Harry Osborn was out of control as well.

III

THE BEST-LAID PLANS . . .

PETER KNEW IT WAS an insane time to visit his aunt May. But he also knew what he wanted to do regarding Mary Jane, and he was convinced that if he didn't discuss it with someone, then his resolve might wither and fade with the coming of the morning sun. If, on the other hand, he discussed it with Aunt May, then he would have voiced the decision that was rattling around his brain. Speaking would give it life that might well outlast the dawn. Besides, how could he be thinking about committing himself fully to Mary Jane if he couldn't even commit himself fully to the idea to begin with?

So it was that he rolled up to May Parker's apartment on his motor scooter at an ungodly hour, when the entire Queens neighborhood was sound asleep. Cautious as ever, certain he was unobserved, he picked up the scooter as if it weighed nothing and carried it through the front entrance of the apartment building. There he rested it against a wall while he found Aunt May's doorbell on the residents' list.

He hated that she'd had to move out of the old house in Forest Hills. Bad enough that, thanks to him, his uncle

Ben had been murdered by a two-bit thief that he, Peter, could have stopped well before the fatal incident. Because of that, May had wound up in dire financial straits, forced to sell the place that had been her home for as long as Peter could remember.

She acted as if it were a blessing. *How long was I supposed to putter around in the empty house?* she said at the time. *It deserves a young family just starting life, not an old woman whose family years are behind her.* Peter never answered her, suspecting the question was rhetorical. But he felt a touch of melancholy just the same and sometimes wondered if there was ever going to be an end to the things over which he felt guilty. Aunt May had forgiven him for his admission that he had had some culpability in his uncle's violent passing (although naturally he had left out the more "incriminating" aspects of the tale). When was he going to forgive himself?

He pushed the doorbell of Aunt May's apartment and silently promised to focus on more positive thoughts for the time being.

May Parker was startled out of her slumber by the urgent ringing of her apartment buzzer. She squinted in the darkness, disoriented, and was startled to see that the glowing numbers of the digital clock on her nightstand read 2:00 A.M. Her natural assumption was that someone had died. Why else would she be woken up at this hour?

She got out of bed, tossed on a robe, shoved her feet into the bunny slippers that Peter had gotten her for her last birthday, and made her way to the intercom. She banged one shin on the coffee table as she did so and swore in a way that would have prompted her to scold her nephew fiercely if he had uttered the same word. But she figured that if one had lived as long as she had, one was entitled to a few allowances.

Nursing her sore leg, she limped the rest of the distance to the intercom and tapped the button. "Who is it?" she asked, fully expecting it to be some drunken idiot pushing the wrong button.

To her astonishment, a familiar voice said, "Peter."

"Peter?"

Immediately she buzzed him in, then steeled herself for whatever disastrous news he had.

It had to be simply catastrophic. He was dying. Mary Jane was dying or already dead.

There was a knock at the door, and although she assumed it was Peter, May still peered quickly through the peephole. There he was, holding his motorcycle helmet and backpack. He looked concerned but determined.

Prepared for the worst, she threw open the door and waited, holding her breath.

A grin split Peter's face. "I've decided to marry Mary Jane."

May thought she was going to pass out—not from being overwhelmed by Peter's announcement, but from relief that all her worst-case scenarios were without foundation. Then, ever so briefly, she considered smacking Peter upside the head for scaring the living daylights out of her at two in the morning.

Out of her boundless love and forgiveness, she did not do so.

"Oh my," she managed, and then, when nothing else came to her because her mind was still processing the information (and banishing images of funerals), she fell back onto her default response to any startling news: "This calls for a cup of tea."

Any hesitancy or remorse Peter had felt over rousing Aunt May from her slumber instantly dissipated when he saw how genuinely happy she was for him. As he sat at her kitchen table sipping tea, he chatted about how much Mary Jane meant to him. How his life somehow just made more sense when she was a part of it. It wasn't just for May's benefit in understanding his elation. It was for his own as well.

Even now, he was still talking himself into taking the big step, and he figured that if there was any fault in either his logic or emotions, Aunt May would point it out. "You're too young" or "Are you sure you've considered all the ramifications?" or other similar helpful bromides would undoubtedly fall from her lips if she had any concern over Peter's course.

If Aunt May sensed Peter's nagging second thoughts, or if she did really believe it was the wrong move, she said nothing to that effect. Instead she continued to smile and listen attentively. She yawned once or twice, discreetly covering it with the back of her hand. Peter chalked that up to her being so interested in what he was saying that she was making the effort to stay awake. After all, scientifically, that's what yawning was: the body's attempt to intake a sizable portion of oxygen all at once to refresh the brain lest fatigue set in. Peter felt that no one should ever be insulted if someone yawned in his or her presence. It's actually a compliment: it meant one was worth the effort of trying to stay awake for, as opposed to nodding off.

Peter finally ran out of things to say and realized that he had "presented his case." He paused, waiting for Aunt May's opinion.

She added a bit more hot water to refresh her tea and stirred it thoughtfully, composing her thoughts.

Then, as if her mind were a million miles away, she looked at the engagement ring on her finger and smiled wistfully. "You know, the day your uncle Ben asked me to marry him, we were both scared and excited and"—she laughed at the recollection—"*very* young. And I loved him so fiercely." She added that last with a touch of fiery pride.

"And you said yes, right?"

"No," she replied, which startled Peter. "I wanted to say yes, but I said no. I wasn't ready. Neither was he. So we took our time. Looked forward to it. Didn't want to run into something with nothing to count on but love." She rested a liver-spotted hand atop his and said gently, as if delivering bad news that he wouldn't want to hear, "Love is not enough, Peter. There's so much more beyond it that has to be considered."

"Come on," he said with an uncomfortable laugh. "I know that."

"When Uncle Ben and I were married, we had a little more security."

So that's what this was about. Here all of his concerns and doubts stemmed from uncertainty over his feelings. Trust Aunt May to approach the question from the most pragmatic aspects. "I have security. I have a job," he reminded her.

"You need a steady job. With benefits."

He had to admit that much was true. There were wider aspects to consider. If Peter was single, whatever happened to him was really his own lookout. If he was married, then his problems became Mary Jane's problems. What if he was seriously injured in a battle? A broken limb . . . a stray bullet that got lucky? Yes, he healed quickly, but you couldn't heal a bullet. He couldn't be in need of hospitalization or a doctor's care and have no medical insurance. Plus what about more everyday considerations? What if they were married and Mary Jane became pregnant? It could happen. Happened every day. The cost of a pregnancy and hospital stay without medical coverage . . . it could break them. *Would* break them.

As all this raced through his mind, Aunt May looked fixedly into his eyes and continued, "A husband has to be understanding and put his wife before himself. Can you do that, Peter?"

With this question, at least, Peter felt confident. "Of course I can," he said with utter conviction.

She smiled. Apparently, as far as Aunt May was concerned, if Peter was on solid ground with that aspect of it, everything else would fall into place. "Then you have my blessing," she said, and he hadn't realized until that moment he was actually looking for it. Once she gave it, though, it felt right. It felt good. "And," she said, "I hope you've considered a proper proposal." Again she looked at her engagement ring, reminiscing, and when she spoke, she could have been describing something that had transpired just yesterday. "Uncle Ben had it all planned. We went for a walk, and he laid me down under a juniper tree, and he said . . ."

She paused, then deepened her voice to sound like Ben's. "Close your eyes and make a wish." She chuckled and continued, "And I did. And he said, 'Open them,' and I did. And he was holding this ring."

It wasn't especially large. Quite the opposite, actually. Then again, May Parker was never the showiest of women and would have considered a large, gleaming rock too gaudy. Plus, that it was given to her by Ben probably made it huge in her eyes. "This ring, dazzling, in front of me. I thought it was the sun." She looked at it with a trace of sadness. "We'd be married fifty years come August if . . . if someone hadn't been . . ." Her voice dropped, and in a husky tone, clearly trying to compose herself, she sighed, "Oh, God," as if annoyed with her own weakness. She clenched her hand into a fist, then let out a soft sigh like a cleansing breath. "So," she said, "make it very special for that lovely girl. Do something she'll never forget." She hesitated only for an instant, then she pulled the engagement ring from her finger and held it out to Peter. "And give her this."

Peter was stunned by the generosity. His instinct was to protest, to say that he couldn't. How could he possibly take one of her fondest memories of Uncle Ben? Then he realized that, with or without the ring on her finger, the memory would remain intact. Furthermore, if Peter had learned one thing in his life, it was never to argue with May Parker when she had a particular determined look on her face—as she did now.

Giving in to the inevitable, he took the ring from her with great care and in a hushed tone said, "Thank you, Aunt May."

She nodded once, the deal sealed, and then her eyes sagged slightly. She pulled herself back from fatigue and said, "It's late. You better go on home."

Peter gathered up his things as May cleared the china from the kitchen table.

As he headed for the front door, Peter's gaze fell upon the old, small upright piano on the near wall. He remembered with great amusement all the times that, in his youth, Aunt May had sat with him and forced him to practice. She had disdained the need for a piano teacher. "Why spend good money to have someone teach him something that I already know," she had sniffed whenever Ben had suggested someone else be brought in to show Peter the ropes. Peter had come to despise the instrument, far preferring to stay up in his room and read his books since he knew he was good at that. Now, though, as an adult, he had come to appreciate May's intentions in widening his horizons.

As a gesture of appreciation, he slid onto the piano bench, sat with his fingers poised over the keys, called up the strains of Debussy's "Clair de Lune" from those long-ago lessons, and started to play.

It was . . . uninspiring.

Frighteningly enough, Peter remembered "Clair de Lune" as one of his stronger pieces, so he shuddered to think what the *William Tell* overture must have sounded like to adult ears. As it was, he stumbled through the first few bars as best he could. Aunt May kept a smile plastered on her face, but he could see her eyes wincing with every misplayed note, of which there were more than a few.

Peter's musical effort was mercifully cut short by an irritated banging on the floor from the poor devil living underneath, who didn't apparently feel like being serenaded, badly, at whatever time in the morning it was. Pulling his hands away from the keyboard as if it had caught fire, Peter said in a lame attempt at self-defense, "Needs tuning."

Aunt May grinned as she held the door open for him. Peter pulled his helmet on and she patted him on the arm as he passed. "After you're married, feel free to visit me. Only come a little earlier."

He hugged his beloved aunt, the woman who had raised him, and headed out the door, feeling far lighter in spirit than he had in weeks.

The feeling stayed with him all the way back to his Manhattan apartment. Although naturally he was paying attention to the road the entire ride, he was still unaware of the passage of time. His mind was awhirl with images of Mary Jane accepting his proposal, of their marriage, honeymooning, having children, growing old together. He savored every one.

Life was good.

Almost too good, his ever-sour subconscious warned him, but he dismissed that sort of thinking. As he pulled his bike up to his apartment building, killing the motor, he decided that he was going to embrace the power of positive thinking. Perhaps things went wrong because he expected the worst-case scenario at any moment. He had even temporarily lost his powers because of his uncertainty and lack of desire to live up to his responsibilities. There was no reason that he couldn't shape his life to be as positive as he wanted it to be simply by being determined to make it happen.

He stepped off the bike, removed his helmet, and checked his watch. Four in the morning. He didn't feel at all tired. Perhaps he should do some webswinging to . . .

Nah. How about something normal for once? Drink a glass of milk, watch TV, or read a book until your eyes get heavy. Something like that. You've been prioritizing Peter Parker's life for once, and that's been going pretty well for you. Smartest thing would be to keep doing exactly what you're doing, and not switch over to Spider-M—

His spider-sense went off.

He acted completely on instinct, as he always did in such matters. He leaped toward the building, figuring to hit the wall and scurry up it, buy a few precious seconds, get a clearer idea of what was happening and where it was coming from.

It was one of the rare instances when his instincts betrayed him.

Airborne as he was, he had no protection, no recourse, as something slammed into him. The ground spun away from Peter with dizzying speed as he arced upward, heading toward the stars that he had been admiring from a distance only a few hours before.

He twisted around, trying to see who or what had grabbed him. He heard the high-pitched whine of a powerful engine and suddenly found himself staring—not into a person's face—but into a demented-looking, and hi-tech almost familiar mask, covering the lower part of his attacker's head.

The Goblin?! The Green Goblin! But he's dead! I saw him die! Am I dreaming? Did I fall asleep? Am I still in the web hammock with MJ and I drifted off? This can't—

The buildings were a blur beneath him as Peter, an unwilling passenger, continued to angle sharply upward. This "New Goblin" grabbed Peter by the hair, yanking his head back. Peter gasped, trying to comprehend what was happening, with the sharp pain and the stinging feel of the wind in his face reinforcing that this was no dream. The New Goblin drew his free arm back, ready to strike, and fearsome blades sprouted from the wrist of his armor. Peter tried to pull away, but he had no leverage. Snagged as he was, immobilized as he was, Peter couldn't offer more than token resistance as the blades sliced across his chest. It shredded his shirt, raising a thin line of blood, and he cried out in agony. If he hadn't managed to pull back even the marginal amount that he had, it would have ripped open his torso.

The Goblin repositioned himself and tried to bring the blades around again, but the pain galvanized Peter. He snagged the Goblin's arm, strength against strength, holding the lethal weapon at bay. The Goblin was cackling dementedly, but there was a slight hesitation, the briefest uncertainty. Grabbing the opportunity to do some damage, Peter swung his foot up and kicked the Goblin hard in the chest. The Goblin lost his grip on Peter's hair, although Peter was certain he felt some strands pulling loose from his scalp.

Peter twisted clear and flipped himself over the Goblin's head. He let himself go into free fall just to get some distance. He afforded a fast glance behind him and saw that the Goblin was astride a different vehicle than he had been the last time. It wasn't a bat-winged glider, but instead something that looked more like a supercharged hi-tech snowboard. The armor was also different, far more minimal . . . a few pieces slapped together.

Peter kept his arms and legs straight and dove like a parachutist. The ground spun below him, but he'd been in far more dizzying circumstances than this. In fact, the effect was almost calming, the first chance he'd had to compose his thoughts since this unwarranted, insane attack had begun.

Obviously, whoever his assailant was, this new Goblin knew that Peter was Spider-Man. His secret identity was blown. At the moment, though, his biggest worry was not to get killed; everything else could just wait.

Believing he'd managed to put enough distance between him and his attacker, Peter fired a webline and snagged a nearby building. He started to swing toward it, then his heart fell as he saw the Goblin swoop down near the adhesion point of the webbing to the building. Then the rest of him fell along with his heart as the Goblin sliced through the webbing with one fast flick of his blades. Cut loose from his momentary salvation, Peter started to fall again, tumbling out of control. Knowing that the Goblin could keep repeating that trick—that he could follow Peter all the way down, cutting through weblines until Peter was out of building and out of time—he didn't have any other choices and so brought his arm up to fire yet another webline.

He didn't even get the shot off. His spider-sense warned him, but he couldn't do a damned thing about it as the Goblin slammed into him, sending him tumbling literally heels over head and crashing into the side of a nearby skyscraper.

If it had at least been glass, Peter could have smashed through it and perhaps escaped to the inside. No such luck—instead he impacted with solid brick and mortar, embedding the left side of his body in the side of the building. Peter knew he could pull free, but it was going to take him a few moments to extricate himself.

The Goblin soared down toward him, and Peter wondered if he was going to have even those precious few seconds. If the Goblin came in hurtling a pumpkin grenade or swinging his blades or . . .

But he didn't. The Goblin slowed and then stopped, hovering nearby. The move surprised Peter. The Goblin had him cold, but he wasn't pressing the advantage? Why? Did he want to toy with him? Convinced that Peter couldn't get away, was he determined to make Peter suffer? Or was it that he was reluctant to make the final move *because* it seemed Peter was a goner? If it was the latter . . . if the Goblin was conflicted . . .

It couldn't be . . .

Of course, it had to be. There was no one else . . .

As if intuiting what was going through Peter's mind, the Goblin touched some sort of mechanism in the palm of his gloved hand. The mask slid back, and the coldly furious face of Harry Osborn glared at him.

"Harry?" Peter whispered. Inwardly he wasn't surprised. He'd figured it out. Knowing it, however, wasn't the same as being confronted by the harsh reality.

"You knew this was coming, Pete." The friendly nickname sounded like an obscenity on his lips.

Harry abruptly angled the "Sky Stick" forward, slamming his fist at Peter in one rapid motion. Peter barely managed to yank his arm clear. He heard and felt a tearing of cloth, and part of his jacket sleeve was left behind, but better ripped clothing than a shattered face. Leaping aside, Peter just avoided Harry's punch, which smashed brick and crumbled some of the mortar to dust. Peter, landing on another section of the wall some feet away, gaped at the destruction.

Whatever Norman Osborn had done to himself to acquire accelerated strength, Harry had clearly done it as well. And the action had muddled Harry's mind just as it had Norman's.

Or . . . perhaps not. It might have been wishful thinking, but it still seemed to Peter as if Harry was moving slowly, hesitating at key moments, reluctant to deliver a final, lethal blow. Holding out a slender thread of hope that his erstwhile friend could be reasoned with, Peter called out to him, "He was trying to kill me! He killed himself!"

"Shut up!"

Harry shoved his hands into the section of the broken wall that Peter was still perched upon and ripped it clear of the building. Peter went flying, his arms pinwheeling, his jacket flapping wide . . .

Aunt May's engagement ring flew out of his pocket.

It was the merest luck that his peripheral vision noticed it, glinting in the night. He twisted around in midair, grasping at it. Ironically, it was the only thing that saved him, because Harry dive-bombed right where Peter would have been had he been trying to get back to the wall. But Peter was moving in a completely different direction, toward the tumbling ring, and so Harry missed him clean.

Peter desperately fired a webline at the diamond ring. As accurate as he typically was, because both he and the ring were falling and it was so small a target, the webline whizzed a fraction of an inch to the side of the ring.

Don't take your eyes off it! Don't—

As if he were swimming through air, Peter lunged toward the ring, oblivious to all else.

This time it cost him.

Harry sped down toward him and sideswiped him hard. Peter was knocked violently to one side. He was completely disoriented, with no idea which way was up or down. A dozen different tactics ran through his brain like a computer sucking down data, and none of them seemed as if it would work. Despair seized him, and then he slammed into another building. His arm went out instinctively to break the fall; even then it only partly shielded his head. He cracked his skull and was positive that he could actually hear his brain sloshing around inside his cranium. Blackness started to envelop him.

For the first time since this had begun . . . possibly for the first time since he had acquired his spider powers . . . Peter Parker was seized with the belief that he was going to die.

His life flashed before his eyes.

And then everything went dark.

IV

THE LONGEST NIGHT
(PART 1)

THE RUSHING OF AIR past Peter's face roused him to the outer fringes of consciousness. He hadn't recovered enough to completely register what was happening, but he reacted with desperate reflex.

He twisted around and blindly fired a webline. He had absolutely no idea which way he was shooting it, and no clue how close to the ground he was—if the webbing went straight up, he was a dead man.

For the first time since the assault began, Peter's luck held up. His webbing snagged something. He didn't know what it was, but as long as it wasn't moving, that was good enough for him.

From high above, he heard a roar of disapproval. The Goblin had apparently been watching his descent, satisfied to observe Peter's final splat from a distance. So Peter was actually far enough away that the Goblin didn't have an opportunity to cut the webline.

Peter snapped back upward like a bungee jumper, and as his vision cleared, he saw that the webline had snagged on a stone gargoyle perched atop the corner of a building.

He landed on the ledge and held on to the gargoyle for a moment, steadying himself.

Then he remembered the ring.

Desperately looking around, stretching his already heightened senses to their limits, he spotted it. Ten stories below, the glittering ring ricocheted off a parked car with a hollow *tink,* bounced into the street . . .

. . . and tumbled straight toward a sewer grating.

No. God, please, no, not that.

Shoving his back against the wall for balance, he fired webbing from both arms at the grating. The webbing sprayed out across it, completely covering the openings. Seconds later the diamond ring rolled onto the grating but came to a halt, ensnared in the webbing.

Peter let out a sigh of relief, but he had no time to dwell on his brief triumph. The Goblin was diving down toward him, a pumpkin bomb in his hand. He threw it, and Peter leaped clear of the building side. The bomb slammed into the gargoyle and blew it off the ledge, sending the entire statue hurtling toward the ground.

Seizing the opportunity, Peter landed a short distance away even as he fired a webline, snagging the gargoyle. He swung his arm, whipping the statue around. Perfect timing—Harry had wrongly assumed that Peter was going to prevent the gargoyle from falling to the street. Instead Peter snapped the statue around as if it were a mace and sent it slamming into the Goblin with such force that it caused him to lose control of the Sky Stick. Harry pinwheeled across the Manhattan skyline, howling with fury.

Still holding the webline, Peter swung the statue up in

a smooth arc that sent it tumbling onto the roof overhead. He then released it and skittered to the ground, moving with reckless speed. Peter hit the street still running, stumbled for a second, then righted himself and sprinted to the sewer grating. He plucked the precious ring from the webbing, shoved it in his pants pocket—and then for good measure webbed the pocket shut.

Peter looked around to figure out where the hell he was and realized that the battle had carried them many blocks south into Chinatown.

For some reason a Woody Allen comment crossed his mind: *I'm astounded by people who want to "know" the universe when it's hard enough to find your way around Chinatown.*

Chinatown was an endless maze of narrow streets and alleyways. Peter had gotten lost there on two separate occasions and had always considered it one of the perks of his powers to be capable of swinging *above* Chinatown and not have to worry about it anymore.

That wasn't possible now, as the cackling of the Goblin informed him. Harry had obviously pulled out of his tailspin, descending toward Peter at high speed.

It was a blessing to be here. In the open space, bounding between buildings, Peter had had no chance. The Goblin *(Harry, dammit, it's Harry, stop thinking of him as the Goblin)* had all the room to maneuver and could hammer him relentlessly while Peter had nowhere to hide and no means of avoiding the attacks except through healthy dollops of luck. Down here, though, in the confines of Chinatown, his agility and quick thinking might give him the edge he needed.

At least, that was the theory.

Knowing that his life depended on his being right, Peter vaulted into the nearest alleyway and started running down it. For a moment he wondered if Harry would figure out what his strategy was and refuse to be drawn into it. He needn't have worried. Without hesitation, Harry descended into the alleyway on his Sky Stick and went in pursuit of his best friend.

"You can run, Pete, but you can't hide!" Harry crowed, and laughed once more.

The alley couldn't have been more than four feet wide. Peter ran as fast as he could, his heart pounding against his chest. Harry stayed right on him, never more than a few yards back. Peter's spider-sense managed to keep him ahead, but just barely. He moved right, left, never slowing, vaulting over garbage dumps, trash heaps, and the occasional unconscious drunk.

Peter cut a corner tight, entered a street that was as narrow as the alley he'd just left, and kept going. He ducked as a blast of concussive force seared the air over his head. Then the ground under his feet exploded, sending him flying and crashing through a storefront display window.

Harry dove down toward Peter, his right fist crackling as it prepped another concussive blast.

Peter seized a string of Chinese firecrackers from the ruined storefront display window and frantically threw them just as Harry unleashed another blast. It struck the firecrackers in midair and the entire array exploded directly in front of him. Noise and great gouts of color erupted all around Harry, confusing him, causing him to roar in fury, and then Peter was off again.

"You don't get away that easy, Pete!" Harry shouted, and kept on coming. Peter sprinted down another alleyway, which connected to another and yet another. Harry didn't slow; in fact, he was gaining, and Peter was starting to get out of breath. His endurance was superhuman, but it wasn't infinite.

A Dumpster sat dead ahead. Peter grabbed hold of it as he passed by, turned fast, and with an impressive display of strength sent the whole thing hurtling upward toward the Goblin. Garbage and assorted decaying food filled the air, momentarily blinding Harry (and, likely, grossing him out a bit). Peter headed down yet another alleyway in this labyrinthine neighborhood, his mind racing, trying to come up with *any* more ideas as his energy flagged.

He looked up—clotheslines were strung above him. The upper section of the alleyway was going to be too difficult for Harry to maneuver, so he was going to fly low. Quickly Peter fired his webbing at a spot about five feet overhead and affixed it to the wall opposite. He drew it taut, and in the darkness of the alley, the gossamer web strand practically disappeared.

He heard Harry coming in fast, gunning the engine of the Sky Stick. Peter started running again—Harry had to see him to make the trap work. Peter was halfway down the alley when Harry came roaring around the corner, practically a blur to Peter's eye.

Without slowing, Harry sped down the alleyway toward Peter, holding a pumpkin bomb in one hand and announcing that this was it, Peter wasn't going to get away this time.

Harry never came close to spotting the webline.

He hit it at full speed, the webbing cutting across his chest. Harry was knocked clean off the Sky Stick. The device kept going, bereft of its operator. Seconds later it crashed to the ground, tumbling several times before sputtering to a halt.

Harry fared far worse.

He bounded back with as much force as he'd expended when he hit the webline. Because it had taken him in his midsection, he flipped over and landed on the pavement headfirst. Peter gasped in horror. Yes, the armor would absorb some of the damage, but that was still Harry's body in there suffering the high-speed concussive impact. The human body could only take so much jolting around. A neck or back could easily snap, armored or not.

Peter saw his friend lying in a heap on the ground and, to his own frustration, found himself hesitating. It could be a trick. Harry could be playing possum, lying there to draw him in close, biding his time for Peter to lean over him in concern—and then Harry could gut him. Send his intestines spilling out into the alleyway and laugh in glee at the stupid expression on Peter Parker's dying face.

Peter's hesitation seemed to him to last an age. *If that's how I die, then that's the way it goes, but I've got to see if he's all right.*

Disdaining caution, Peter vaulted to the fallen Harry and checked him over. No warning of imminent danger from his spider-sense—Harry wasn't faking anything. Peter pulled the mask away and saw that Harry's eyes were closed, his face pale, a thin line of spittle trailing down the side of his face.

"Harry?" he said, but didn't wait for a response. Yanking the gauntlet off, he checked Harry's pulse.

Nothing.

"Oh my God," he whispered, unable to believe it. There was no way Peter could endure the knowledge that he had killed his best friend and single-handedly put an end to the Osborn family line. He put his head to Harry's chest.

Still nothing. The silence of the grave.

"Oh my God! Harry!" There was no whispering it now, and even as Peter howled his dismay, he started pumping Harry's chest. He had never been more grateful for that course in CPR that he had taken at the Y some years ago. He had been driven by terrible concerns that he might find his aunt or uncle collapsed on the floor one day, and he wanted to be certain that he would know what to do. Of course, he could never have envisioned back then, back before his life became the insane spectacle that it was today, the use to which he would be putting the training.

Even as he applied the pressure to Harry's heart, Peter's mind was racing. First rule of an accident: don't move the victim. You could cause all manner of greater damage in doing so.

But he didn't have a cell phone to call an ambulance, and even if he did, Peter didn't know where the hell he was. He couldn't begin to describe their location beyond "somewhere in Chinatown."

He thought he felt a stirring in Harry's chest, but he couldn't be certain. CPR was simply a stopgap to keep someone alive until the paramedics showed up. None were going to be coming in this case . . . or at least not in time.

Seeing that he had no choice, Peter slung Harry over his shoulder in a fireman's carry. Taking two quick steps, he fired a webline upward and bounded to the top of a building. He needed height, he needed to be able to see what was in the vicinity. The instant he hit the roof, he fired another webline and started swinging. *Uptown, head uptown,* he frantically told himself. He knew uptown better than he did downtown, and besides, downtown tended to be more deserted at this hour.

Peter had never moved with less consideration for his own safety. Even with the web-slinging skills he had developed, swinging one-handed was remarkably dangerous. Rather than alternate arms, he would fire a webline, swing to its apex, release, fire another one, and keep moving. The advantage was that it resulted in great, distance-eating arcs. The disadvantage was that if he miscalculated, he could wind up smeared all over a building or on the side of an ill-timed passing truck.

As he swung, he scrambled to recall everything he'd read about brain damage that could set in from lack of oxygen. What was it? Three minutes? Five minutes? How long before irreparable harm was done? How long before, even if Harry were brought back to full respiration, he would wind up being a vegetable?

Peter spotted a huge red cross six blocks west. Instantly he headed in that direction. Time had slowed to a crawl, even though he was moving faster than anything else in Manhattan. In seconds, he was within sight of the emergency room, taking only the time required to yank the rest of the Goblin armor off Harry. Thank heavens there were passable street clothes underneath. Peter just didn't feel the need to answer certain questions right then.

Peter dropped to the street a block from the hospital and sprinted the rest of the way. He had no idea how much time had elapsed since Harry had been injured. He wasn't even sure if the tortured young man slung over his shoulder was still alive. But he had no choice. He couldn't let Harry die. And if, despite his best efforts, Harry didn't make it . . .

Don't think about it. You always get in trouble when you think about things. Just run. Running, you're good at.

He was moving so quickly that the automatic doors to the emergency room almost didn't open in time. Peter charged in, shouting for help, and a nurse and some guys in green shirts came running toward him. Part of him was surprised that it was really just like what one sees on television. Within seconds, Harry was being loaded onto a gurney and the doctors were doing triage. Peter was so numb that he didn't even remember Harry being lifted off his shoulder.

He watched as they shoved the gurney through a large set of double doors. They were shouting complicated medical terms, all at the same time, and it was so fast and loud that Peter couldn't follow any of it. But none of it sounded good. He took a step toward Harry, and then his way was blocked by a doctor or orderly or paramedic or someone who was shouting into his face, "What happened? Tell us what happened!"

Peter said the first words that came to mind: "Hit and run." Miraculously, that seemed to satisfy the person who'd been demanding answers. Either that or Peter looked and sounded so much like someone in shock that they simply figured they weren't going to get any better answers out of him.

"In shock" would have been the correct diagnosis for Peter. He was still processing that Harry had followed his father's path so completely, all driven by a desire to kill Peter, and hadn't quite made it to the notion that Harry might not survive the night.

The inquiring someone had vanished, and Peter—moving like a sleepwalker or a man in a trance—walked through the double doors. Harry was lying on the gurney a few feet away. They had yanked out the defibrillator paddles from a crash cart and positioned them on Harry's chest.

"Clear!" a doctor shouted. Verifying that no one was touching Harry's body, the doctor triggered the paddles and Harry's body violently spasmed. Peter watched, trying not to panic and not succeeding.

"No response," said the nurse, checking the readings.

"Recharge and go again!" the doctor snapped.

At that moment, someone noticed that Peter was standing in a restricted area, and two orderlies descended upon him. He offered no resistance as they pushed him from the room. The door swung shut, blocking his view of what was going on.

He felt stricken and terrified and guilty . . . but not guilty because he had caused the injury that had landed Harry in the hospital. No, it was guilt because Harry knew Peter's secret, and if Harry died, then the secret died with him.

The terrible truth was that Peter's life would be much easier if Harry Osborn died here in the emergency room. That realization produced not only guilt, but self-loathing. What kind of person was he, to dwell on the notion that someone's death would be personally convenient?

The kind of person who's concerned about other people. What if Harry recovers and he decides the best way to get to you is through your loved ones? Why not? Norman figured out that I was enamored of Mary Jane and played upon that. If Harry dies . . .

No! He's not going to die! Peter angrily cut himself off. *He's going to make it! And . . . and we'll get it all worked out somehow.*

How?

Somehow! Now shut up!

He leaned against the wall, feeling as if his soul weighed a hundred pounds. He glanced at the clock. Still well before dawn. Peter rubbed the bridge of his nose, fighting fatigue, and decided that this had to be the longest night of his life. He briefly wondered if anyone was having a worse night than he was.

V

THE LONGEST NIGHT (PART 2)

DR. T. ALAN CHAFIN hated his job.

What the hell was he, a scientist of his standing, doing testing a particle accelerator in the middle of the night? He should be home in bed, spooning with his wife, who was beginning to make loud noises about feeling like a widow thanks to the hours that her scientist husband was keeping. He would keep assuring her that things were going to change, and in one respect, he was right. They did keep changing. They kept getting *worse,* thanks to the increasing paranoia of Quest Research's upper management.

Ever since that incident when the test of their new mechanized war suit was destroyed by some lunatic on a glider, Quest had been frantic about the prospect of industrial sabotage. So Quest had chosen increasingly remote places to build research facilities and opted for strange times of night to conduct the actual tests. The belief was that atypical procedures were required if they were going to stay one step ahead of those who were going to spy on, or trash, their endeavors. That this policy was beginning to weigh heavily on their staff didn't factor into the equation.

"Alan? You okay?"

The question came from his assistant, Ashley Michel. She was diminutive, but with a solid frame, brown hair, and brown eyes. Chafin forced a smile and said, "Fine, Ash, fine. Just working hard on keeping everything together." He sat back in his chair, which was woefully uncomfortable, and continued, "So . . . where do we stand?"

"Capacitators are at seventy percent." Looking over the instrumentation, Ashley checked the dials with her customary meticulousness. She was well-known for her almost obsessive attention to detail; if the readings were off by so much as a fraction, she would notice it. She wiped a hank of her perpetually unruly hair from her face. "Estimate full charge in . . . three minutes, seventeen seconds."

A third technician, Donnie Blaswell, nodded confirmation. Not that anyone expected Ashley to be wrong. "Do you think we'll manage it this time?" he asked.

The other scientists looked at young Blaswell with amusement. Donnie's energy was legendary around the facility. He was referred to as Too Much Coffee Boy since most of his enthusiasm was attributed to an excess of caffeine. Curiously, Donnie didn't actually drink coffee, but that did nothing to dissuade the nickname.

"You mean really accomplish total demolecularization?" asked Chafin. He shrugged. "Does it matter?"

"Well, of . . ." Donnie looked surprised and pushed his glasses up on the bridge of his nose. "Of course it matters. I mean . . . total demolecularization . . . it's . . ."

"They'll weaponize it," Michel said sourly. "Just you wait."

"They keep saying it's going to be just for molecular research," Donnie protested, but he didn't sound entirely convinced.

"They can keep saying a Big Mac is filet mignon, but it's still gonna taste like a Big Mac," a fourth scientist, Sean O'Shea, commented. He was walking into the lab and heard the tail end of the conversation. Tall and lean, he filled the room with his presence and said with quiet authority, "Gentlemen, ours is not to question why, and so forth and so on, you know the drill. Let's get our baby up and running, shall we?"

He always referred to the project as "our baby." Chafin suspected it was because he was more comfortable calling it that than "our future weapon of mass destruction."

Giving in to the inevitable, Chafin propelled his wheeled chair across to his station with impressive agility, sliding across the floor like an accomplished skateboarder. "You heard the man," Chafin called out. "Let's get ready to roll."

His love for his job had not increased.

Flint Marko felt his freedom slipping through his fingers like sand.

For a brief time . . . a wonderful time . . . Marko had been certain that he had lost his pursuers. He was quickly disabused of the notion, however, as he heard the sounds of barking dogs in the distance.

Damned police. Damned lawmakers. Why couldn't they leave him the hell alone? Why did they insist on pigeonholing him into the role of the bad guy? Why couldn't they see shades of gray in their black-and-white world of cops and robbers? It was like some big kids' game to them, and he was the prize.

He had eluded them sufficiently to get out of New York, jacking a car and driving into one of the more remote areas of the New Jersey marshlands. But he'd had to fill up the tank. While the pump was filling the car, Marko had gone to the bathroom, and when he came out, it was just his crappy luck that a cop car had likewise chosen that exact moment to pull in to gas up. The instant that the cop in the passenger's seat glanced Marko's way, he knew he'd been made. He hadn't even bothered to go back to the car. He'd turned right around and bolted for the back of the service station. The howling protest of the cop car's siren assured Marko that he'd been absolutely right.

The back of the service area opened onto a steep drop-off, which, in turn, led into a heavily wooded area. Marko vaulted over the low mesh fence that lined the perimeter of the service area and rolled down into the brush. By the time the cops managed to get to the top of the hill, he was already sprinting into the woods.

"Police! Stop where you are!" one of them shouted, and a warning shot snapped a branch off a tree just to his right. He ignored it. Instead he vanished into the concealing forest and ran headlong without the slightest care as to which way he was going or where he was going to end up. The only thing that mattered was that he got as far away from them as possible.

The ground had slowly become boggier, and as the trees thinned out, the grass got taller. He was no longer able to run with assurance; instead every step felt like a tough slog. There was a full moon, thank God, but every time it went behind the clouds, he found himself tripping and sprawling over random branches, stones, and depressions in the ground that seemed to be there purely to make him fall.

A gentle wind blew into his face, and only when he heard the sounds of the barking dogs behind him did he realize he'd had yet another piece of crummy luck. Because the wind was coming at him, it meant he was upwind of the dogs, and they'd have an even easier time tracking him. But how had they gotten his scent? Obviously: he'd left the car behind in the service station. They'd sniffed around on the seat, on the steering wheel, the gas and brake pedals. That would have been more than enough to put them on his tail.

The grass was now chest high, the ground spongier than ever. Marko was soaked in sweat, his breath labored. The marsh air was so thick with moisture that he felt as if he were trying to breathe water. Still the dogs grew closer. How the hell were they managing that? They were lower down to the ground than he was; how could they be moving faster? It didn't make any sense.

He glanced back to see how close his pursuers were, half-expecting them to be no more than five feet behind, and slammed headlong into a fence. He staggered back and fell into the marsh grass. Sputtering and furious over this dead end, he scrambled to his feet and saw—in a dim outline as the moon once again scampered behind a cloud—the closely woven mesh of a cyclone fence.

Marko had no time to retrace his steps, and certainly no time to move down the length of the fence to find a way around it. It could run a mile or more, and by that time they'd have him. *One choice is no choice,* his grandmother used to say. She'd had such high hopes for Flint when he was a child. He wondered what she'd say now.

Actually, he didn't wonder. He knew.

Flint forced himself to take one deep breath to steady his nerves, then he sprinted toward the cyclone fence once more. He vaulted as high as he could and his fingers snagged into the upper links. His feet scrambled for purchase and found some minimal support, but it was mostly the strength in his arms that enabled him to pull himself up and over.

Just as he reached the top of the fence, lights hit him from behind. Powerful flashlights, maybe even searchlights. There were shouts of "Halt! Freeze!" and other orders that Marko was only too happy to ignore.

He clambered over and threw himself to the other side. Marko landed heavily, but the spongy ground cushioned the fall. As he got to his feet, he noticed for the first time that a sign was posted on the side of the fence from which he'd just come. He hadn't taken the time to read it—probably a standard KEEP OUT warning, as if he cared.

Marko started running once more. He discovered that he'd injured his ankle in the fall and was now limping badly, just to add to his aggravation. He heard the dogs barking at the fence, their claws scratching the links. He risked yet another glance, fully expecting to see the police scrambling over the fence after him. Instead they were remaining right where they were, on the other side, and were angrily shouting for Marko to come back before it was "too late."

Too late? Too late for what? For them to catch me? Screw that.

To his surprise, the marsh grass suddenly disappeared, giving way to a paved, pitch-black field. Something had been constructed here. A private airfield, perhaps. Yes, that made perfect sense. He had stumbled upon a private airfield, and this might be the biggest break he'd ever gotten. All he needed was to find a pilot with a private plane and "convince" him to transport Marko out of here. He was certain he could do it; Marko was a pretty persuasive guy when he wanted to be.

His luck was finally turning. Even his ankle was starting to feel a little better.

That was when the ground went completely out from under him.

With no warning at all, Marko suddenly found himself tumbling down a massive concrete slope, curved like a gigantic bowl. He desperately tried to find a way to slow his downward skid, but the walls were perfectly smooth. He kept falling, rolling end over end, until finally he skidded to a halt in the bottom of the structure.

Marko went headfirst in a large pile of sand. He pulled his head out, sputtering, coughing up granules that had gotten between his lips, his teeth. Getting to his feet, he looked around, trying to get his bearings.

Suddenly a massive light kicked on above him. He had

no idea what it was. Oh, Lord . . . what if he'd foolishly broken into, not an airport, but a prison? Wouldn't that be just too freaking perfect if—in his determination to escape—he wound up back in jail?

Marko looked up, shielding his eyes, uncertain of what he was going to see. His jaw dropped. Now that he was looking at it, he still didn't know what it was.

It appeared to be about three stories tall and bore a passing resemblance to an agitator in a washing machine. The upper section began to turn, slowly at first, then faster. Three mechanical arms extended above Marko and started whirling. They formed a high-speed arc around him. He tried to find a way out, but the metal arms were moving by him so quickly that he couldn't get past them. It was like being trapped inside a helicopter with propeller blades that were tilted down, blocking escape.

On the far side of the bowl, a servomotor whined as a bank of observation windows were being covered by reinforced steel blinds. The noise was sufficient to draw Marko's attention, and he desperately waved, trying to get the notice of whoever was in there. If the windows sliding into place and blocking any further view of Marko's predicament was any indicator, then Marko had failed spectacularly in his endeavor.

At that moment, as Marko felt the hair on the back of his neck standing straight up and heard the energy around him building up toward what sounded like some sort of detonation, he really, really wished he'd read that sign before jumping the fence.

Knowing that the sign screamed DANGER! HIGH ENERGY

PARTICLE PHYSICS TEST SITE! KEEP OUT! would not likely have made him feel any better.

Inside the research facility, the technicians studied the arrays on their computer screens. "Capacitators charged," Ashley Michel said, satisfied at the results she was getting.

"Right," said Chafin, confirming it. Then he saw something that didn't look quite right, and he leaned toward Blaswell. "Donnie, got a little fluctuation on one."

Adding his own concerns, O'Shea said, "There's a change in the silicon mass."

Donnie considered the possibilities and reasonably concluded, "Probably a bird." It made sense. Stupid birds saw the pile of sand at the base of the particle accelerator gun and didn't know it was there to measure molecular bonding. They thought it was someplace convenient to build a nest and lay their eggs. "It'll fly away when we fire it up."

The others nodded, satisfied with the explanation. Chafin called out, "T minus three and counting. Three . . . two . . . one . . ."

"Initiating demolecularization," announced Michel, and she activated the cycle.

The spinning arms crackled with electricity as the centrifugal force whipped up the sand around Marko. A centralized energy blast triggered an electronic ripple effect that began to spread, bathing Marko and the particles of airborne sand. Marko and the sand began to glow.

Had Marko been capable of perceiving things on a

microscopic level, he would have seen the particles of sand—single granules no larger than a period in a sentence—being broken down into their atomic components. Glowing from the intensity of the particle gun's radiation, the sand atoms slid between the atoms of Flint Marko's atomic structure, affecting Marko at a fundamental, molecular level.

Like any human, Marko was a carbon-based life-form. But that was about to change, as the glowing silicon atoms of the sand slammed into Marko's carbon atoms, knocking them out of their orbit and taking their place in his molecular structure.

It was not an isolated occurrence. The inorganic atoms of silicon dioxide—sand—penetrated Flint Marko's entire body. None of his physical makeup was spared, and he staggered under the barrage. The heaviness in the air that impaired his breathing increased until his lungs felt as if they were full of sand. Now he couldn't breathe at all. He put a hand to his chest as the sand whirled around him, peppering ever molecule of his body like a dust devil.

He twisted in place to see if the mechanical arms were slowing, if there was any way out of this. He watched in disbelief as his hand started to transform into sand.

Transform.

Into sand.

Reflexively he grabbed at his chest and felt Penny's locket nestled against it. There was no practical reason for what he did then; it was entirely instinctive. He yanked the locket free and threw it low. It bounced once, twice, and under the whirling arms, clear of whatever was happening to him.

Only in the final seconds of reflection before his hideous fate overtook him did he realize why he'd done it. His desire to protect his daughter was so overwhelming that he couldn't allow even an image of her—an image that had smiled out at him every time he had opened the locket and peered in—to come to harm. At that moment he realized he was never, ever going to see her again. That knowledge, more than the horrific transformation he was undergoing, caused him to throw back his head and scream.

Nothing emerged from his mouth except a geyser of sand.

If Flint Marko had been able to see himself, he would have witnessed his features starting to dissolve. Like a million years' worth of erosion happening all within a few seconds, his head became sand and his face began to slide off. Eyebrows, nose, his eyes, his mouth open in a silent howl of protest and then falling away, leaving his face inhumanly blank and featureless, like a department-store mannequin. *Please, no . . . she needs me . . . Penny needs her father . . . I can't die now, I can't.* Then seconds later, his entire body fell apart and was whisked away into a small whirlwind of air that looked like a sandy, brown cyclone.

"Shut it down?! Now?!?" Chafin was outraged at the timing. He was on the phone with a guard at the front gate and couldn't believe that the call had even been put

through to him. They were busy men involved in serious work—work that was finally giving them proper readouts for the first time. "You can't be serious! Why are you even calling me?"

"Because the police are here," shot back the guard from the front, sounding both irritated and nervous. "They said they're pursuing some criminal and that he's somewhere here on the base. And I didn't think it was a good idea to have them stumbling around in the dark while you're testing whatever the hell it is you guys are testing in there."

"Of all the—"

Suddenly the anomalous readings that had been reported came back to Chafin. The readings that had carelessly been chalked up to a bird. Yes, it could still have been a bird. But if a man had been down there by the gun, it would have generated the exact same readings, which could have meant . . .

Oh hell.

"Shut it down!" Chafin abruptly shouted.

Everyone gave him stunned looks, their expressions demanding explanations. There was no time to provide them. *"Shut it down! Now!"* he screamed, the urgency in his voice giving them all the impetus they needed. The particle accelerator deactivated within seconds.

As the readings spiraled to normal, Chafin realized that he was gripping the receiver so tightly that his knuckles were getting white. He forced himself to relax and said, through gritted teeth, "All right. Send them back here. But I want an escort with them at all times. Make sure they don't touch anything. We don't need them contaminating the field."

He slammed down the phone without waiting for an acknowledgment and sat back in his chair, shaken to the core. The others approached him, looking bewildered. "What happened, Al?" asked Michel. "Why'd we shut down? Everything was going fine. It was the best—"

"What would happen," Chafin said, ignoring the question and instead responding with one of his own, "if a human subject were trapped in the field that the gun generated?"

The scientists looked at each other quizzically. "Are you thinking of looking for a volunteer?" asked Donnie. "Because I don't think it's a good—"

"What would happen?" Then, as an afterthought, Chafin added offhandedly, "Hypothetically speaking."

There was a moment of silence, and then Ashley Michel said, "The subject would be dead, I suppose. If everything worked correctly, his molecules would essentially bond with the air, so he would be functionally discorporated."

"How do we know he wouldn't bond with the concrete of the pit? Or the sand?"

"We don't," Michel said reasonably. "But either way, he's dead, so what difference would it make?"

"None," Chafin admitted. "Probably none."

"Al, what's going on here?" demanded O'Shea, taking charge of the situation as the senior technician. "Are you saying there was a person down there during the test?"

Chafin pictured what the poor devil's final moments

would have been like. Would he even have understood what was happening to him? How long would his consciousness have held on? Would he actually have felt his body falling apart around him? Would he have felt nothing . . . or everything?

"I hope to God not," was all Chafin could say.

The police searched the entire grounds. They paused at the top of the large, bowl-shaped pit with the ominous-looking tower, like something out of a James Bond film, protruding from dead center. At first they wondered how in the world they were going to get down there and inspect it, then concluded that shining the searchlights down would be sufficient. There really wasn't any sort of cover where Marko could hide. Still, one of the technicians, a twitchy-looking guy with the name CHAFIN on his ID, had said they might want to check it out. Furthermore the dogs were sniffing around one of the edges and whimpering in an odd manner.

The lights played all along the interior and came to rest on the pile of sand at the bottom. There didn't seem to be any sign of Marko, and the sand certainly wasn't deep enough for Marko to have buried himself under.

"Where'd he go?" wondered one of the cops. The others shrugged. They continued to shine the light down there for long moments, making absolutely certain there wasn't some hatchway or other means of egress that might have eluded them at first glance. Finally, satisfied that wherever Flint Marko had made off to it wasn't here, they turned their attentions elsewhere. Curiously, they practically had to drag the dogs away, since the stupid mutts seemed determined to haul the cops down into that pit in pursuit of nothing more than a pile of sand.

A pile where, had they looked very, very closely, the police would have seen the glint of a half-buried locket that had slid back down from the edge and come to rest in the sand, as if returning safely home.

VI

DEAD FATHERS

LYING TO THE POLICE officer had been the toughest thing for Peter, but he had done it with confidence and aplomb.

As he sat in the waiting room, apprehensively watching the sun crawl over the horizon and wondering if Harry would be alive to see it, he decided that—in retrospect—it hadn't been that difficult after all. He was still so shaken after the night's events and revelations that his vagueness had come across to the cop as genuine shock. The hospital had naturally summoned the police officer when Peter had informed them that Harry was the victim of a hit and run. The cop had sat opposite Peter, notepad in hand, and asked him to recall everything he could. His expression had appeared neutral, but Peter could tell the cop—an older uniformed officer with a lined face who had seen far too many innocent people hurt in his career—was eyeing him closely, looking for some indication of drug or alcohol influence. Was this really a random accident, or a couple of doped up young guys who got themselves in big trouble?

In Harry's case, of course, it really was closer to the latter. But they could run all the drug/alcohol tests on Harry's blood they wanted, and they still weren't going to detect whatever the hell it was that Harry had put into his system that had transformed him into the New Goblin. As for Peter, clearly articulate and earnest as the day was long, he was so obviously not under the influence of anything that the cop relaxed in short order and simply listened.

What he heard was a story that Peter kept deliberately vague. They'd been up all night cramming for school—or more accurately, Peter had been cramming and Harry had been helping. They were hungry, there was nothing in the fridge. They'd decided to go out, see if they could find an all-night eatery. Harry had started to cross the street; Peter had looked away to see if he could spot someplace down the street. Then came the screeching of tires, the hideous thud, and he'd looked back. There was Harry lying in the street, a car speeding away. A dark car. Blue, he thought, but hard to be sure. No, he hadn't gotten the make or license.

"You shouldn't have moved him," the cop said in a severe tone. "Could've done him more harm than good."

"I didn't know that," Peter said, looking down, as he had been much of the time. Now he looked up, though, and said with absolute sincerity, "I hope to God I didn't kill him."

The cop allowed a gentle, almost paternal smile and said, "You've got the best doctors in the world right here at this hospital. If anyone can help your friend, they can."

Peter suspected that they said that at every hospital, but he accepted the reassurance for what it was worth.

The cop was now long gone, after giving Peter his card

and asking him to contact him if he remembered any more details. Peter continued to pace nervously. He glanced at the clock on the wall to see how much time had passed and realized with a start that he was supposed to have gotten together with Mary Jane for a late breakfast that morning. He quickly phoned her and got her machine. Assuming that she was in the shower or otherwise occupied, he left a terse message, a *Reader's Digest* version of what he'd told the cop.

Then it was back to waiting, until finally he saw a doctor exiting the intensive care unit. Peter instantly recognized him as the doctor who had asked him earlier what had caused Harry's condition. Peter rushed over, moving so quickly that the doctor was startled and stepped back in surprise. "How is he?" Peter blurted in a rush.

"You a relative?" asked the doctor.

Peter considered claiming that he was. But then the doctor might start asking for ID, and it could get embarrassing. Besides, Peter was sick to death of lying. "His best friend," he said. The doctor made a face that indicated Peter had no business inquiring, and that the doctor shouldn't even be speaking to him, so Peter added, "His parents are both dead. He's an only child, so . . ." He took a deep breath and let it out. "I'm all the family he's got."

The doctor clearly considered what Peter was saying, then nodded once as if satisfied. "He's going to be okay . . ." he said, and Peter immediately felt as if a huge weight had been lifted from his shoulders. Then he grew tense as he sensed a *but* coming. Sure enough: "But there's been some memory impairment. Particularly his short-term memory. Right now he can't remember the accident or much of anything that's happened to him recently." His tone shifted from clinical to sympathetic. "You can see him now if you'd like."

Peter was apprehensive, unsure of just how much Harry had forgotten. Perhaps he didn't recall the details of the battle, sure, but did he remember the events that had led up to it? "Is it permanent?" he asked.

"Could be," said the doctor, and he started to move away, clearly heading somewhere else. "Only time will tell." As an afterthought he called over his shoulder, "Keep it brief. I want him to rest."

Peter watched him go and, steeling himself for the worst-case scenario, entered the ICU.

He asked an orderly to point him in the direction of Harry Osborn's bed, since all the sections were curtained off, and he didn't want to start poking around. The orderly scowled a moment, and Peter quickly said the doctor had given him permission for a short visit, even though visitors weren't typically allowed in the ICU. The orderly obviously wasn't sure if Peter was lying, but apparently didn't feel like calling him on it. Instead he simply pointed toward one curtained area, then added, "Make it quick."

Peering around the curtain, Peter saw Harry lying in bed, eyes closed. Tubes were running in and out of him, his chest rising and falling slowly, with a steady beep from the various monitors. *How did it come to this? My God, how did it come to this?* Peter thought bleakly.

He was about to turn away and leave when he saw Harry's eyes open into narrow slits. At first they didn't seem to focus on Peter at all. Then Harry's stare latched onto Peter, and there was a moment of confusion. Peter was certain at that point that Harry had no idea who his visitor was.

But to Peter's surprise, Harry smiled slightly, although in a pained manner, as if the mere stretching of his mouth muscles hurt, and he said softly, "Hey, buddy."

It was the first time in an age, it seemed, that Harry had addressed him in a manner that sounded like . . . old times. Scarcely daring to believe it, Peter—working hard to control his emotions—said in an offhanded manner, "Hey," as if he and Harry had accidentally bumped into each other on the street.

Harry raised a hand to his forehead, taking care not to jostle the tube that was inserted into the hand. "Hit my head."

"Yeah." Peter remained cautious, not wanting to say too much, fearful of triggering some emotion or recollection that could shred the moment. He felt as if he were watching slowly hardening concrete. If he did nothing to disturb it, then it would dry smooth and flat. The last thing he wanted to do was scrawl Spider-Man's initials in there.

Frowning, Harry said, "Doctor said I was . . ." He paused, trying to recall. "Hit and run, he said. Can't remember. Did they get him?"

Briefly, Peter had no idea who the "him" was. He thought Harry was referring to the doctor. Then Peter remembered that a mythical person had been driving a mythical car that he himself had created, and it was important that Harry continue to believe that. "Not yet. They will," Peter assured him.

"Can't remember much of anything. I'm . . . thinking about my dad." He sounded bewildered, as if he couldn't figure out why that would be the case.

Peter didn't know why either, but if it was because Harry was remembering that he had followed his father's lead and become a cackling, flying maniac out for blood, he sure didn't want his friend's thoughts to continue in that direction. "Doctor wants you to rest," he said.

"My dad," Harry persisted. "He . . ."

Peter braced himself.

"He died . . . didn't he?" He looked up at Peter with great pools of sadness in his eyes. "Did he die?"

It was all Peter could do not to let out a wholly inappropriate sigh of relief, then instantly regretted it. How could Peter be glad that Harry's first moment of clarity was the realization that he was an orphan? Reining in his emotions, Peter said, "Yes. He did."

Harry took that in with the air of a tourist who just had some interesting sight pointed out to him. "This is all so weird," he said finally. "It's like I'm looking at my life from a hundred miles away. Like I'm on the outside looking in, and it's happening to some other guy. Know what I mean?"

"More than you can possibly believe," Peter said ruefully.

The curtain was suddenly pushed aside. Peter expected it to be an orderly shooing him out. Instead it was an out-of-breath Mary Jane. Her hair was slightly damp, confirming Peter's earlier supposition as to her whereabouts. He had no idea how she had managed to talk her way into the ICU and chalked it up to the notion that, once Mary Jane Watson was determined to go somewhere, nothing short of a brick wall was going to stop her.

"Hi. Got here fast as I could," she said, except it was all in a rush and came out *HigoderefasdIkood.* She stopped, composed herself, then struck a casual pose that was amusing in its breathtaking artificiality. With a sideways flip of her hair, she said chipperly, "Hello, Harry."

A genuine, huge grin lit up his expression. "I know that face," he declared.

She walked over to him and took his untubed hand gently in hers. "How you doing?"

"I don't know," he said honestly, and frowned. "Last thing I remember I was fine . . . somewhere."

"The doctor says you're going to be okay," she assured him, answering for Peter the question of how MJ had gotten in here. She'd obviously caught up with the attending physician and had had little trouble managing to sweet-talk him. Hell, he was probably down in the gift shop at the moment buying her flowers. "That's all that matters."

"It's good to have you back," Peter said, meaning that in a way that neither Harry nor Mary Jane was going to fully appreciate.

Patting the back of Harry's hand, MJ whispered, "Get some sleep."

Harry was starting to fade. "Thanks for coming . . ."

A nurse stepped in, mastering an expression that allowed her to look both compassionate and yet firm. "I'm sorry, I have to scoot you out," she said to them. "He needs to rest."

She certainly had good timing. Peter had ascertained everything he needed to know, at least for the time being. It was a good idea to get out now while Harry was still thinking of Peter as his friend, rather than the evil creature who had killed his father. Let the former impression sink in and become the lasting one. "See you tomorrow," he told Harry.

Harry nodded slightly, sinking toward sleep, and half-raised his hand in farewell. As Peter and Mary Jane stepped around the curtain and headed out, he could hear the nurse say to Harry, "You have lovely friends."

"My best friends. I'd . . . give my . . . life for them," Harry said, each word suffused with fatigue. Then, a few moments later, he heard Harry say, both by way of informing the nurse and coming to terms with it himself, "My father died."

Peter closed his eyes tightly against the sting of tears he felt welling up in them. For the life of him, he didn't know whether he wanted to cry out of sympathy or relief.

The bottom of the pit where the particle gun had been tested remained in shadow for a good part of the morning. As noon approached, the continually rising sun finally stretched its rays to the bottom, chasing away the shadows and illuminating a bit of glinting metal that was a little girl's locket.

The sand lay there in a pile.

The police officers were long gone, reluctantly reporting to their superiors that a golden opportunity, not to mention man-hours, had been wasted. Flint Marko had gotten away somehow.

The scientists had never mentioned the anomalous readings that might have been a major clue as to Marko's whereabouts, or more accurately, lack of whereabouts. The scientists' caution was understandable: they were balancing the fate of one random thug against an intense investigation into exactly the type of work that was being done in the facility. Police reports were matters of public record, and the scientists simply didn't need too much information leaking out for anyone's consumption, specifically journalists.

The project had temporarily been shut down while the scientists concentrated on studying the readings and results of the previous night.

Thus, no one was around to see the sand in the bottom of the pit beginning to stir. At first glance it would have seemed that a vagrant breeze was responsible. Moments passed and then the sand started to undulate in a way that could not be explained by anything in nature. Stray particles from all over the pit started moving, seemingly of their own volition. They streamed toward the center area, and other streams joined in, like multiple branches of a river. More and more came together, particles that had been blown or carried as high as the top of the pit. Soon every grain of sand in the area had met in the center of the pit, forming one large pile.

The pile began to move.

Slowly at first and then more quickly, the growing

mound began to take the shape of a man. Initially it was little more than a crude form, like a featureless sculpture made by a five-year-old. Then the face began to define itself. A mouth appeared where there had been none before, then thin lips. The mouth wasn't closed, but open wide, frozen in the shape of a scream, as if it were constructing itself in accordance with the last memory it carried. No voice emerged from it, and then tongue and teeth became visible, although still little more than vague outlines. There was a loud gasping for breath, but it was more habit than anything else since there weren't truly any lungs to suck the air into.

Like an hourglass running in reverse, the sandy form began to bear a resemblance to an unfinished sculpture of Flint Marko. It was doubtful that anyone in his family would have recognized him. In fact, it was unlikely that Marko himself would have been able to gaze at a reflection of the flat, featureless creature that had seeped into existence and know it to be him.

At that moment, Marko was scarcely able to comprehend his own existence. He felt as if he were looking in a million directions at once, as if every molecule (*particle, grain*) of his body (*form*) was infused with its own little piece of his consciousness. Worse, each wanted to go in a different direction. Just trying to hold his body together was like undertaking the notoriously problematic job of herding cats. It was all Marko could do to focus sufficiently and form the sketchy outline of a human being.

His awareness had likewise been scattered to the four winds, but as he physically pulled himself together, his shattered consciousness began to reassert itself. He held up the extended, crudely shaped, sandy stumps that constituted his arms and stared at them *(how are you staring? You have no finished eyes. What part of you is seeing this? All of you. Every particle of your body is aware of every other part. It's just a matter of figuring out how to use it. You have to. Penny needs you to)* with only the slightest dawning of comprehension *(there was a thing above you. The thing that made a noise like a million screaming bees. It did something to you. It made you a freak. Penny's father is a freak. Oh my God, oh my God, what will Penny say, oh my)* of his predicament. He looked down *(you don't need to. You already know what you're going to see because that part of your body is already seeing it)* and saw that his body ended at the waist. He was merged with the ground. To an observer, it might almost have appeared comical. He looked like some poor sap who had fallen asleep at the beach, and some kids had come along and buried him *(except this ain't no day at the beach. Haw! Laugh. That's right. Laugh, clown, laugh, so you won't scream, because if you start screaming, you're never gonna stop)*.

("He always cried.")

The disdainful words of his wife came back to him, and he knew them to be true because he was crying now at the freak he had become. His shoulders were slumped, and they began to shake with great racking sobs, but there were no tears. He had no tear ducts. Or eyes. Or bodily organs of any sort. His existence was completely impossible, and he couldn't shake the feeling that he'd be better off dead, except he wasn't entirely sure that he wasn't already dead. This might just be some bizarre form of hell on earth, and he was suffering this torment for everything he had done wrong.

Then the glint of something shining in the sunlight caught his *(no eye, you have no eye, not one, not two, nothing you freak, you)* attention. It was buried in the outer perimeter of the sandy base that formed his lower body, and he seeped tentatively toward it. Spiraling into hopelessness, he drew desperate succor from that glint and everything it represented.

It lay half open in the sand, and he reached for it. He found that his crudely shaped hand was unable to grasp it. It slipped through his fingers *(like sand, isn't that just too sick for words)* and for a moment despair threatened to seize him once more. He pushed it away, determined not to allow that to happen. There was no way that he was going to be so close to the locket and everything it stood for, his one link to humanity, and fail.

Burning with furious intensity, he closed his hand. He remembered the story about the sculptor who claimed that the secret to his art was simplicity itself: all he needed to do was chip away everything that didn't resemble the image he had in his mind. Marko now followed that same philosophy. He visualized exactly what he wanted his hand to look like. He didn't stop until he could see it perfectly, and then he willed the vague, mittenlike appendage at the end of his hand to mimic it. Fingers began to form, and they were still made of sand, but they were clear and distinct and—most important—hard. Tentatively, almost afraid to find out whether it would work, he reached down and gasped with joy as the newly created fingers deftly picked up the locket. He raised it so that it was at eye level and gazed at the image of the smiling, young girl within.

In a gravely, raspy voice, Marko said softly, "Penny."

Just speaking her name aloud was enough to galvanize his determination. He had been given a second chance at survival. More, he started to realize that he had been thinking of his status all wrong. Yes, he was a freak, but that didn't mean that it made him less than a man, less than human. If he could pull himself together, so to speak, he could become far more than either. Penny's picture, her name said aloud, the thought of what he could accomplish on her behalf, provided all the incentive he required; indeed, all that and more.

Marko became emboldened, as if he were truly alive for the first time in his existence. He had no internal organs, no blood, no heart. But the locket substituted for that most vital of organs as he clutched it against his chest tightly and drew strength from it. Willing himself to stand, he started to rise, the sand beneath him coming together to form rudimentary legs.

I'm doing it, I'm doing it!

He celebrated his success too soon, as the sandy columns proved inadequate to support his weight. He crumbled like the tower of a child's sand castle. Moments earlier that would have been enough to cause him to break down in despair, but it was now no longer the case. He was convinced he was going to triumph over his present circumstances. That it was simply a matter of when, not if. Marko took a mental step back and envisioned once more what he wanted the lower half of his body to do. The legs reformed, this time more dense than before. Quickly, before he could topple once more, he willed feet to come into existence. They did so, supporting him and providing balance where he'd had none earlier.

He stayed there for a time, just making certain that he could keep this up. He didn't want to rush his first step. He had plenty of time. After all, no one ever saw sand on a beach in a hurry, did they? Human rules and priorities no longer applied to him. He was of the earth now. Immortal? Quite possibly. Like unto a god? Too soon to say, but it couldn't be ruled out.

He took an unsteady step forward. It was difficult recapturing muscle memory when one didn't have any actual muscles anymore, but he was going to do his best. He couldn't help but think he probably bore a strong resemblance to Frankenstein's monster, lurching forward with his arms outstretched to help maintain his balance, staggering one step at a time. That was only temporary, though. Soon he would be walking relatively normally. He would sculpt his body so that it was indistinguishable from what it had been before. Yet anyone who thought that he or she could approach him, deal with him, treat him the way that Flint Marko had been treated before, was going to discover that there had been a major paradigm shift.

To his ex-wife, he had been a figure of contempt upon whom she could blame everything wrong with her life. To the cops, he was just a dumb con, a slob who had gotten lucky in eluding them for as long as he had and deserved to rot in jail.

Only Penny had seen the real Flint Marko. Only Penny

loved him, and yet she was the one that a cruel god was intent on removing from the world. Now it seemed, though, that God wasn't as cruel as Marko had been supposing. Marko had been given this amazing gift, and he was going to use it for all it was worth.

He was going to use it to help Penny, reward her for her love and devotion.

Penny Marko's dead father had risen from his grave, and heaven help anyone who got in his way—for if they sowed the storm, they would reap the sandstorm.

VII

PRIORITIES

MARY JANE WATSON SPRINTED up the stairwell in Peter's apartment building, clutching the newspaper to her chest. She was doing everything she could to keep herself together, furious over her self-pity and inability to remember what was important. Mere hours ago she had been at the hospital where Harry Osborn might well have died. Yet he had survived, and wasn't that really far more important than the contents of the paper she was holding? Didn't one really have to prioritize in life and—

She stopped, gripped the stairwell railing as a wave of nausea passed over her, and realized she was coming close to throwing up because she was so upset. She waited until the impulse was gone, then made it the rest of the way up the stairs. She banged on the door and heard a distracted "Yeah?" from within. Obviously Peter was studying. He always sounded as if he were speaking to her from the surface of Mars when his mind was occupied with his schoolbooks. Normally she found it charming.

This day she found nothing charming.

"It's me," she said. Peter had given her a key to the

front door of the apartment building in which he lived, but she needed his aid to come into the apartment.

"Hey! Come in!" his voice came.

She rolled her eyes in annoyance. "You know I can't open the door!"

"Pull, lift, and give it a good shove." He still sounded distracted. Clearly he was in the middle of studying and didn't want to be bothered to get up. At that moment she would have kicked the door open if she weren't afraid of breaking her leg. She wasn't ruling out the possibility of kicking *him,* though.

"Just come on and help me!" Her tone of voice made it clear that she was fed up, and if he didn't get off his ass and open up, she was going to turn around and leave, and it would be a cold day in hell before she saw him again.

Obviously she had managed to convey her mood exactly, because she heard the sound of a chair being pushed back from the desk (yep, studying), and moments later Peter swung the door open and looked at her quizzically. She held up the newspaper in response. Clearly he didn't understand, because he said, "What?"

"The review," she replied icily.

"The review! I forgot!" He hit his forehead with the base of his hand and obviously thought he knew what the problem was. He assumed she was annoyed with him because he'd forgotten that her play's opening-night notices were going to be hitting the streets. She was holding the *New York Times,* unarguably the foremost paper in setting critical perception for New York City. Indeed, most of the other papers were irrelevant. The *Times* could make or break you. "How was it? Great?"

She felt her throat constricting with fury. "They hated it. They hated me."

Peter looked as if he thought either Mary Jane had read it wrong or he had heard her wrong. "They can't hate you," he assured her, as if she had said something on par with announcing that Congress had endeavored to repeal the law of gravity.

In response, she turned to the Arts and Leisure section and began to read aloud. She uttered each word in a tense, clipped manner. " 'The young Miss Watson is a pretty girl, easy on the eyes but not on the ears. Her small voice didn't carry past the first row.' "

"That's ridiculous," Peter assured her. "I was there."

"You were *in* the first row."

"So something was wrong with the acoustics. Or the sound guys didn't have you wired properly. Any one of a hundred technical things, none of which have anything to do with you or your performance." Seeing she wasn't mollified, he took the newspaper from her, tossed it aside, and put his hands gently on her shoulders. "Listen, you have to know you were great. This is something you just have to get used to. You can't take it so personally. I've been through it. Spider-Man gets attacked all the time—"

"Spider-Man isn't your real name! At least you have something to hide behind! I don't!" Here Peter was nattering on about his alter ego? How could he not understand? "This isn't about you; it's about me!" she snapped at him, probably more angrily than she should have, but she didn't care. "It's about my career!"

"I know. Exactly," he said, as if they were on the same wavelength when she knew they weren't. "And all you have to do is believe in yourself and pull yourself together and get right back up on that—"

She clamped a hand over his surprised mouth. "Don't give me the horse thing." He nodded in mute acknowledgment, and she removed her hand, but she was no less frustrated. Why was someone as intelligent as Peter being so dense? "Try to understand how I feel. I look at these words and it's like . . . like my father wrote them."

Understanding dawned on Peter's face. He knew full well that Mary Jane's father had lived for tearing her down at every opportunity. When she had wanted to embark on her acting career, her father had been her first and loudest critic. She had been determined to prove him wrong in his negative assessment of her abilities. Now it was looking as if her father was correct.

Peter took a moment to regroup and started to open his mouth to reply, when the police radio he kept on his desk crackled to life. Keyed in to the emergency frequency, it only went active when something truly major was hitting the band. That happened now, and Mary Jane saw Peter wince as the voice—static-filled since Peter's eavesdropping connection wasn't exactly legal—announced, "All units in the vicinity of Fifty-sixth and Madison, report. Large crane out of control. Approach with caution, Fifty-sixth and Madison. Pedestrians in danger."

Instantly, Mary Jane felt conflicted. Part of her wanted

Peter to ignore it, to focus on her. On the other hand, how could she be that selfish? Yes, her career was on the line, her ego was on the line, but so were lives. Careers could be rebuilt, shattered egos restored, but dead was dead. If Peter could save their lives . . .

She hated this. She hated that she couldn't even seek solace from her boyfriend without it turning into a major soul-searching referendum on her priorities as a woman and a human being.

Peter stared at her, waiting for some clue as to what she was thinking. She gave none. She just gazed at him with an impassive face. She didn't even give him the slightest twitch of an expression when the sound of a siren blew in the front window. As if he were prompting her because she'd missed a cue, he said hopefully, "Go get 'em, tiger?"

He never even considered staying for me.

But . . . what did you want him to say? "Don't worry, honey, let people's lives be at risk. This is more important."

Except this is more important, to me at least.

My God, how can you even think that?

She lowered her head, feeling frustrated, feeling ashamed, feeling angry that she had come seeking emotional support, and all she had gotten was more frustration and conflict. First the review had belittled her talent. Now she herself was belittling her values as a person. A little more support like this and she'd be ready to throw herself off the roof.

There was a sound at the window and she turned and realized that, as she'd been standing there zoning out in distraction, Peter had changed into his costume and was standing at the open window, his mask in his hand, one foot on the sill.

"Wait for me?" he asked, hopeful.

Mary Jane made no reply, since she had no clue as to whether she would.

He pulled on his mask, fired a webline, and swung away. Mary Jane stared for a long time at the open window, at the emptiness that it represented. There was something tremendously symbolic in that.

She remembered when she'd sprinted here in her wedding dress, convinced that she had been running toward something. Now she began to wonder if instead she'd simply been running away from something else. She felt lonely, directionless. Support from critics hadn't been there for her professionally; support from Peter hadn't been there emotionally.

Yet she felt guilty for feeling this way, and perhaps that was what rankled her most of all. She wondered if this was how a doctor's wife felt, always playing second fiddle to the needs of her husband's patients. That wasn't really the same, though. A successful doctor's wife had a home, and friends, and at least she didn't have to worry about her husband being killed on the job. She supposed she was closer to a policeman's wife. Even then, though, an entire support system was in place: other spouses of cops who understood the risks, plus a salary, benefits.

Mary Jane was in a unique club. She had no one to whom she could talk about her feelings, no one to share her frustrations or concerns. She had thought she had

Peter, but it was Spider-Man who really had Peter, had possessed him, taken him over. She had believed she could understand, had wanted to be supportive. But she desperately needed to be the focus of Peter's world. Not all the time. Just occasionally she had to know that she came first.

She glared at the radio that was continuing its distress warning and had an epiphany—she would never, ever come first. Total strangers would always be more important to Peter than she was.

It both galled and mortified her that she was angry about it. What the hell kind of match was such a selfish girl with such an unselfish guy?

Mary Jane walked over to the desk where his open science books lay, afforded them a quick glance, crumpled the newspaper, and dumped it in the trash can. She headed for the door, pulled it open, then turned and glanced back at the room once more, wondering if she was ever going to set foot in it again.

Something curious caught her eye. Peter, a typical guy, had left clothes strewn around, and she noticed his dress shoes lying in the corner in the shadows. One of them had a huge chunk of what looked like black tar on the sole. She wondered what in the world Peter had stepped in.

She picked the shoe up and glanced around to find a rag to clean it off, then stopped herself and wondered just how much of a glutton for punishment she was. Peter had ditched her to go off and be a hero; she was an emotional wreck over it, and she was going to fix his shoes in the midst of all that?

Mary Jane shook her head at her own foolishness, tossed the shoe aside, walked out the door, and closed it behind her.

The shoe landed in the sunlight near the radio. The radio blared loudly, and feedback caused a high, shrill tone to cut through the air. As soon as that happened, the ebony substance on Peter's shoe pulsed, flexed, then peeled itself off the sole. It left a small part of itself behind, but didn't seem especially slowed by it. It moved quickly away from the sunlight, away from the radio, undulating across the floor as fast as it could. Within seconds it had made it to the cool, quiet darkness of the closet, slithering inside and taking refuge in the shadows once more.

Unaware of the unearthly drama unfolding in the apartment she'd just left, Mary Jane was walking down the hallway when she found her way blocked by Ursula, the wafer-thin daughter of Peter's landlord. Mary Jane had spotted her before, looking at Peter with the puppy-dog eyes that only a teen girl with a hopeless crush could possibly effect. *Just hold out hope, kid. Maybe someday soon you'll be old enough so you can have your heart cut in half too.*

"Hi, Mary Jane," Ursula said with forced perkiness.

"Hi." MJ started to step around her, in no mood for conversation.

Ursula didn't move aside. MJ didn't think she was being rude; she was just oblivious to the fact that Mary Jane wanted to leave. "How's Peter?" Ursula asked.

"He went out."

From the blinking surprise in Ursula's face, Mary Jane instantly realized she'd given the wrong answer. Who knew how long Ursula had been standing there? She would have known that Peter hadn't gone past her. And she was too credulous to consider the possibility that Mary Jane might be lying and Peter was still up in his apartment. Still, she sounded dubious as she said, "He always goes so fast."

"Very fast." Seeing that Ursula wasn't moving anytime soon, and surrendering to the inevitability of a conversation, she forced herself to appear interested as she asked, "What are you up to?"

"Not much. Washing dishes at a jazz club." Since that clearly wasn't especially interesting, she added, "The waitresses sing. I can't sing. Can you sing?"

Of all questions to ask.

She thought of Peter's excuses as to how the critics got it wrong. But she also considered that, if she'd read that review about someone else, she would have taken the critic's assessment at face value. *So why then, but not now?*

Making one of the most difficult admissions she'd ever uttered, Mary Jane said, "I don't know."

VIII

THE EYES OF EDDIE BROCK

UNAWARE THAT ALL HELL was about to break loose, the photo shoot in the law offices of Miller and Ingersoll, Esq., continued blissfully along with music blaring and photographer clicking.

The offices had been rented for the day—no big deal since both attorneys were in court—by the publishers of an office supply catalog. Three comely models . . . a blonde, a brunette, and a redhead . . . were draping themselves over the latest-model office copier and desperately trying to make mundane photocopying look sexy.

They were oblivious that, just outside at a construction site, a crane operator had been hoisting a massive steel girder above the street. Warning lights had flashed on the control panel within the cab, and the crane operator had struggled desperately to bring things back under his command. His efforts were well-intentioned but futile, and he had screamed into the microphone connecting him to the foreman, "I've lost control! Shut it down!"

His foreman tried to do just that, but was thwarted by the very problem that had caused the controls to go out of whack in the first place: a short in the transformer. Sparks flew out of it, several of them bouncing against a sign with an interchangeable number slot on it that read: SEVENTY-NINE DAYS ACCIDENT FREE! leaving small scorch marks. The foreman had yanked the shut-off override switch and, instead of shutting down the crane, had received a sizable jolt that blew him backward.

The crane began to swing wildly, and all its erstwhile operator could do was watch in horror and wish for a miracle.

Meanwhile, the three models alternated chatting about guy matters while tossing smiles at the photographer. The brunette was an exotic-looking Latina named J. J. Sachs, with a mane of curly, black hair and olive skin. She exuded sexuality the way that other mere mortals exuded sweat. The redhead, Wendy Goldstein, had a slightly round face and short-cropped hair. Of the three, she was having the toughest time making upbeat expressions. Clearly, a good deal was on her mind, and the smile that she plastered onto her face at the photographer's command seemed forced.

The blond model attempted to forestall any problems that Wendy might be having by offering advice. The blonde was Gwen Stacy, Peter Parker's lab partner at Empire State University, and as she struck a pose in which she was caressing the photocopier, she urged Wendy, "Don't fight with him. It doesn't fix anything."

"But that's all he wants to do," Wendy complained.

"Well, tell him if all you do is talk about the relationship, there's no time to have one."

"Everybody hold it!" called Ernie Schultz, the heavyset

and increasingly annoyed photographer, liking the position they were in. He fired off a few quick shots, but when Wendy opened her mouth to address Gwen, he anticipated it by calling out, "Stop talking! Hold it!" Wendy's mouth snapped shut like a lobster trap, and he continued, "Give me office efficiency but with bedroom eyes. Not sleepy, Wendy!"

Gwen was beginning to feel exhausted. She had no aspirations toward being a model. She'd just answered the call for the gig on the university bulletin board as a means of picking up some extra money. She'd figured, *How hard could it be to stand around and get your picture taken while smiling?* Gwen was getting the answer. Her face was starting to hurt, and she was certain that her smile looked as artificial as it felt. She was copping a feel on a photocopying machine, for heaven's sake. How was someone supposed to get enthused about something like that?

Clearly Ernie was getting a sense of her frustration. He lowered his camera and said impatiently, "Look, I know you're new at this, but you're not giving me what I need. I need"—he groped for the right words—"I need mystery . . . I need . . ."

"A new personality?" Gwen suggested with wide-eyed innocence.

Wendy and J.J. choked back laughter, but the photographer completely missed the veiled insult. "Yes!" he declared as if the Holy Grail had just been presented him. "Some life! Some . . ."

He had been peering through the viewfinder, trying to compose a different shot, and now he was looking up in annoyance. "Now what's that thing doing in my background?"

His "background" consisted of a New York skyline visible out the wide windows behind them. Gwen turned to see what he was talking about, and at first she wasn't clear on what she was seeing either. It was moving quickly, but the shadows of the skyscrapers were obscuring it and she couldn't . . .

Then her eyes widened in horror as she saw the massive arm of a construction crane swinging toward them at high speed. Dangling beneath it was a teetering girder.

Gwen was paralyzed with denial, certain the thing wasn't going to hit. Or perhaps she was dreaming of something that she had seen in an action or disaster movie.

She remained that way for several precious seconds until her mind processed reality. Then, as the wildly swinging girder hurtled toward them, she screamed, *"Get down!"*

Everyone dove to the floor as the spinning girder shattered the window. Glass flew everywhere. Gwen kept her eyes shut, terrified of being blinded by flying shards, as small pieces of broken window littered her hair. The girder kept going, smashing lighting fixtures, sending sparks flying, and annihilating a row of desks, reducing them to splinters. Then, just as quickly and surreally as it had appeared, the girder was whisked out the window.

Ernie Schultz, Gwen, J.J., and Wendy slowly got to their feet. Standing in the middle of the office wreckage, they quietly marveled at not only the amount of destruction, but that they were still alive to see it. Still stunned, they picked their way through it, inspecting the damage. Impressed by the photographic possibilities the devastation offered, Ernie snapped off a few shots.

A high-pitched whistling of wind filled the wrecked office. As one, they turned and saw a massive shadow sweeping over them.

"It's coming back!" shouted Ernie.

Having no desire to press their luck and uncertain they'd be fortunate enough to survive a second pass, the four bolted for the door. The girder suddenly dipped, swung low, and slammed into the building one story below them.

That was way too close, thought Gwen.

Ernie was leading the way or, more likely, was just trying to save his own ass, as he threw open the door and charged through. Wendy was right behind him, with J.J. and Gwen bringing up the rear.

Suddenly the entire office violently tilted, as if it were constructed on a gigantic seesaw. The girder must have taken out the structural support columns in the floor below them, and now the entire office structure where they were was pitching downward at a forty-five-degree angle.

J.J. had been sliding as well, but she had grabbed hold of a metal strut in the floor that had been ripped open by the girder's initial pass through. She threw her arm out, trying to snag the sliding Gwen . . . but Gwen went right past her.

The open window yawned before Gwen as she went toward it, grabbing at the smooth floor and unable to find purchase. She tried slapping her open hands flat on the floor, perhaps in the vain hope that she might suddenly acquire adhesive powers like Spider-Man. This only slowed her down for a few seconds. Meantime, pencils, cans of soda, and rolling chairs skidded past her, tumbling out the smashed window and falling to the street below.

She would inevitably have followed, save that a ringing telephone of all things grabbed her attention. It had fallen off one of the smashed desks, and the cord was jacked into the wall. She snagged the receiver as she slid past, and receiver, phone unit, and Gwen all started to slide toward oblivion. Miraculously the cord, all of $2.49 at RadioShack, remained affixed to the wall, stubbornly refusing to release its hold.

Everything that wasn't bolted down slid past Gwen and out. Clinging wildly, she heard a tinny voice coming through the phone receiver.

"Hello! Hello?!" she screamed.

The voice on the phone came back at her with sunny cheerfulness that didn't exactly match the moment. "You've got the rockin' sound of WKRQ! If you can name our last two "Two for Tuesday" songs, you could be our grand-prize winner!"

"Help! I can't hold on!" she shrieked at the receiver.

"Right you are!" chirped the DJ. " 'Help' and 'I Can't Hold On'! Pack your bags, 'cause you're going on a trip!"

With a remarkable, if morbid, sense of comic timing, the telephone cord chose that moment to give up the ghost. It snapped, and Gwen continued toward the open window. It waited for her like the maw of a great beast, knowing that sooner or later patience would pay off, and it would swallow her up.

She slid right out the window but, at the last second, snagged a jutting piece of the steel window frame.

Dangling in midair, her legs pinwheeling as if she were riding an invisible bicycle, Gwen Stacy hung one hundred stories above the street.

In an insane digression, her mind flashed to when she was a little girl and had leaned too far out the bedroom window of her Queens home. Before she could tumble out, a hand reached out and grabbed her. The terrified child, realizing how close she had come to seriously injuring herself, sobbed into the chest of the man who had saved her. "I'm sorry, Daddy!" she had wailed, afraid that she was going to be punished. Instead her father had simply held her close, whispered that it was going to be okay, that her being all right was the only thing that mattered, and he assured her in that low, gravelly voice of his, "I'll never let you fall."

The frightened little girl in Gwen Stacy now irrationally wondered where her father was, and if he was going to make good on his promise.

Half a dozen police cars were already on the scene when police captain George Stacy leaped out of his vehicle. He was tall, with an angular face and eyes that alternated between being kind and understanding or fiercely penetrating and threatening, depending upon whether he was dealing with a victim or a suspected criminal.

Now they were filled only with concern.

A police officer, DeFalco, rushed up to him. "They got some kind of short up there, and they can't shut down the crane."

"Get Con Ed on the phone," Captain Stacy ordered. "Have them kill the power to the whole block."

"Yes, sir!"

"And get me a rescue team up there!" he shouted.

People screamed as debris started hitting the streets. The crowd, pressing forward like curious sheep to get a better look, almost stampeded trying to get back out of the way, as various pieces of office furniture tumbled from high above and either crashed to the pavement or ricocheted off parked cars. Car alarms howled in protest as the vehicles' roofs and hoods were crushed by plummeting furniture.

The crowd scampered backward. Stacy looked at the falling debris and thought, *Dear God, please, no bodies.*

Dear God, please, let's see some bodies.

Fresh-faced, short-cropped-blond Eddie Brock, camera equipment hanging from a strap around his neck, with an expression like a starving dog seeing fresh meat dangled in front of him, came rolling up to the site of the crane emergency in a yellow cab. He'd practically had to throw himself in the taxi's path to grab it.

Anyone else would have considered it a fluke that Brock, tossing back drinks in a local bar, had seen the unfolding crisis on a news report and realized it was only ten blocks away. But Eddie Brock didn't believe in luck—he believed in destiny, and he further believed that he was destined for greatness. And no cab with the pathetic excuse of being off duty was going to deter him from getting over to the scene of an accident as fast as humanly possible, camera at the ready.

As he clambered out of the cab, telling the driver to keep the change, he slapped his *Daily Bugle* identification on his sweater so that the police could tell at a glance that he was not one of the mere masses. He was a man with a job to do, same as they had. With any luck, neither of them would get in each other's way while they were doing it.

Brock approached the scene with a very different mental attitude from Captain Stacy's—he was looking for the most dramatic shots. He heard someone shouting, "Get that taxi out of here!" but the cab was already on its way out. Brock sidestepped a police rescue team and brought his camera up, looking for something truly juicy. He fired off several quick shots of the girder flapping around in midair, but he knew even as he did so that it was boring. The almighty newspaper axiom was *if it bleeds, it leads.* The ideal situation would be to get a shot of someone plummeting to his or her death. That was page-one material. That was the stuff that Pulitzers were made of.

Never once did Eddie Brock question the ethics or morality of his way of thinking. Why should he? It wasn't as if he had set these events into motion. People were going to die or not as the fates decreed. But there was no escaping that pictures of their plunging demise were going to be incredibly memorable. The most memorable pictures in the world depicted innocent people suffering, like the famous shot of that screaming, naked Vietnamese girl fleeing her burning village. Eddie Brock desperately wanted his own piece of immortality, and if it came at the expense of someone else's mortality, well . . . he could live with that.

Scanning the building exterior, he was suddenly certain he saw a tiny form high above. It wasn't falling, but it was on the verge of doing so. He pulled out his extreme telephoto lens, brought it up to his trained eye, and zoomed in on what now appeared to be a helpless blonde fighting for the last few seconds of her life.

Good. That was good. Dying females were even more compelling than dying males, and this looked to be a gorgeous one too—

He lowered the camera, all the blood draining from his face.

"My God, that's Gwen!"

Shock pounded through his brain. No longer was this some anonymous woman whose death might, if photographed properly, help make his career. This was Gwen Stacy . . . his Gwen.

Briefly, he considered not taking the picture.

Then he brought the camera back up to his eye and refocused.

He watched in helpless frustration, but snapping shots the entire time, as bits of metal started flying past Gwen's head. The rivets that connected the window frame to the building were popping out one by one. Suddenly Gwen opened her mouth and was undoubtedly screaming. Eddie couldn't hear it, of course, but he saw her mouth open wide as in the famous Munch painting, and then the metal frame tore away from the building. It swung thirty feet outward and left Gwen dangling high above the intersection. There was no way she was going to be able to hold on, and nowhere for her to go even if she managed to do so.

Brock's mind was blank. He was entirely on autopilot as he continued to make a visual diary of Gwen Stacy's last moments. He was so absorbed with what he was seeing that when he heard a triumphant whoop of joy from the crowd, he assumed it to be people who were excited over witnessing an imminent death. *Sick bastards. I don't know how people can live with themselves.*

All the while he kept shooting.

Gwen's fingertips slipped from the girder, and with a shriek, she started to fall.

She won't be alive when she hits the ground. A fall from that height . . . she'll be dead long before. It'll be merciful. Quick. On film forever. You'll be immortal, Gwen. Even though you'll be dead, I'll make sure you're immortalized.

A flash of red and blue hurtled across Brock's field of vision, blocking out his shot. Confused, Eddie switched from a tight angle to wide . . . and was astounded to see that Gwen was in the arms of Spider-Man.

He realized belatedly that the crowd had been responding to the sight of the web slinger hurtling through the air and intercepting Gwen. Spider-Man scooped her up, and she threw her arms around him.

Everything had happened so quickly that it had been

barely seconds between the time that Brock had shouted, "My God, that's Gwen," and an older-looking, uniformed cop approached him with a strange look on his face. Brock fully expected the cop to try to shoo him away from the scene.

Instead the policeman said, "Gwen?" Not understanding, Brock simply nodded in confirmation, and the cop grabbed the camera from Brock. The strap was still looped around Eddie's neck, nearly causing him to strangle as the stranger peered through the lens to see for himself. The cop gasped and said in confirmation upon seeing her, "That's my daughter!"

Brock made a gargling noise, pointing at the strap that was cutting off his air, and the cop promptly released his hold. As Eddie cleared his throat, the officer stared at him in confusion. "Who are you?"

"Eddie Brock Jr., sir," Brock managed to say. He smoothed the front of his sweater. "I'm dating your daughter." He forced a smile as Captain Stacy simply stared at him as if he were a new type of fungus. "She's told me all about you."

"Really. She hasn't mentioned you at all," Captain Stacy said, not sounding particularly condescending. He was simply stating it as fact, attributing nothing to it in his voice. It was still enough to make Eddie feel cut off at the knees.

Apparently giving Brock no further thought, Captain Stacy headed toward where Spider-Man was descending to street level. Spider-Man set Gwen gently down upon the ground. She almost toppled over from a combination of dizziness and, most likely, fear. Not fear of Spider-Man: she was gazing at *him* with awe and amazement. Certainly the near-death experience itself, however, was enough to make anyone woozy. But before she took a spill, her father was there, catching her by one arm and supporting her. She looked in wonderment at him and said in an almost dreamlike voice, "I knew you wouldn't let me fall."

Suddenly Spider-Man was leaping skyward and began spinning some sort of webbing net directly above the crowd. Brock didn't understand why, and then a hail of concrete descended upon them from above. Scattered debris from the crumbled floor high overhead continued to rain down, and the hastily spun web held firm as the wreckage fell harmlessly on it. It sagged a bit under the weight but didn't break. It was impossible to say how many fatalities there would have been if Spider-Man hadn't adroitly protected the bystanders.

Satisfied that the people on the ground were safe, Spider-Man landed on a lamppost and stared up at the crane, which was still moving out of control. He was actually scratching his head, trying to figure out the best way to approach the problem . . . when every light on the street suddenly went out. The power shutdown caused a sound that was almost like a body's great exhalation of relief, and then the runaway crane came to a slow, grinding halt. A ragged cheer arose from the crowd.

Eddie Brock quickly made his way over to where Captain Stacy was steadying his daughter. Brock had never seen any man look so relieved in his entire life. The moment he drew within earshot, he called to Gwen,

"Beautiful! Pulitzer Prize!" He tapped his camera. "Wait until you see that shot, Gwen. The light on your hair was golden."

Gwen gave him that same *Who are you?* look that her father had given him only moments before. Only then did it occur to Eddie Brock that he had just admitted to snapping shots of Gwen during what had seemed to be her tragic and violent death. Perhaps that wasn't the smartest thing to be crowing about.

Spider-Man dropped lightly to the ground near them, turned to Gwen and asked, "Are you okay?" Even his voice wasn't what Brock had anticipated from a bigger-than-life hero. He had thought Spider-Man would have some deep, classic, booming hero voice, like a Shakespearean actor or something. Instead Spider-Man just sounded like . . . like some guy.

Gwen, however, did not appear to be disappointed by either his voice or his height. Instead, with a look that bordered on adoration, she said, "I'm fine. Thank you, Spider-Man."

Desperate to insert himself into the moment, Brock called out, "Hold it, Spidey! Smile!"

Spider-Man turned and looked in his direction as Brock snapped away. "Are you smiling?" Brock asked.

Spider-Man continued to stare at him.

"Just kidding," Brock said, feeling foolish and not knowing why he did. He squared his shoulders and, as he continued to take pictures, said, "Name's Eddie Brock. I'll be taking shots of you for the *Bugle* from now on."

Spider-Man tilted his head slightly, like a curious dog. "What about that guy, Peter . . . what's his name?"

"Strictly amateur," Brock replied dismissively. "Wouldn't know an f-stop from a bus stop. His stuff makes you look bloated. Little chunky."

Spider-Man appeared to consider this, then he fired a webline and swung off across the cityscape. A huge, rousing cheer went up as he departed.

None of them saw Spider-Man, several blocks away, stop on a ledge in front of a window and study his full profile in reflection. He placed his hand flat on his stomach, then sucked in his gut.

"Chunky?" he muttered, and decided right then and there that this Brock guy was not going to be on his Christmas card list.

In the offices of the *Daily Bugle,* Betty Brant—secretary/personal assistant to editor and publisher J. Jonah Jameson—was riding herd on a typical day of barely controlled insanity.

Jonah was in one of his moods, which was to be expected since it was a day ending in the letter *y.* Just to make Betty's life even more exciting, Jonah's recent physical had not been a happy experience. Jameson's wife had provided Betty with a list of things that Jonah should avoid, according to doctor's orders. The word *stress* was at the top, triple underlined. Betty had laughed uncontrollably until she realized that Mrs. Jameson was dead serious. Betty pointed out that, in her defense, Jonah's wife had unwisely chosen to present the list on April 1st and Betty had reasonably concluded it was a joke.

So now Betty was the official and unwilling monitor of Jonah's food and mood and was starting to think that she should ask for a raise that was commensurate with what was being expected of her . . . like, say, a million dollars a year.

Ted Hoffman, the much beleaguered head of promotion, strode toward Betty's desk with the jaunty manner he always exhibited before going in to see Jameson—a direct contrast to the way he typically acted upon departing. "Boss is gonna love this campaign!" he announced as he breezed past.

Betty was always impressed: Hoffman was like that bop 'im bag she had had as a kid. The four-foot-high, inflatable punching toy with the weighted bottom and the clown face painted on. No matter how hard you slugged it, it would always roll back to standing and have that same determined smile. That was Hoffman. However many times Jameson flattened him, he rolled with it and came right back next time for more abuse.

Moments later, the fast-moving form of Eddie Brock tried to make it past Betty's desk. He had a portfolio tucked under his arm. As if his going into Jameson's office were a done deal, he said chipperly, "Hey, Betty-Betty-Bo-Betty . . ."

Betty generally tried to be as accommodating as possible, but in Brock's short time with the newspaper he had gotten under Betty's skin with amazing ease. The most aggravating thing was that he wasn't even trying; he thought he was being charming. Nor did it help that he kept trying to set her name to various songs. Last time it was "Betty My Love," and now it was "The Name Game," of all things. She hated that damn song.

"He's busy," she said more curtly than she would normally have.

As if he'd always intended to do so, Brock skidded to a halt in front of her desk and said suavely, "Oh, I'm here to talk to you, beautiful."

Points for effort. She'd give him that much. Nothing fazed the guy. Her nostrils flared, and she frowned. "What's that smell?"

"It's called Nice 'n Easy." He made as if to sniff the air around her. "What's on you?"

"It's called Go Away," she replied, although not without a small smile.

Brock was undeterred. "Where'll we go? China?" He made a clicking sound with his tongue that was intended to be suggestive.

Before Betty could tell him where to go, the thoroughly expected bellowing emerged from behind Jameson's door. The door was thrown open, and a terrified Hoffman scampered backward out of the office. He almost tripped, but Brock caught him. Betty was about to remind Hoffman that he was no longer carrying the easel that he'd brought into the office when Jameson appeared in the doorway, mustache bristling. He tossed Hoffman's easel after his fleeing form while shouting, "That's the dumbest idea you've ever had! And you've had some doozies!"

"Blood pressure!" Betty called out, trying to get her voice over Jonah's outraged roaring.

Ignoring her, which was certainly nothing new, Jameson turned on his heel and headed back into his office. Seizing the opportunity, Brock headed toward the open door.

"Hey!" Betty shouted, half out of her chair. "Where are *you* going? I said he's busy!" She moved so quickly that she banged her knee on the underside of the desk and grabbed it as pain shot through her leg. Just to make things even better, the phone rang. With a moan, she sank back into her chair, picked it up, and said, "J. Jonah Jameson's office," through gritted teeth.

The hell with it. If Brock wants to be face-to-face with Jameson that badly, let him. I hope he gets what he deserves.

Brock, buoyed by boundless determination, strode into Jameson's office armed with his portfolio, displaying the confidence of a lion tamer facing down the big cats with nothing but a chair and a whip. In this case, the big cats were Jameson and city editor Robbie Robertson, who already seemed deep in conversation when Brock walked in. Jameson's head thrust forward in a manner not unlike a cobra's, and he glared at Eddie. "Who are you?" he demanded.

In a low voice, Robbie said, "You hired him last week. Freelance."

"I did?" Jameson sniffed the air. "What's that smell?"

"It's Brock, sir."

"Stupid name for an aftershave."

"That's *my* name."

"They named you for an aftershave?" asked Jameson, now hopelessly confused.

Brock took a step back, both mentally and physically, and said, "I'm Edward Brock, Jr."

"Who?"

Since the introduction seemed to be a lost cause, Brock pulled a photograph out of the portfolio and slid it across the desk. Looking for something to steer the conversation—if one could call it that—away from his name, Brock looked at Jameson and said, "Wow, can I just say I really like that shirt? Here . . ." He pointed to the photograph. "Crane accident. Check out the light source."

Jameson slid the photo over to Robbie and glanced at his sleeves. "He likes my shirt," he said with a touch of wonderment, as if no one had ever complimented his wardrobe . . . which, Brock had to admit, was probably the case.

Robbie barely had to look at it to recognize the quality of it. "We can use it," he said firmly.

"How much do you want for it?" demanded Jameson, all business.

"Whatever you think is fair, sir."

"What? Fair?" Jameson glowered, clearly suspicious that this was a trick response or perhaps the opening salvo of a lengthy negotiation. "What's your name again?"

"Brock, sir," sighed Eddie. "Edward Brock, Jr." He enunciated it slowly, hoping that it would imprint on Jameson's gray matter this time.

In the brief silence that followed, as Jameson studied the picture and obviously calculated an amount that he believed the picture was worth—and then would no doubt halve—Brock heard a brief exchange on the other side of the office door. A voice said, "Hi, Betty," followed by Betty quietly replying, "Hi, Pete. You better get in there. New guy."

Great. I show up and get "He's busy. You can't go in." This other guy shows up and he's told to hurry right in. Nice to see that our Miss Brant plays favorites. Got to remember that.

The door flew open and a young, intense-looking guy entered. He was holding a manila envelope in his hand.

"Parker, you're late," snapped Jameson, and Brock immediately realized that *this* was Peter Parker, his main competition. Brock smiled widely, knowing that Parker had already lost this round before he'd even entered the game. "Maybe too late," continued Jameson, confirming Brock's suspicion. "Bruckner here brought me a pretty good photo."

Eddie rolled his eyes and was about to correct Jameson as to his name for what seemed the tenth time when Peter extracted a picture from the envelope and said, "I got you this."

Peering at the photo, Brock couldn't believe it. An aerial shot of Spider-Man spinning the web that protected the crowd?! "How'd you get that shot?" he demanded. "I didn't see you there. How'd you get that high?"

"I climbed. Nearly fell off the flagpole."

"Flagpole?" Brock had an excellent memory for scenes—his cameraman's eye gave him a photographic

memory. He didn't remember a flagpole there. Was it possible he missed it? He didn't think so. But how else . . . ?

"Which picture do we use?" asked Robertson.

Brock tensed. His was the better composed, with that intense human drama of Spider-Man saving the girl. But Parker's had a broader sweep.

Jameson, however, didn't hesitate. "I like Bernstein's."

Brock exhaled in relief. Who gave a damn whether Jameson could remember his name, so long as it was correct in the photo credit and on the check.

Robertson, holding both photos, nodded once in confirming Jameson's decision. "It's better," he acknowledged, and Brock was sure that he was looking sympathetically at Peter. So Robertson also played favorites. Well, that was going to have to change.

"Cheaper too," Jameson announced. "Congratulations, Brooks." *(Brock, you idiot, Brock!* Eddie thought.*)* "We're gonna go with your photo. Fifty bucks."

Eddie nearly choked. That wasn't even enough to cover expenses. He'd underestimated Jameson—$50 was maybe a quarter of what the picture was worth. He considered telling Jameson to shove it, but Parker's presence took that option off the table. The competition was in the room, and Eddie wasn't about to torpedo his long-term chances for the short-term satisfaction of telling off J. Jonah Jameson. Instead he swallowed his irritation and gave a genuine fake smile. "All right, JJ, then I'm your man." He leaned over the desk to extend a handshake to Jameson. Jameson stared at the hand as if wondering why

Brock was pointing this thing in his direction. Brock quickly turned the open hand into a fist as if he'd always meant to and thumped it firmly on the desktop for emphasis. "I know more about what makes a good picture than any photographer in town. Photography is not about, no offense"—he nodded to Parker—"*flagpoles*. It's about lighting, composition, drama."

Eddie saw that Jameson was nodding, looking interested. Although Eddie was taking a huge risk, he decided that now was the time to get aggressive. "I want a staff job. I have a girl that I intend to marry. And I have this kind of stupid little dream of working for one of the greatest newspaper editors of our time: J. Jonah Jameson."

Jameson was soaking it up like a sponge. "We do have an opening. Johnson quit. Remember?" he said to Robertson.

"You fired him," Robertson reminded him.

"Whatever."

Peter Parker, however, was clearly not about to roll over. "Wait a minute," he protested. "I know what makes a good picture. And I've been here a long time. If there's a staff job, Mr. Jameson, I think I deserve it."

Robertson, that great player of favorites, said, "He's right, Jonah. Peter's been with us for years. He does great work."

Looking from one to the other, Jameson growled, "You want a staff job, and you want a staff job. Anyone care about what I want?"

Hoffman, displaying the resilience of a Whac-A-Mole, stuck his head in and said, "I do."

"Shut up! Get out!" Jameson snapped, and Hoffman immediately did so. Jameson turned his attention back to the two photographers. He shoved an unlit cigar in his mouth and rolled it from one side to the other a few times. "I want the public to see Spider-Man for the two-bit criminal he really is," he finally said. "He's a fake. He's full of stickem. Catch him in the act. Spider-Man with his hand in the cookie jar." He paused for dramatic effect, then concluded, "Whoever brings me that photo gets the job." When neither Brock nor Parker initially moved, Jameson snapped, "What are you waiting for? *Go go go!*"

"I'm on it, boss!" Brock announced, and headed for the door.

As Eddie went, Peter Parker was one step behind him, which was just how Brock liked it. But he was surprised when Parker said in an unusually intense voice, "You'll never get that picture."

"Oh, we'll see." Brock fired a smug grin at Parker as if it were a done deal, eyes blazing with determination. "We'll see."

IX

UNEASY HOMECOMINGS

PETER PARKER WALKED THROUGH Times Square, frustrated by the situation in which he now found himself.

There was only one way that he could give J. Jonah Jameson what he wanted: by setting up some sort of false picture and criminalizing his alter ego. He couldn't see himself doing it. No way.

Peter was skirting the line of ethics as it was, taking photographs of himself in action and selling those to the *Daily Bugle.* He always told himself that it wasn't really fraud. He wasn't setting up the situations that Spider-Man got himself into—he was simply providing photographic documentation of events. He didn't see it as being morally any different from writing an autobiography and being paid for it. But faking a photo of Spider-Man doing something corrupt? That crossed the line. No job was worth it. Besides, if he did transform Spider-Man into a criminal by making it look as if Spider-Man had done something illegal, wouldn't that impede his other identity's effectiveness? Things were turning the corner in public perception; why roll matters back to suspicion and apprehension? Bottom line, the citizens of New York had no reason to fear Spider-Man; giving them one would be criminal in and of itself.

If Peter required any further proof of that, it came as he stopped and looked up at the news scrolling across the JumboTron screen high above. There was footage of Spider-Man swinging away from the site of the crane incident, with people waving excitedly at his departure, and the words: SPIDER-MAN TO RECEIVE KEY TO THE CITY.

This was wishful thinking on the part of city administrators. No one had contacted him about such a thing since, naturally, they had no means of doing so. Instead he'd heard and read about the intended ceremony in the local news. The mayor said that they were going to make this presentation, and their hope was that Spider-Man would see fit to join them. If he didn't, the key would be donated to the Museum of New York and be put on permanent display.

Peter hadn't bothered to call and say he'd come; the chances were that every crank in the city was doing exactly that already, no doubt hoping some sort of monetary reward came with the honor. In fact, he'd more or less decided that he would not show up. As Peter Parker, he was seeking ways to bring in regular income. But being Spider-Man wasn't about chasing wealth and fame.

Still, with Jameson's latest mad-on about Spider-Man and being so anxious to prove the web slinger a menace, Peter couldn't resist the thought of Spider-Man being lionized by the very public to which Jameson wanted to criminalize him.

Peter continued to go back and forth about it as he

headed over toward the hospital where Harry Osborn was preparing to check out. By the time he arrived, he hadn't yet made a decision. He gave it no further thought as he went to Harry's room and found his friend dressed and ready to go.

Harry still looked a little unsteady, even weak, but the hospital had pronounced him fit to travel and decreed that bed rest in his own home was the best thing for him.

Hospital policy insisted that Harry be brought to the hospital doors in a wheelchair, and Peter was only too happy to oblige. "Good thing I survived, huh, Pete?" said Harry with an amused snort. "Otherwise you wouldn't have Harry Osborn to push around anymore."

Peter laughed at that. It felt good to be relaxing with his old friend. The more time that passed, the more Harry acted like his old self, the more it convinced Peter that maybe the worst really was past them.

Harry's limo driver was waiting for them, and the ride over to the town house was amazingly carefree. They reminisced about their time in high school, and how Peter had bailed Harry out when it came to science. When talk turned, as it invariably did, toward Norman Osborn, Harry was fairly restrained. Peter supposed that was natural—the poor guy was trying to cope with so many losses at once.

Once they arrived, Peter helped Harry through the main foyer and into the small elevator that would carry them to the penthouse floor. Harry inserted the key that would bring them up there, and the elevator shuddered slightly before it wheezed to life and hauled them to the top floor. Bernard, Harry's butler, was waiting for them, and he opened the ornate gate that blocked access to the penthouse itself. Harry and Peter stepped off the elevator, Peter hovering near Harry's elbow just in case his friend was seized with momentary weakness.

"Welcome home, Harry," Bernard said as he stepped aside. "Thank God you're all right."

Harry nodded slightly in acknowledgment while Bernard relieved Harry of his small suitcase. "Thank you, Bernard."

The penthouse was split-level, and Bernard headed upstairs where he would unpack Harry's suitcase for him. Peter shrugged off his backpack and removed from it a large, round, crudely gift-wrapped object. Harry didn't notice it at first since he was gazing around the penthouse as if seeing it for the first time. Peter figured that, in a way, he was. Harry had lived here all his life, but it had always been his father's house and Harry was just in residence. Now Harry needed to reacquaint himself with the fact that it was *his* home, not Norman's. That alone was going to require some adjustment. "Brought you a homecoming gift," Peter said, hoping to take Harry's thoughts away from that morbid direction.

Harry took it from him and opened it, but the smile on his face indicated that he knew what it was before he even unwrapped it. "It's your old ball," he said, and sure enough, it was. A battered, slightly underinflated basketball with the name PARKER scrawled on it. "Thanks, buddy." He dribbled it a few times, then tossed it to Peter in a reasonably good pass. "We were pretty good in the backyard."

"C'mon. We were terrible," Peter good-naturedly reminded him, and threw the ball back. "Whatever made us try out for the varsity team?"

"Cheerleaders."

Peter nodded, recalling. "They *were* cute."

Looking thoughtful, Harry asked, "Do I have any girlfriends?"

"I don't know."

"You don't?" Harry raised his voice and called out, "Bernard! Do I have any girlfriends?"

"Not that I know of, sir," Bernard's crisp tone replied from upstairs.

Harry passed the ball back to Peter. They moved through the giant front hallway, ricocheting the ball back and forth between them, dribbling and acting as if they were on a basketball court. The steady bouncing sound of the basketball echoed through the vast hall. "Hey, this is a cool pad," Harry decided, clearly liking the idea that he could play basketball indoors without fear of remonstration.

"Sure beats my place."

"And"—Harry bounded the ball to Peter once more—"it looks like I'm not hurting for money, right?"

"Harry, you're loaded!" Peter said with a laugh.

Harry considered this and then grinned. "I think I can turn this 'no girlfriend' thing around."

Their impromptu basketball game carried them into

the main salon, and Harry froze. Peter followed his gaze to see what Harry was staring at and shouldn't have been surprised.

There, hanging on the wall, was a large, formal portrait painting of Norman Osborn. The eyes appeared to be fixed on Harry. Peter wondered if Norman's gaze followed you around no matter where you stood in the room.

Harry stared back as if expecting the real Norman to peel himself off the painting. "He always appreciated how you got me through high school," he said, his voice subdued, as if they were at a museum . . . or a wake. "I wish I could remember more about him."

No, you don't, Peter thought. Flipping the ball from one hand to the other, Peter said uncomfortably, "He loved you. That's the main thing."

He bounced the ball back toward Harry then, hoping to distract him. He failed utterly as the ball bounced past Harry and smacked into a pedestal supporting an antique vase that looked to be from the Ming dynasty. Peter was horrified as he saw the pedestal tilt from the impact and the vase begin to fall. He was too far away to do anything about it short of leaping all the way across the room or else firing some weblines to intercept it.

Harry, however, moved quickly . . . *far* more quickly than he should have been able to. Instantly he grabbed the ball to prevent it from bouncing around and hitting other breakables while, at the same time, snagging the falling vase out of midair with the other hand.

Amazed at his prowess, Harry stared at both the ball and the vase, and then at Peter. "Wow! Didya see that?"

Oh, yes, Peter most definitely had and was extremely uneasy over having done so. The last thing he needed was Harry wondering why he could move faster, and with greater strength, than ever before. Quickly Peter did the best he could to hide his growing anxiety as he said cheerfully, "Guess you still got the moves."

"I guess so!" Carefully Harry placed the vase on the pedestal, then flipped the ball back to Peter. "Varsity, here we come!"

"Little late for varsity. How about the NBA?"

"Damn straight! And if I can't get on in tryouts, I'll just buy a team and put myself in the starting rotation."

"If that doesn't get the girls, nothing will," Peter agreed, allowing relief to flood through him. The two friends continued passing the ball back and forth as they headed out of the room.

Curiously, when Peter passed a full-length mirror, he felt a twinge of warning from his spider-sense. He had no idea why. Perhaps it was because he saw the portrait of Norman Osborn reflected in it. That had to be it. The thing would be enough to give anyone the creeps.

Mary Jane Watson had come to think of the Broadhurst Theater as her home away from home. Considering the amount of time MJ spent there, she should have been paying rent. And the cast . . . the wonderful cast had become her extended family.

That business with Peter earlier today had been difficult. She'd finally forced herself to realize that maybe

Peter couldn't understand simply because he wasn't an actor. Acting was a profession like none other, and seeking solace from Peter might well have been the wrong move because it was beyond his ability to comprehend. As she had told him, when he went out into the public eye, at least he had anonymity. For Mary Jane, stepping out on the stage and singing was the equivalent of stripping naked, standing in a store display window, and inviting passersby to take their best shot. She could explain that to Peter, and he could comprehend it intellectually. But he couldn't really sympathize the way that her castmates would.

Looking forward to much understanding and empathy from her extended family, Mary Jane walked into the theater foyer in the hopes that the day was going to take a much better turn.

She was understandably confused, then, when she saw another actress standing center stage, singing "Falling in Love."

At first MJ thought it was her understudy getting some rehearsal in, but then the rest of the cast came in on cue, moving to their marks. Both the producer and the director were seated in the center of the theater, and the director was clapping his hands briskly together as a way of bringing everything to a halt. The cast obediently stopped, as did the music. "Stop on the fifth step, Helen! Then hold it for a beat, then hit it!" Next to him the producer nodded in agreement.

Helen nodded and the music—provided for rehearsal by a pianist—started up again. Helen opened her mouth to start singing, but then stopped as she spotted Mary

Jane standing in the back of the theater. The director and producer turned to see where Helen was looking, and the director looked visibly startled when he saw Mary Jane there. So did the rest of the cast. "What's she doing here?" he whispered to the producer, his voice carrying despite the low tones. "Didn't anybody call her?"

The cast was huddling together now as if expecting a storm to come rolling in. Mary Jane moved to the top of the aisle and simply gaped, like an orphan watching a Thanksgiving feast through a window while snow fell upon her. There were her "dear friends," Linda Curtis, Solomon Abrams, the rest of them, all staring back as if she had no right to be there. *You can't go home again.*

Clearly feeling he had to take charge of the situation, the director walked toward her, an apologetic look on his face. "We tried to reach you . . ." he began.

The reality of what Mary Jane was seeing finally began to sink in. *They're cutting me. Cutting me because of one critic.* "One critic?" she said aloud.

The producer had now come up and said, "*All* the papers." Realizing how harsh that sounded, and having no desire to make Mary Jane feel worse than she did, he added sympathetically, "If you'd like, we can say you became ill."

That wasn't going to be simply a cover story—it was everything Mary Jane could do not to vomit right there in the middle of the theater. She wondered if her legs were visibly trembling, because it sure felt as if they were.

"Sit down, Mary Jane," the director urged her. "Let us explain."

She didn't want his explanations. She wanted to get as far away from this place as possible.

Without a word, Mary Jane turned and walked out. No, not walked: ran. She didn't want to exit to house left—that would take her out past the box office, and she had no desire to see people in line to purchase tickets. Instead she headed in the other direction, through the side exit that opened out onto a narrow alleyway. The doors slammed heavily behind her, like a guillotine blade, severing her ties to the group of strangers whom she had briefly considered family.

Clutching her small overnight bag tightly under her arm, she headed down the alley and stepped out onto Forty-fourth Street.

Instantly there was a chorus of cheers, applause, whistling. Was the reception for her? Perhaps the producer had been spooked by the crummy reviews, but at least the fans had . . .

. . . their backs to her. They were looking in another direction entirely.

They were looking up.

Mary Jane did the same, although she didn't really have to. She knew what everyone was going nuts over.

Spider-Man.

There he went, webbing his way across the skyline. In the distance she could hear sirens wailing. He was off on another mission of mercy, and everyone adored him for it.

Mary Jane never wanted to hate someone more than she did at that moment . . . and had never been more incapable of doing so.

Filled with frustration and self-loathing, and determined not to let anyone see her cry, Mary Jane headed back to the place that she called her apartment, but was still not home. "Home is other people," she said aloud.

And some guy passing her—probably a writer, from the aesthetic look of him—promptly corrected her by saying, "Hell. 'Hell is other people.' Jean-Paul Sartre."

"I guess he'd know."

He stared at her a moment. "Do I know you from someplace?"

"No," Mary Jane said quietly. "No one knows me at all." Without another word, she headed away from the Broadhurst as quickly as she could.

X

GRANDSTANDING

PETER PARKER WAS CERTAIN that he had never seen a more gorgeous day than the one facing him this crisp morning. Absolutely no clouds, sky a perfect blue. He had spent time with Harry the day before, and everything seemed okay with him. Granted, he hadn't been able to get in touch with Mary Jane. But when one considered everything that they had been through and had survived—both in their relationship and in their lives—certainly they'd be able to get through this. For God's sake, it was a single review from some loudmouthed critic. She'd get past it. With the perspective of distance, she'd realize that she was making too much of it.

Everything was going to be all right.

Because this was his day, baby. His day.

He was down by City Hall, moving past the displays of banners and balloons that had been created to celebrate the greatness that was—let's face it—him. Police lines had been set up for crowd control of the vast number of people assembling for the celebration. It was a heady experience. Peter was completely blown away by the positive energy and outpouring of support. He couldn't believe he'd seriously considered skipping the entire event. Every single person there was wondering the same thing: Was Spider-Man going to show up? Peter Parker was the only one who knew the answer to that, and he was loving every minute of it.

In the old days, he would be frustrated as the public and media trash-talked Spider-Man, and he'd feel so tempted to rip the mask off and shout, *Hey! Look! See? I'm just an ordinary guy under here, not the monster everyone's making me out to be! So cut me a break, would you, please?!* Those were the times that he despised the need to keep his identity a secret.

Now, though, he was getting a kick out of being the only one here who knew what Spider-Man's plans were.

A discordant blatting of musical notes cut through his thoughts—a high school marching band was tuning up. And there had to be something like a thousand people of varying ages and sizes attired in homemade Spider-Man outfits.

Peter brought out his camera and started clicking away. He didn't care whether Jonah bought them or not. If nothing else, he could create a scrapbook so he'd always have a visual record of the greatest day of his life.

A small boy in a Spider-Man costume, noticing that Peter was taking pictures, ran toward him with some sort of large plastic device on his wrist . . . a lever attached to a canister. The kid pushed the lever and a small gout of what appeared to be Silly String spurted out from it. Peter recognized it for what it was: a homemade web shooter. Peter tried to contemplate what it would be like building a functioning mechanical webshooter if he didn't possess organic spinnerets. He couldn't even begin to imagine how he would make such a thing.

The kid tried to fire more "webbing," but the can made a fizzing noise. Obviously he was out of ammo. Peter glanced right and left, saw that no one was paying attention, extended his right arm, and fired a quick burst of his own webbing. It leaped out from his forearm and splattered on the kid's shoe, creating a small patch of web on it. The boy's eyes went wide as he correctly figured out what had just happened, and he turned and shouted, "Mama! I just saw Spider-Man!"

By the time his mother came to the kid's side and looked where he was pointing, Peter had already joined a group of teenaged Spider-Man fans and easily mingled in. The boy's mother would just assume her son was referring to a particularly effective costume.

In the large plaza area directly in front of City Hall, Peter spotted Gwen Stacy standing near the proscenium, studying a piece of paper as if it had been produced by divine hand. The way she kept closing her eyes and murmuring to herself, Peter surmised that she was attempting to memorize the contents. In her other hand she was holding a large golden object: the fabled key to the city.

Gwen looked in his direction, except she wasn't looking at him; she was just randomly turning his way as she continued moving her lips in memorization. Then she focused on him and realized he was standing there, waving. Her face brightened. "Hiya, Pete!"

"Nice key," he said.

She nodded, looking distracted as she did so, and held up the piece of paper she'd been studying. "Trying to put the right words together. How do I introduce somebody who saved my life?"

"Keep it simple. Maybe just, 'Here he is, folks, your friendly, neighborhood Spider-Man.' " He glanced around, saw various important-looking individuals coming together at the base of the proscenium. Things were about to start rolling.

Any lingering doubts that he had about making a personal appearance were finally put to rest by the hopeful look in Gwen's eyes. It would mean so much to her to be able to tell Spider-Man how she felt. And . . .

Okay, admit it. Admit your darker feelings to yourself at least. The way that Mary Jane was looking at you so accusingly, so full of hurt the other day. You were trying your best, honest to God you were, but it wasn't enough. And there are some days when you just get fed up with the notion that your best doesn't measure up. So here's Gwen Stacy, and all she has to do is mention Spider-Man and her eyes just . . . just light up with gratitude and excitement.

And don't you frankly deserve some of this? After all these years, finally being appreciated for everything you have to offer? Aren't you finally getting your due, and what the hell is wrong with being pleased about it and feeling entitled to . . .

He shook himself out of his reverie and added, "Then . . . list some of his great achievements!" before heading off into the crowd.

• • •

Gwen watched Peter go and smiled. What a nice guy he was. No Spider-Man, of course, but not everyone could be. Hell, hardly anyone could be.

She headed toward the stairs that led up to the stage, and suddenly a voice from behind her shouted, *"Boo!"*

A startled Gwen jumped as she spun to face the speaker, only to find herself staring down the lens of a camera. A series of rapid clicks told her that her slightly frightened expression had been preserved for posterity, and she wasn't the least bit happy about it. And unsurprisingly, the photographer made no effort to capture the scowl that quickly followed. Tossing her long, blond hair out of her face, she snapped, "Eddie, I don't have time. I'm working on my speech."

Eddie Brock lowered his camera and asked, "Need any help?"

"Not now."

She headed for the stage. Eddie followed, not taking the hint. "I'll see you tonight, right?"

"Not tonight."

"Why not?" he persisted. "We had a great time."

"We had coffee, Eddie."

"But you let me kiss you good-night."

Gwen, becoming totally fed up with this conversation, turned and faced Eddie, with one foot on the steps that led up to the stage. "It was just a little kiss, Eddie. It was nice. Excuse me."

As Gwen headed up the steps, she wondered about the kind of luck she'd been having lately. It certainly was running to extremes. On the one hand, she'd encountered Eddie Brock in a casual meeting at a Starbucks near ESU. They'd had a pleasant enough conversation, happened upon each other yet again at the same Starbucks (except now she was wondering whether it wasn't happenstance and Eddie had simply been staking out the place after their first encounter), spent some more time together, and he'd brought her home that one night . . .

She shouldn't have kissed him. Gwen was all too often a creature of impulse. But he'd seemed nice, and even a little needy, and so it had happened just before she'd walked into her house. It was nothing much to her, and frankly, he'd tasted a lot like coffee. Apparently, though, it had meant way, way too much to Eddie, and now his actions were bordering on obsessive. How could one compare her stupidity in kissing him with his stupidity in stalking the daughter of a cop?

Contrast that experience to nearly plunging to her death, only to be miraculously rescued by a masked man on a string of web.

She wondered why in the world she couldn't meet a nice, decent, down-to-earth kind of guy, someone comfortably between the two extremes.

At which point Peter Parker's face suddenly came to her mind. She turned and looked back toward the crowd, thinking that maybe she should have invited him up onto the stage with her. If Eddie saw Gwen next to another young guy, it might send him a message. Besides, Peter was smart, reasonably good-looking, and wonderfully normal with his feet solidly on the ground. Maybe the answer was right there in front of her, and she just had to see it.

Unfortunately, Peter was nowhere to be seen.

Why are you doing this to yourself? Mary Jane wondered for what seemed the umpteenth time as she moved through the crowd. And for the umpteenth time, she had no sure answer.

She had spent the rest of the previous day and much of the night staring at the telephone, trying to decide whether to call Peter. Her phone rang a couple of times, but she shut off the volume on her answering machine so that she didn't have to listen to the message being left. She didn't want to talk to anyone unless it was on her own initiative. After a sleepless night, she had finally picked up the phone and dialed him, only to discover he wasn't there. Then, turning on her TV, she'd seen live news coverage of this Spider-Man love-in. Of course.

So she had come here, not knowing why, but feeling the need to be with Peter. To see him. To tell him . . .

. . . that she'd been fired? That his perceptions of her abilities had been colored by his love for her, and because of that she couldn't count on him to give an unvarnished assessment of her talent?

And . . . was that really such a bad thing?

"Hey, beautiful, can I take your picture?"

Mary Jane glanced over her shoulder and, sure enough, there he was, focusing on her. If he'd only shown up a few minutes later, she might have gotten her thoughts in order. As it was, the best she could manage was a halfhearted smile. Peter lowered the camera, picture still not taken, then approached her and stopped half a foot away, as if she had a force field around her. "Hope you're not still mad at me," he said.

"No, Peter, I'm proud of you."

He smiled then, pointed the camera, and took a picture. Then he stepped in closely and said in a low voice, "I'm planning to swing in from over there." He pointed behind her. Mary Jane, in the meantime, glanced down at the camera's tiny display screen. The digital picture that he'd just taken was still on it—there she was, all right, but behind her was a banner reading: SPIDEY THE MIGHTY. She wasn't sure, but it looked as if her image was slightly blurry while the banner was perfectly clear, as if he had had to decide which to focus on and had opted for the sign. Then the picture blinked out and went back to "view" mode.

Perhaps she was overthinking it. Or at least she hoped she was.

"Give them a good show," she urged him.

A marching band played an opening fanfare, complete with drumroll, and Mary Jane sensed the anticipation rising in the crowd. Peter was already fiddling with the top button on his shirt, and as he started to move away, he called to her, "Hey! I made a reservation for dinner tomorrow! I left you a message."

Hearing that, Mary Jane knew she had to confess everything. Heaven forbid Peter would go to meet her at the theater and find her name missing from the marquee and posters, as if it had never been there. But she couldn't bring herself to tell him now, not when he was in such a fantastically upbeat mood. Sensing her conflict and unhappiness but not knowing why, Peter obviously concluded that she was still upset about her bad press . . . which, technically, she was, but not for the reasons he was assuming. "And don't worry about that review," he urged her as a parting shot. "We'll laugh about it tomorrow."

He moved off toward a building across the street. No one noticed, since all eyes were focused on the stage some distance off.

"Yeah," was all she could bring herself to say.

With Peter gone, she felt like a balloon with the air out of it. She tried to pay attention to the festivities. The band had segued straight from "New York, New York" to a marching version of "The Eensy Weensy Spider," a tune she'd never have thought lent itself to a brass band.

Mary Jane was suddenly overwhelmed by everything she was seeing. Everyone was so happy, and she was so miserable. She had no place here, as if she might drag down the mood of the entire crowd with her sorrow.

Deciding she couldn't stand to be there anymore, Mary Jane turned to leave and found herself face-to-face with an equally startled Harry Osborn. He had a small bandage on his head and a slight but fading discoloration under his eye: the only souvenirs of his hospital stay.

"Hey, MJ!" he said with an enthusiasm so contagious that she couldn't help but smile in return . . . the first genuine smile she'd made in what seemed like ages.

"Harry!"

"Where's Pete?" he asked, glancing around. Naturally

it made sense that he would assume Peter would be here. Even with his memory on the fritz, he was aware that a news event with Spider-Man present would be the ideal function for his photographer buddy to attend.

"Taking somebody's picture, I guess," she said, trying to sound casual, and worried that instead she came across as forced. It didn't appear to register on Harry, who just seemed so grateful to be alive that Mary Jane was basking in his positive aura. "I'm so happy to see you! You look so good, Harry."

"I never felt better," he replied, chipper. "Very strange feeling, not knowing exactly who you are. A bump on the head and I'm free as a bird."

Except it was obvious to Mary Jane that Harry knew who he was; he was simply bereft of the sadness that had shrouded him the past months. Harry had a clean emotional slate, and she envied him for that. "Hey, bump *me* on the head, will you?"

Playfully he tapped her lightly on the forehead with his knuckles. Then he looked around, taking in the celebratory atmosphere, and that—combined with the music being played—appeared to trigger a recollection. "Hey, Peter said you were in a play!"

"You were there, remember? You sent me flowers."

"I did?" He looked momentarily confused, then shrugged it off, his newly cheerful nature simply unable to sustain anything other than feeling upbeat. "I'll come tonight!"

"You can't," she said quickly. She saw the surprised look on his face. Clearly he thought that she didn't want him at the show for some reason, and she was stuck. Mary Jane lowered her voice and said, "I was let go."

"What happened?"

"I wasn't very good." She tried to make it sound lighthearted, but the misery in her voice was palpable.

"Don't say that. Man," he said, frustrated, "I wish I could remember so you'd believe me when I said you must've been good, and they're all nuts. But I know I've seen you in other stuff, and I know what you can do. You *are* really good."

"I don't know," she sighed. She was slightly buoyed by his confidence in her, but still shaken by all that had happened. "Sometimes I think I am, but then I'm not sure."

The crowd around them had started chanting, *"Spider-Man! Spider-Man!"* It made it almost impossible for them to continue the conversation. Harry stepped closer to Mary Jane and practically shouted in her ear, "You know, this is embarrassing, but I once wrote a play for you in high school."

"You wrote me a play?" Mary Jane couldn't have been more surprised if Harry had sprouted a third eye on his forehead. Even when they'd been dating, he'd never struck her as the creative type. Obviously he felt so self-conscious about his work that he couldn't even bring himself to show it to anyone.

"I forget how it went," he said with a shrug. "It was some silly romantic thing."

"Harry!" She touched the side of his face affectionately. "That's the sweetest thing!"

"Well, y'know, I'd still put you in my play."

It was comments like that—the surprising moments of tenderness that Harry Osborn was capable of displaying—that reminded her of why she'd gone out with him. Granted, it had all soured because of Harry's father, but Norman Osborn was gone, and that part of Harry that had acted so badly toward MJ was also gone. . . .

Well. Wasn't this an interesting development?

A female voice boomed over the sound system. After a brief squeal of feedback that was quickly adjusted for, the attractive blonde on the podium said, "I'm here today because I fell sixty-two stories and someone caught me. Someone who never asks for anything in return. Someone who doesn't even want us to know who he is."

The girl—whom Mary Jane knew was Gwen Stacy since she'd certainly had her name and picture plastered in enough places since her near-death experience—continued, "So, I ask you, when you're dropping without a parachute, or your store's being robbed, or your house is on fire, who is it that breaks your fall and puts out the flames and saves your children?"

Peter Parker, thought Mary Jane. *Peter Parker, who always has time to be the guy you're here to worship, and never time for me . . . and I'm such a creep for being upset about that . . .*

"Spider-Man!" bellowed the crowd.

Atop a nearby building, Peter Parker—clad in his red-and-blue costume—listened to Gwen Stacy's introduction and decided that it was a hell of a lot better than the quick *here he is* that he'd suggested.

The crowd shouted Spider-Man's name, and he murmured to himself in amazement, "They love me."

"And who," Gwen was saying, "with astounding courage puts his life on the line every day for justice and fairness?"

"Spider-Man!" they screamed yet again.

"Then let's hear it," said Gwen, expertly playing to the crowd, "for the one, for the only, for the fabulous, the sexy . . . *Spider-Maaaaaan!*"

The music swelled; the crowd roared. Had there been a roof, the energy level would have been through it.

And all that from people who still didn't know if Spider-Man was actually going to show up. It was a celebration of more than just the hero; it was all about the city's appreciation for him.

Well, then . . . how could he possibly let down his adoring public?

Firing a webline, Peter swung out high over the crowd. It took only seconds for people to spot him, and if the cheers had sounded loud before, they were now positively thunderous, spectators just out of their minds with glee.

He drank it in hungrily, greedily, like a man dying of thirst coming upon not simply an oasis, but an Irish pub. He was giddy with the adoration; it was intoxicating.

And like a man who was genuinely drunk . . .

. . . he went further than he should have.

Gwen Stacy clapped her hands in delight as she saw Spider-Man hurtling down toward her. She had prepared an entire second half of the speech in the event of his being a no-show, although she hadn't been looking forward to it. She knew what the crowd wanted, and it wasn't a longer speech. They wanted their hero, in person, live, large and in charge.

Now they were getting their wish.

Spider-Man swung high above, twirling his body as he soared in an upward arc. It was pure showing off. Not that it mattered in the least; the crowd was eating up every moment. Someone had written a catchy little song about Spider-Man that had been in heavy rotation on the local radio stations. The marching band struck it up, and Spider-Man now dropped down at dizzying speed. There were gasps, some of shock and fear that he was going to hit the ground like a rock, and some in excitement as they anticipated his pulling out of it just in time. The second contingent were naturally correct as he fired a webline behind him that snagged the top of the City Hall archway.

Spider-Man lowered himself so that he was upside down and facing Gwen. Face-to-face, Gwen put her arms around him and posed for the battery of cameras that flashed away.

Under his mask, Peter was grinning like a lunatic. Suddenly, to the sound of wolf whistles and cries of "*Kiss him!*" Gwen gave him a kiss on his masked cheek.

With his ego swelled almost to bursting by the unparalleled adulation of the crowd, Peter proceeded to seize the moment full-on.

"Go ahead, lay one on me," Peter told her.

Gwen looked startled, but not in a bad way. "Really?"

"They'll love it."

She leaned in toward him and pulled down his mask so that it cleared his mouth. Then she kissed him with a startling ferocity that Peter wouldn't have expected from the normally sedate Gwen Stacy.

For an instant it took him out of the moment, and he remembered that improbable, deliriously romantic kiss he'd shared with Mary Jane while rain poured down upon them in buckets. That kiss seemed long ago and far away, and this was very much happening in the here and now. All he was thinking about were the shouts and cheers, and that his head was probably going to explode any moment.

The thoughts of that rain-soaked kiss also caused him to dwell on Mary Jane, but he wasn't concerned. She was a working actress—he'd watched her kiss other guys onstage, and it hadn't bothered him because he knew that she was performing a character. That's all he was doing as well.

Certainly Mary Jane would understand all that, right?

Mary Jane watched with her eyes wide, filled with disbelief, hurt, anger. What the hell was Peter playing at? Was this some sort of . . . of sick game to try to make her jealous? As if she hadn't been feeling low enough, inadequate enough . . . now this? *Now this?!*

Harry, like everyone else around him, was focused on what was happening onstage. "Wow! Hope Pete's getting a shot of this," he said.

Not like the shot I'm going to want to give him.

The band had switched to a punchy "college fight song" version of that infernal Spider-Man tune, as if their hero had just scored a touchdown. Mary Jane, unable to take it anymore, felt tears stinging her eyes. She turned away and wiped the moisture from her face, praying that it wouldn't cause her makeup to run.

She couldn't imagine this day getting worse.

She was about to discover just how limited her imagination was.

Gwen was only partly playing to the crowd as she affected a swoon. She stepped away from Spider-Man, swaying a bit, and grasped the standing microphone as if it were the only thing preventing her from falling over. "Wow!" she sighed.

A shadow fell over her.

At first Gwen thought that some errant clouds had moved in and blocked out the sun, but, no—the sky was clear. Meanwhile the shadow continued to spread, darkness covering the crowd, Spider-Man, the entire district.

People began to scream and point, and then Gwen saw what was causing it. Even when she did, it made no sense. She could imagine something like this in the middle of the Sahara, but not in downtown Manhattan.

But there it was, unmistakable: a cloud of sand, hundreds of feet high, barreling toward them, blotting out the sun and hurtling at high speed down the narrow canyons of the city.

Spectators started to run, prepared to stampede over whoever was in their way to get clear of it, and then suddenly—impossibly—the sandstorm made a sharp right three blocks shy of overwhelming the celebration. Rounding a corner as if it were a combination of sandstorm and tornado, the sand cloud disappeared, although a distant roaring could still be heard.

"What *was* that thing?" Gwen asked, forgetting that she was still at the microphone and her question was going out to the entire crowd.

Spider-Man's determined declaration of, "I don't know, but I'm going to find out!" resulted in another roar of support from the crowd. He bounded upward, fired a webline, and swung off after what would more than likely turn out to be some sort of weird atmospheric condition.

Yet the science student in Gwen told her that it couldn't possibly be that simple.

Her inner science student, as it turned out, was absolutely right.

XI

SON OF A BEACH

FLINT MARKO WAS BRIMMING with confidence. It was a pleasant feeling, one that he was unaccustomed to, given the usual assortment of people criticizing him, beating him down, or at least trying to.

Now, as he strode down the streets of New York City, he looked back on all the people who had made his life miserable, people who had loomed so large in his day-to-day existence. Cops, wardens, his wife, teachers, his parents . . . especially his father. Indeed, the crappy way his father had treated him had compelled him to be the best parent he humanly could for Penny's sake.

It was odd. All those loomed-so-large people now seemed small, pathetic . . . even irrelevant. How could he ever have been so concerned about them? They were nothing. He was now a giant, bestriding humanity like a colossus, and if they didn't like him or despised him or thought he was beneath them . . . what did it matter? All they could do was shout at him or try to tear him down, and that just wasn't going to be happening anymore. Not to Flint Marko.

Because Flint Marko was no longer there. He had left

the building, gone on to a better place. The man that he was now—the being that he was now—had as much in common with Flint Marko as Flint Marko had in common with an amoeba. Thinking of himself as merely Flint Marko would be limiting.

He scratched his ear thoughtfully, wondering . . . if he wasn't Flint Marko, who was he? A few grains of sand fell out of his ear. Feeling as if something was still in there, he pounded firmly on the side of his head as he tilted it, and a stream of sand poured out. That wasn't surprising—as he had trimmed away excess sand so that his features would appear more and more normal, the grains had simple retreated into his body. Because of that, he now had too much sand between his ears. Once he'd extracted it, though, he felt a lot better.

Some blocks away he heard music and cheering. He snorted and wondered if it was to celebrate his return to New York City and somehow doubted that was the case.

He walked past two policemen who were sitting in a cop car. Marko barely afforded them a glance as he kept on going. He heard one of them say, "Isn't that the guy from the prison break?" and the other replied, "Fits the description. *Hey, you! Halt!*"

Marko didn't feel like bothering with them. They were too little and simply not worth his time. Walking quickly across the street, he ducked behind a construction truck. The police officers, pursuing him on foot, split up and came around the truck from two different directions, knowing there was nowhere for him to go.

To their confusion, they came from either side and met

on the other end of the truck. There was no sign of him. However, a large tarp covered the back of the truck, and the two cops looked at each other and nodded together. Clearly they thought they had him.

Seconds later, one of them had whipped the tarp aside and both of them had their guns leveled, fully expecting to see Flint Marko charging them in a hopeless attempt to escape.

There was nothing there except a truckload of sand.

One of the cops grabbed a shovel and stepped forward, about to push it into the sand. That was when Marko suddenly thought, *Why am I hiding? Why am I waiting for them to go away? Why am I afraid of them? That's the old way of thinking. That's Flint Marko's way of thinking. I'm not Flint Marko anymore. I'm not a man of flesh and blood. I'm a man of sand.*

Yes. I'm . . . the Sandman. And the Sandman lies down for no one.

Before the cop could start probing, a giant sandstone hand thrust upward, launching him into the air. He soared a short distance and came down hard on a car windshield.

A patrol car rolled up and several more cops sprang out. *It's like a clown car,* the Sandman grimly thought, and he decided to make clear to them just how hopeless the situation was. He rose, having merged his form with the load of sand that was already in the truck, and towered over them, twenty feet high and growing with every passing second.

The cops stepped back, goggle-eyed, and went for their weapons. Instantly Sandman was filled with concern . . .

but not for himself. Unlike the cops, he knew their bullets would be useless against him. They were in a populated area, and flying bullets didn't discriminate between criminals and law-abiding citizens. He had an image of a little girl, not unlike Penny, standing up at her window somewhere to see what all the noise was about and getting an errant slug square between the eyes.

He opened his mouth to tell the police they should put the guns down, but no voice came out. He was still working on being able to speak without normal vocal cords or a tongue when the cops opened fire. Bullets tore through his chest and out his back. He looked down and saw daylight streaming through the holes.

"Don't!" he finally managed to say. *"I said don't!"*

You'd think they'd have learned. Instead they kept shooting. He couldn't believe that he was more worried about citizens being hurt than the cops were.

His physical form imitated his thoughts, and he transformed into an angry sandstorm that blasted down the street. Overwhelmed by the force and fury of it, the cops were knocked flat onto their backs, clawing at the air, unable to breathe. Nor were the police cars spared Sandman's wrath as they were flipped over from the sheer power of his onslaught, their wheels spinning.

Seeing no point in continuing to screw around with the fools who thought they had a chance in hell against him, Sandman blasted down the narrow canyons of the city. He never knew how much free-floating dirt and dust there was in New York. He gathered it all to himself, like a nurturing father, and grew larger and larger until he was a living sandstorm sixty stories high. People ran screaming from his advance, which was fine by him. He wasn't out to kill anyone—he simply wanted to help his daughter, and having cops wasting ammunition on him wasn't going to accomplish that.

Satisfied that he had left his pursuers behind, Sandman reconstituted himself, drawing in the grit tighter and faster until he looked like a stationary whirlwind. Seconds later the sand and wind faded, leaving him standing there looking at his hands. They appeared fairly normal and he smiled with satisfaction. It was taking him less time to sculpt himself to human specifications. Clearly he was ahead of the learning curve.

He smiled as he stood outside his target: an armored car outside the First National Bank. The words MANHATTAN SAFE ARMORED CAR CO. were emblazoned on the side, along with the assurance that the company had been PROTECTING NEW YORK SINCE 1925. That was laughable. They didn't give a damn about New York. They cared about protecting New York's money. Not exactly the same thing.

As he stood there, the armored car—oblivious of his presence—roared to life and pulled away from the curb. Either they had just discharged their contents, so the car was empty and useless . . . or else they'd just made a pickup, in which case it was ready to be picked like an overripe grape.

With a single thought, he caused the grains of his body to separate slightly, making him light as air. He vaulted to the top of the truck and instantly brought them all back together tighter than they originally were. Far denser than a normal human, Sandman landed with a heavy thud atop the roof, the paneling creaking and groaning beneath his feet.

He heard a voice from within—a guard, no doubt—saying, "There's something on the roof," followed by an electronic crackle of static. The guard was probably communicating to the driver via walkie-talkie. Fine. Let him call for help, for all the good it would do him.

Sandman stared at his right arm, willed it into the shape he wanted it, and was pleased to see it reform into a giant sandstone mace. He raised it high and then slammed it down, tearing into the rear of the armored car and shredding it like tissue paper.

The one guard inside looked up at him with a face that had gone the color of curdled milk. Then Sandman spotted what he'd been after: the huge sacks of bank cash piled in a corner like so much laundry. Jackpot.

Sandman glanced back to the guard just in time to see the shotgun being pointed at him before it went off.

He tried to avoid the blast out of reflex and was only partly successful as the left side of his face was blown away. Howling in fury at the pain he didn't feel, Sandman let his cohesion go. The guard was instantly besieged by a tidal wave of sand, smashing him against the Plexiglas partition that separated the cargo section of the truck from the cab.

The driver turned, his eyes wide in alarm, as he saw the back section fill impossibly fast with cascading sand. The partition was designed to withstand direct shots from bullets, but not the sheer unyielding amount of weight that was piling up against it now. A ribbon of cracks appeared in the Plexiglas, and before the driver could think of what he should do, the partition shattered and sand gushed into the cab. The driver let out an alarmed shriek, but the sound was overwhelmed by the roar of Sandman's onslaught. Pouring into the cab without letup, sand buried the driver up to his neck.

It also buried his foot on the accelerator, pressing it to the floor.

Even enveloped as he was by sand, the driver desperately fought to keep the armored car on course. He was only partly successful.

The armored car careened wildly down the street, sending pedestrians scattering. A taxi veered to get out of its way, but the speeding truck dealt it a glancing blow and sent it skidding to the side.

Sandman, meantime, had reformed part of his body into its human proportions, even as the rest of the sand kept the driver immobilized and the armored car moving.

Only a short time earlier he had been so concerned about the safety of others in regard to flying bullets. But the more he used his power, the more he found such concerns to be quaint, even irrelevant. He had the power of a god . . . and what use did gods have for worrying about the safety of mere mortals?

He could do anything now . . . anything . . .

A jaunty voice broke through his musings on omnipotence. "What sandbox did you crawl out of?"

Sandman looked up and saw the masked face of

Spider-Man staring down at him. The wallcrawler was leaning against the rear doors of the armored car, apparently having dropped through the hole that Sandman had created. He had a cocky demeanor, like a blue-and-red-clad Bugs Bunny, that immediately irritated the hell out of Sandman.

"Don't you know there's a penalty for early withdrawal?" Spider-Man demanded.

"Back off," snarled Sandman, and just to underscore how serious he was, he extended his arm and swung a sandy fist at Spider-Man. Moving faster than Sandman would have thought possible, Spider-Man ducked under it, punching Sandman in the gut.

It had about as much effect as the cops' bullets—his fist went right through Sandman's body. Sandman instantly reacted, transforming his fist into the shape of a hammer and slamming Spider-Man not only into the truck's rear doors but through them, tearing the doors right off their hinges.

One of the doors clattered to the street and tumbled away; Spider-Man landed atop the other. The door, still moving at the same speed as the armored car, skidded and sent up a shower of sparks. The annoying insect fired a webline and, affixing his feet to the door with his astounding adhesive powers, "surfed" down the street behind the car, dragged along at top speed.

Other cars were scrambling to get out of the armored car's path. The armored car swerved, mowing through a line of parked cars, sending each of them flipping up and over, and Spider-Man had to surf left, right, left again, dodging the tumbling vehicles as they crashed down on either side of him.

Sandman witnessed a van fly toward Spider-Man, who somersaulted over it and landed back on his still moving "wakeboard." A Gremlin, of all things, now hurtled toward him end over end, and Spider-Man practically bent backward, like a limbo dancer, allowing the car to pass harmlessly over him.

Sandman admired Spider-Man's agility, if not his brains. Deciding that watching the wildly gyrating web slinger had provided enough amusement for one day, Sandman climbed out the top of the armored car, hauling as many of the cash bags as he could carry. Out the corner of his eye, he saw his pursuer suddenly vault from his makeshift wakeboard onto the top of the armored car, squaring off yet again in this ongoing and ridiculous attempt to impede him.

Just ahead of the out-of-control armored vehicle, oblivious of the world around her, a woman crossed the street to her car while chatting away on a cell phone. She opened the driver's door of her parked car. The armored car was barreling straight at her—in about five seconds there would be nothing between the hurtling truck and the open door of her car.

She was standing directly under a lamppost. Without thought, Spider-Man fired a webline in a long arc that soared over the top of the lamppost, descended, and snagged her from behind. In the instant before the armored car struck, the webline drew shorter, and the startled woman was yanked upward. The armored truck smashed through the open car door, sending it flying with such impact that it landed a block away. The woman dropped to the ground seconds later, looking around dizzily, clearly uncertain as to what had just happened.

Spider-Man was torn with conflict. Clearly this . . . this human sandpile had to be stopped. But so did the armored car before it killed someone, and at least he had some clue how to go about that.

Taking a huge risk, he dropped into the speeding armored car, ignoring the scowling face of the sand guy as he went. He spotted the one guard, pressed up against the shattered Plexiglas, and the driver, who was buried up to his neck.

Spider-Man also saw that the problem of stopping the armored car was about to be solved. It was heading toward the solid side of a building.

With only seconds to act, he grabbed the one guard under one arm, hauled the driver out from the sandpile with the other, and threw them both out the back of the ruined car. Even as he did so, he spun webnets faster than ever before. They formed slings around the guards, snagging them both.

Spider-Man was about to leap clear when the leftover sand beneath his feet grabbed at him. He looked down in confusion, buried in sand up to his ankles. He tried to pull free, yanking with increasing desperation.

Just as he managed to extricate his feet, the armored

car hit the curb, flipped completely over, and slammed into the side of the building.

Ironically, the pile of sand in the cab saved him. Spider-Man was propelled forward on impact, but all the sand in the front that had nearly smothered the driver cushioned the blow. The rest of the armored car crunched in behind him, and he tightened himself into a ball, tucking his head down for maximum protection.

Even after the car had been halted in its suicidal course, Spider-Man stayed there for long seconds, scarcely able to believe he was still alive. His whole body ached, the world around him spinning.

Hauling his battered body forward, hand over hand, Spider-Man pulled himself out the open back of the car and tumbled with a distinct lack of gracefulness into the street. The armored car was a smoking wreck, and a bit of flame burned on the underside. He snuffed it out with a few quick web shots; the last thing anyone needed was for the whole thing to erupt in a massive fireball.

He looked over toward the guards just long enough to ascertain that they were all right. There was not, however, any sign of the money, nor of the sandy freak that had made off with it.

Spider-Man immediately fired a webline that hauled him to a high perch, giving him an unobstructed view of the surrounding area for blocks in all directions. He tried to catch a glimpse of his opponent, but there was none to be had. He was long gone.

He briefly pondered the insane opponents that had

surfaced since the first day he had put on the Spider-Man costume—the Green Goblin, Dr. Octopus, the Goblin redux . . . and now this human sandpile.

"Where do all these guys come from?" he wondered aloud, then grimly thought that the *Daily Bugle* was going to have a field day with *this*.

Peter Parker couldn't have been more correct. The next day's *Bugle* headline blared: SANDMAN! SON OF A BEACH! EVEN SPIDEY CAN'T STOP HIM! Even more irritating was the smaller headline, which had a picture of Spider-Man receiving the key to the city from Gwen Stacy, with the words: GIVE BACK THE KEY! plastered beneath it.

Reading the front page in his apartment, Peter threw it down in irritation. Then he looked in the mirror, straightened his tie, and pulled on his sport jacket as he muttered, "It was a draw."

He was still aching from the pounding he'd taken at the hands of the guy everyone was calling Sandman. An obvious enough name, and certainly appropriate, since he'd come close to hammering Spider-Man into unconsciousness. But Peter healed quickly and was determined to soldier through the pain for Mary Jane's sake. This was going to be an important evening, and he didn't want to risk anything ruining it.

Pulling his wallet out of his jacket pocket, he checked the contents and wasn't thrilled. He went to a drawer where he kept what he laughingly referred to as the Parker family fortune and extracted a few more bills. He stared at it, looked at the money in his hand, then took the whole pile and shoved it in his pocket. From his other pocket he extracted Aunt May's engagement ring. It was tiny, granted, but if he held it up just right in the light, it dazzled.

As he headed for the door, he had a vague sense of unease. At first he thought it was simply butterflies in his stomach over his plans for the evening, but then something drew him to the closet.

He glanced in and saw nothing except his sparse wardrobe and deep shadows. Peter supposed it was understandable that he was getting increasingly cautious in his old age. If sand could have it out for him, then it was entirely possible that, the next thing he knew, shadows would be out to get him.

Laughing inwardly at the notion, Peter headed out the front door, shutting it tightly behind him . . . and never noticing that one of the shadows in his closet was moving ever so slightly.

XII

PROPOSAL ON THE ROCKS

THE CONSTELLATION RESTAURANT WAS a reasonably upscale rendezvous that was within Peter's financial limits, albeit barely. Originally, Peter had been concerned that he wasn't going to be able to put thoughts of yesterday's debacle behind him, but was now pleasantly surprised to find an increasing spring in his step as he approached the restaurant. During evening hours, an elevator in the front lobby operated express from the ground floor to the Constellation, and Peter stepped into it feeling positively elated. Whatever shellacking his confidence might have taken at Sandman's hands yesterday was all washed away in a flood of good feeling that this evening would turn out well.

Prompted by the cheery ding of the elevator, he stepped out on the top floor and glanced around with uncertainty. He'd never been to this restaurant before, but Mary Jane had spoken of it highly; this was supposed to be her night, and that was all the incentive he'd needed. A wandering violinist passed by, playing a sprightly rendition of "Flight of the Bumblebee."

Peter moved toward the reservations desk, where a

maître d' peered down his nose at him and said, *"Bonsoir. Le monsieur a-t-il une réservation?"*

"I'm sorry, I don't speak . . ." Peter was already feeling out of his depth.

His eyes crinkling with carefully cultivated French disdain, the maître d' reminded him, "This is a French restaurant, non?"

"Oui."

Heaving the sigh of one who does not suffer fools gladly, the maître d' said, "Name, please?"

"Parker. Peter."

He skimmed down the list, then nodded. "Ahhh, here we are. Parker. For two. You are the first."

"I have a request. My girlfriend will be coming. I have this . . ." Peter fumbled around in his pocket and experienced a brief, horrified moment when he thought it had somehow discovered a hole and had slipped away . . . before his fingers finally settled around it. He withdrew Aunt May's engagement ring and held it up. "This ring . . . and I want to . . ."

This seemed to cause the maître d' to perk up. "You want to pop the question tonight?"

"Right. I want to do something special."

"Ah," said the maître d', thumping his open hand to his chest as if he were trying to prevent his heart from bounding out of it. "I love it. Romance." He paused, then added, "I *am* French," as if that were in doubt.

"When I signal you," Peter said in a conspiratorial tone, "if you bring the champagne with the ring . . ."

". . . at the bottom of her glass."

Peter gave him a high sign. "Perfect."

"Magnifique," replied the maître d', and for good measure, he made one of those popping noises, like a champagne cork, by bouncing his hand off his mouth.

"Also," said Peter, pulling a slip of paper from his inside jacket pocket, "I thought at the same time, if the violins could play this song . . ."

The maître d' glanced at it and, to Peter's relief, nodded in approval. "Their favorite."

Peter handed the ring to the maître d', who held the diamond up for closer inspection. If he thought the size was unimpressive, he at least had enough discretion not to say anything about it. "Take good care of the ring," said Peter.

"With my life," the maître d' solemnly intoned. He gestured for Peter to follow him to the table. *"S'il vous plaît."*

"Oui," Peter once again utilized one of the four French words he knew.

It appeared to be enough. "I like you," said the maître d' as he lead Peter past other tables, where elegantly dressed, sophisticated diners were enjoying an evening out. One or two glanced his way, found nothing about him particularly remarkable, and went back to their conversations.

A waiter quickly stepped in to pull Peter's chair back for him, which took Peter by surprise. In the places where he typically dined out, the most interaction he was used to from a server was a bored query of "Do you want fries with that?" He sat down, and the waiter eased his chair in behind him. It was one of the most comfortable chairs that Peter had ever sat in.

He watched the maître d' move off and noticed that a bread basket had been placed in front of him. At least he thought it was a bread basket—it was filled with artistically designed, braided breads and unusual crackers. He wasn't sure if he was supposed to eat them or admire them from a distance. Glancing around, he saw that all the fashionable people seemed to be eating them, although amazingly there were no crumbs to be spotted anywhere.

You swing upside down on threads eighty stories above street level. You can be adventurous enough to have some bread.

He picked up one of the braided sticks and bit into it carefully. It was wonderful, freshly baked.

He waved the stick around in what he perceived was a casual manner and imagined Mary Jane seated across from him. "I ordered some champagne," he said, and realized he was speaking with a French accent. He cleared his throat and continued in his normal voice, "Would you like some champagne?" Then, pretending to see a ring in her glass, he acted surprised as he said, "Oh! How'd that get in there!" He smiled, seeing her getting teary eyed. "Oh, stop. Don't cry."

He acted out the rest of the scenario to his satisfaction, then glanced at his wrist only to discover that he wasn't wearing a watch. Well, that was all right. Certainly she'd be along any minute.

Time passed . . . and more time . . . until he lost track. He was munching on the last of the bread sticks and growing concerned. The notion that Mary Jane might be standing him up never occurred to him. Instead he was entirely concerned that . . . well, who knew what? What if Harry had gotten his memory back and was holding her hostage somewhere? What if she'd run afoul of this Sandman character? What if . . . ?

With great relief, he saw Mary Jane finally enter the restaurant and speak a few words to the maître d'. The maître d' nodded, looking rather pleased, and led Mary Jane over to the table. Peter thought she looked a little self-conscious, but he could understand why. A girl as gorgeous as Mary Jane was always having people looking her way with admiration. It had to be hard drawing appreciative stares wherever you went.

Peter politely rose as the maître d' personally held the chair out for her. She sat down and shifted uneasily, which seemed odd to Peter since there was nothing remotely uncomfortable about the chair.

"This place in your budget?" she asked.

Ah, that was it. Money worries. Peter smiled reassuringly and said, "It's a special occasion. You're on Broadway. You're a star."

"I don't feel like much of a star tonight."

"You're a star in my eyes. You'll be in everybody's eyes now." When she didn't react to that, he reached over and took her hand. "I know what you're feeling, but you'll get used to it. Take me: I'm everywhere." He laughed at the absurdity of it. "I see Spider-Man posters in the windows, kids running around with me on their sweaters. I'm a big Halloween item." He saw a trace of a smile on Mary Jane's mouth over that and, feeling encouraged, continued, "I don't know. I guess I've become something of an icon. 'Spider-Man, Spider-Man.' They kept screaming it. I mean, c'mon . . . I'm a nerdy kid from Queens. So I'm thinking to myself, do I deserve this?"

He hoped he was taking the right approach to the situation. Last time Mary Jane had flipped out on him when he'd started addressing her concerns from his point of view. But he was certain that the way to get through to her now was to make her understand that he could relate to her problems through personal experience. Still, he didn't know how much headway he was making here, and he was about to pursue her worries further when suddenly he saw exactly the wrong person at exactly the wrong time heading their way.

"Hi, Peter!" called a cheerful Gwen Stacy.

You gotta be kidding me. Of all the restaurants in all the boroughs in all New York, she walks into mine.

Peter was suddenly self-conscious. That spur-of-the-moment kiss that had seemed like such a good idea at the time now left Peter feeling extremely vulnerable. Here he'd made this whole big demonstration on the stage, and now the girl with whom he'd performed it was standing there smiling at him, and Mary Jane—to whom he was preparing to propose!—could only scowl.

At that moment Peter would have welcomed an attack from the Sandman just to defuse the situation.

"Oh, Gwen. Hi." He tried not to project anything in his tone or demeanor that might suggest he was doing anything other than politely acknowledging her presence.

"My parents and I were just having dinner here, and I

saw you guys." Gwen pointed toward the doorway, and Peter saw a man and a woman waiting there. They had their coats on, obviously about to leave. They must have been dining on the opposite side of the restaurant, and Gwen had spotted Peter as they were on their way out. It took him a few seconds, but then he recognized the man: the police captain who had been at the scene when he'd saved Gwen.

Her father is a cop? A trained observer of people who could tell when someone was uncomfortable or lying or trying to conceal something? Oh, this is just perfect.

Gwen's parents waved to them, and Peter waved back.

Immediately the maître d', mistaking Peter's gesture for his signal, started toward Peter with the champagne. Peter's eyes widened in panic, and he quickly waved the maître d' off. This caused the maître d' to stop where he was, blinking in confusion like a blinded owl. Meantime Gwen's parents, equally bewildered, continued to wave.

While Peter flapped like a crippled sparrow, Gwen seized the initiative and extended a hand to Mary Jane. "Hello. I'm Gwen Stacy."

Realizing that the two hadn't formally been introduced, Peter quickly said, "Oh, right. This is, uh . . ." To his horror, he blanked on her name for a split second, but recovered quickly and said, "Mary Jane Watson."

"Hi, it's so nice to meet you," Gwen said warmly. "Pete talks about you all the time."

Mary Jane raised a single eyebrow. Never a good sign. "Oh?"

Clearing his throat, Peter said, "Gwen's my, uh, lab cart . . . lab . . . partner in Dr. Connors's class."

Gwen rested a hand on his shoulder, a simple friendly gesture. From the look on Mary Jane's face, though, Gwen might as well have been sliding her hand down the front of his shirt. "Peter's something of a genius," Gwen said blithely. "He saved my life in Chemistry."

"Uh-huh."

Oh, this is so *not good.*

"Oh, and, Pete . . . something else before I forget," Gwen continued, still unaware of the rapidly dropping temperature in the air. "You're Spider-Man's personal photographer, right?" Peter was about to say that wasn't exactly true, but Gwen went right on, "I hope you don't mind my asking, but if you managed to get a shot of our kiss, I'd love it . . . for my portfolio, of course." She laughed lightly and said to Mary Jane, "After all, who gets kissed by Spider-Man these days?"

Mary Jane didn't even glance at Gwen. Instead her gaze was boring through the back of Peter's head as she said icily, "I can't imagine."

The loud, clattering noise in Peter's head was the sound of the wheels coming completely off the evening.

Gwen threatened to keep talking, but then finally—finally—in the brief silence that followed Mary Jane's comment, she realized Peter was hugely uncomfortable, and Mary Jane was steaming about something.

Trying damage control, she said with a desperate smile, "I'll leave you two alone. Loved meeting you." As she started to leave, she called over her shoulder, "By the way, try the rack of lamb. We just love the rack of lamb here."

MJ nodded distractedly, her gaze still fixed on Peter. The eyebrow was still raised. Clearly she was waiting for him to say something.

"She's in my science class. It's not her best subject."

Gwen and her parents waved one final time as they headed out the door. Peter threw a fast wave back and returned his attention to Mary Jane. As a result, he didn't notice that the maître d' yet again mistook the gesture as the real summons for the champagne.

Mary Jane still studied Peter as if he were a slide on a microscope. "Rack of lamb," he asked, doing his best to sound casual and failing miserably. "Do we like lamb?"

Still nothing. Not only had the wheels gone off the evening, it was now skidding out of control toward a cliff, apparently without enough webbing in the world to yank it up short. "What?" he finally asked, exasperation rising within him.

"How come you've never mentioned her?" MJ demanded, and it all came out in a rush. "She's your lab partner. You saved her life. She thinks you're a genius, and she had her polished fingernails all over you, or didn't you notice? And she gave Spider-Man the key to the city! I'll never forget that."

Peter couldn't believe it. What the hell had gotten into her? Mary Jane was acting insanely jealous. Over a *kiss* and Gwen being friendly at a restaurant and a meaningless ceremony, for crying out loud? Had Mary Jane's confidence been that shattered by one lousy review? How in the world was she going to survive as an actress, as a person, if she was that thin-skinned?

And, in truth, Peter was reaching a point where he really, *really* wasn't appreciating getting the third degree. He worked to keep an edge out of his voice, not wanting to exacerbate matters, as he said steadily, "She's a girl . . . in my class."

As if he hadn't spoken (and for all he knew, she hadn't even heard him), she leaned forward and said, "Let me ask you something: When you kissed her, who was kissing her? Spider-Man or Peter?"

"What do you mean?"

"You know exactly what I mean. That was *our kiss.*"

Oh, jeez. What a lunkhead he'd been. It wasn't so much the kiss as that Mary Jane felt something personal had been displayed in a very public forum. Peter had never given that aspect any thought, and he obviously should have. He tried to explain that he now understood and was deeply apologetic, but Mary Jane wouldn't let him get a word in. "Why would you do that? You must've known how it would make me feel. Do you want to push me away?"

"Why would I push you away? I love you. You're my girlfriend." When she continued to stare at him with no further comment, he repeated, "She's just a girl in my class, Mary Jane."

"I guess I thought you were going to . . ."

What? Propose? Apologize? Grow up? Give me thirty seconds and I can do all three.

Instead she rose from her seat. "It doesn't matter. I don't feel very well. I have to go. I'm sorry."

"Hey, wait a minute!" he protested. "Don't do that!"

Too late. She was already headed away from the table. "Please don't follow me," she snapped. The only thing that would have kept Mary Jane there was Peter firing webbing at her feet and gluing her in place—something he was strongly considering.

Peter started to go after her despite her wishes to the contrary, and his path was suddenly blocked by two violinists playing "Falling in Love." When he had imagined the way he thought this evening was going to go, Mary Jane had heard the tune and promptly burst into song, accompanying them. Instead she looked as if she were about to burst into tears the moment the first notes of the song sounded. She walked faster, so fast that she bumped into a table, staggered, and nearly knocked a tray out of a waiter's grasp. All eyes in the restaurant turned toward her, and the moment she was out the door, they shifted toward Peter.

The violinists came in on either side of Peter and serenaded him with the song, which he was now quite certain was going to be a tune he would never be able to stand listening to again. He thought he heard a long, high-pitched scream, and he realized that, yes, indeed, that was the sound of the evening clearing the edge of the cliff and hurtling down, down toward its hideous death.

Holding the champagne glasses and oblivious to how badly things had gone, the maître d' said politely, "May I tell you tonight's specials?"

Without a word, Peter reached into one of the champagne glasses, removed the ring, picked up a napkin, and carefully wiped it off. Meantime the maître d' was prattling on. "We have the watercress soup with an accent of tarragon. We have fresh crab in a Marnier sauce, roast beef with a spark of ginger, and the foie gras conception."

At that moment Peter wanted nothing more than to be invisible to simplify slinking out of here. As the violins continued to play their admittedly beautiful rendition of "Falling in Love," Peter placed the ring in his pocket, picked up one of the champagne glasses, and tossed back the drink in one gulp. It burned in a pleasant manner as it hurtled down his throat.

It was the only thing about the entire evening that had gone down according to plan.

Peter tried to contact Mary Jane several times upon arriving home and got no answer. He hated having to stand there in the middle of the hallway and use the pay phone, but he had no choice—money was too tight for him to spend it on a private phone, or even a cell. "Hello? Mary Jane? Are you there? It's me, I want to talk to you. Come on, Mary Jane, pick up." When he realized she wasn't going to, he hung up with a heavy sigh. It was too late; she'd probably gone to the theater.

As he turned to head into his apartment, the pay phone suddenly rang. Daring to hope that it was Mary Jane, that maybe the evening could be salvaged, he grabbed it off the hook. He did so with such energy that, had it not been for his adhesive abilities, the receiver would have flown out of his hand. "Hello?" he asked, making no attempt to keep the urgency out of his voice.

"Mr. Parker," came a gravelly male voice from the other end, and Peter—crestfallen—was certain it was a bill collector. So he was surprised when the voice continued, "This is Detective Neil Garrett, from the Thirty-second Precinct. I'm calling on behalf of Captain Stacy. He'd like you to come down to the station to speak with him."

Oh my God. He knows. He was able to tell from across the restaurant. I'm dead. I am so dead.

"What's . . ." Peter's voice cracked slightly and he brought it back under control. "What's it about?"

"We've got some new information regarding the homicide of your uncle, Ben Parker."

Peter had always thought it looked odd or unrealistic in the movies when someone stared at a phone in his or her hand upon the receipt of shocking news. Peter's real-life reaction, though, was nothing short of Oscar-worthy, as he stared stupidly at the plastic receiver, his mind reeling, his body paralyzed.

XIII

TRACKS IN THE SAND

Captain Stacy assured Peter that his aunt May had already been called, and that she would be at the station by eleven. Peter made sure to arrive at exactly the same time and met her at the front by the desk sergeant's station.

It all seemed so surreal.

Peter had been convinced that the next time he saw May Parker, it was going to be with Mary Jane at his side, and MJ would be showing the ring sparkling on her finger. In that way he'd finally be responsible for bringing some joy into May Parker's life. Instead old heartaches were being resurrected as Peter and Aunt May were escorted into a small conference room, where Captain Stacy was waiting for them.

Stacy made no mention of encountering Peter at the restaurant the night before, and for that Peter was incredibly grateful. May wasn't stupid: she'd have figured out why Peter had taken MJ to such a fancy place, and she'd be asking all about it. Fortunately enough, the tale of that little fiasco would wait for another time, or better yet, never.

"Originally we thought that this man"—Stacy slid a

mug shot across the table—"Dennis Caradine, was your husband's killer. We were wrong."

"What?" said May, not understanding.

Nor did Peter comprehend. He peered over at the photograph and recognized him instantly as the man whom he had originally let past him at the wrestling arena . . . the man he'd confronted at the warehouse. It was the right man.

Was it that he was using an alias? That his name wasn't really Dennis Caradine? But so what if that was the case? Who cared? Uncle Ben's murderer had met his final justice, and surely that was all that was important.

"It turns out that Caradine was only the accomplice," Captain Stacy told them. "The actual killer is still at large."

What?! This was making less and less sense to Peter the longer it went on. "What are you talking about?" he demanded, and promptly tried to rein himself in, not wanting to sound too aggressive.

"This"—Stacy pulled out a second picture—"is the man who killed your husband."

He placed it between Peter and Aunt May, and Peter fully expected it to be the face of a total stranger.

Instead, the Sandman stared out at him.

"The name is Flint Marko," Stacy said. "He's a small-time crook who's been in and out of prison."

Slowly Peter shook his head. "You've got it wrong," he whispered, barely able to grasp the enormity of what he was being told.

"Two days ago, he escaped. Evidently he confessed his

guilt to a cellmate. And," Stacy continued before Peter could offer up another protest, "we have two witnesses who will corroborate his story. It all fits with our original suspicions. We've never been able to prove it until now."

Peter was rocked back in his chair. A deep pounding pulsed in his temples, and he didn't even hear Aunt May asking, "Would you mind taking these photographs away please?" Instead his mind was whirling with this new information that knocked the props out from under his entire belief system.

For so long . . . for so much time . . . I've been beating myself up, telling myself that I could have stopped the criminal who killed Uncle Ben. That if I had, Uncle Ben might still be alive. And instead . . .

He conjured up a mental picture of Flint Marko walking up to Uncle Ben and ruthlessly blowing him away. Whatever had happened to Marko to transform him into Sandman, it must have been since that night. Recently, in fact, otherwise they'd never have been able to hold him in the first place.

On some level, there should have been relief—a massive burden of guilt should have been lifted. He'd never encountered Flint Marko before and thus couldn't possibly have caused Uncle Ben's death, through inaction or any other action.

Instead . . . instead a deep, dark ball of fury began to build within Peter.

Uncle Ben was doomed from the start? Nothing I could have done that evening would have had the slightest impact on how things turned out?

At least when he had believed himself directly responsible, he felt—strangely enough—as if he had some control over his life. But now he was learning that he'd never had any control at all.

Uncle Ben never had a chance.

Everything that Peter had done in the past two years to atone for his great sin was simply an endless pursuit in the face of an existence that had suddenly become terribly, even blindingly unfair.

Useless . . . all of it useless . . . bad enough I can never bring Uncle Ben back no matter how much I do, but now I could never have saved him in the first place! With great power comes great responsibility? And what if I had no power, huh? That evening, despite all my abilities, I couldn't have done a thing to prevent Ben's being shot and killed. So with no power comes . . . what? No responsibility? I should be able to do whatever I want. . . .

And right then, what Peter Parker wanted more than anything was to get his hands around Flint Marko's throat. Flesh and blood, sand, it made no difference. He wanted to find him and kill him with his bare hands, no matter what it took.

"I'm sorry, Mrs. Parker," Captain Stacy was saying, removing the photographs. "I know this isn't easy, but please be patient. We're doing our job. We'll catch him."

Peter, seething with barely contained rage, said between clenched teeth, "I don't think you're doing your job. I watched my uncle die, and we went after the wrong man. And now you're saying"—his voice began to rise in pitch and volume—"you had suspicions for two years? *Witnesses?* Why weren't we *told* about that?"

"Settle down, son."

Peter stood, bubbling over with fury. "I've no intention of settling down! This man"—he pointed at the back of the photo—"killed my uncle, and he's still out there!"

He headed for the door, ignoring Aunt May's cry of "Peter!" and Captain Stacy's plea to calm down and take a seat. The only thing he was hearing was the pounding in his head that urged him to get out there, to find Flint Marko, to avenge the death of his uncle.

A vengeance that had waited far too long.

As night fell, a sand cloud drifted through the canyon of skyscrapers and toward a medical research facility on Twenty-seventh and Park Avenue. Sandman had gotten the hang of moving without attracting undue attention, keeping the grains of his body far enough apart that—even if people looked straight at him—they would see no more than a faint discoloration in the air.

He sought and found a ventilation duct on the side of the building and seeped into it. He still had no clear idea of how his mind was truly functioning when he was in this form, other than to think that every single grain of sand contained a part of his consciousness. Once inside, he consolidated his body so that it continued to flow as one steady stream of sand.

He moved quickly through the ventilation shaft and found a place where it opened out into a men's restroom. He ran the grains through the duct, pulled himself together until he looked relatively normal, then stepped outside and glanced around for a directory. Not seeing one anywhere, he asked a passing technician—with as polite and harmless-looking an expression as he could muster—where one might find Dr. Ralph Wallace.

"One flight up, room AF15," the technician said. He started to walk away, then turned around. "But he doesn't like to be disturbed during—"

There was no sign of the man to whom he'd just spoken.

As the technician shrugged it off and decided that maybe he'd been working too hard, Sandman eased his way down the ventilation shaft, went straight up, then over, and continued to make his way around until he finally found room AF15. He moved in through the shaft toward the inside of the room . . . and the air duct was shut tight. Apparently Dr. Ralph Wallace wasn't big on air-conditioning. Or maybe he was a germophobe, convinced that viruses floating around from another part of the facility might work their way through the air and infect him.

Sandman was momentarily annoyed, then decided it was another of life's little challenges to overcome. Moving in a different direction, he found a small separation in a connection point and eased his sandy body through it. He discovered that he was inside the wall, moving past electrical wiring that naturally had no effect on him. He found an electrical outlet and seeped through it into the room. As he did so, he managed to short out power—the lights flickered out before coming back on courtesy of emergency backup.

Dr. Wallace, meantime, had clearly heard Sandman's

passing through the vent system, but had no clue what it was. Perhaps mice or something equally charming? He followed the noise to the end of the wall, then said softly, "Is someone there?"

Sandman collected the grains of his body, reconstituted them, and came into existence behind Wallace. The good doctor didn't hear a thing and, after apparently satisfying himself that it was probably nothing, turned around and emitted a somewhat girlish shriek of surprise. "Who are you?!" he demanded, clutching his lab coat as if he'd just stepped out of the shower. "How did you get in here?"

"It's all right," Sandman said, holding his hands up. "It's me. Flint Marko." He waited for Wallace to react to the name, and the doctor did, looking both surprised and alarmed . . . but also curious. "I wrote you from prison about my daughter, Penny. She still needs your help."

Wallace looked worried that, if he didn't say the right thing, Marko might destroy him. He took a deep breath, steeling himself, and said, "I can't help you. I wrote you back. I tried to explain in the letter . . . I didn't have the funding to finish the research . . . the little money you did send barely bought test tubes."

"Well, try this," said Sandman.

He reached down and picked up a bag of money stolen from the armored car. It hadn't been easy getting it in here. Basically, Marko had had to concentrate and absorb the money into his own sandy body, breaking it down molecule by molecule. It was the only way to smuggle it in. The first several bags he'd tried it with, his attempts to reconstitute the cash had resulted in the bills falling apart in his hands. He'd finally managed through practice to make it work. The amount of money lost in the process was incredibly frustrating, but at least he still had an impressive amount.

Wallace stared at the bag for a moment, and Marko saw a thin line of sweat beading his brow. "It won't be enough," Wallace said, which immediately raised Marko's suspicions, since Wallace hadn't even glanced inside. He had no idea how much money was in there. More likely Wallace was terrified at the thought of receiving stolen cash. "It would take teams of researchers, millions of dollars . . ."

"Then I'll get more! All you need!"

"Even if you could," Wallace insisted, "it's highly unlikely we'd find a cure in the short time your daughter has left."

Wallace's reluctance probably stemmed from aiding a known criminal via "ill-gotten gain." But Sandman didn't give a damn about niceties or moralities—to him, the end justified the means. If the end meant that Penny lived, then any means was fine by him. The problem was bringing Wallace, the foremost expert—indeed, the only expert—on this disease into line with Sandman's way of thinking.

Shouldn't be too hard.

"Shut up!" snarled Marko as he slammed Wallace against a window, shattering it. Wallace almost tumbled to the floor, but Marko grabbed him and yanked him forward. Wind whistled in through the broken glass, blowing papers off the counters. He hauled Wallace up until they were practically nose to nose and said with barely controlled fury, "You're gonna help her, Doc. I'll get you the money if I have to level the entire city to do it. Just fine a cure for my Penny!"

"Yes! Yes, I will!" Wallace cried out. "Don't hurt me!"

"Then don't fail me!"

He shoved Wallace well clear of the window, and the research scientist fell to the floor, utterly petrified.

Well, that had been easy enough. A meeting of minds established in just a few seconds through threat and intimidation.

Satisfied with the way matters stood, Sandman released his mental hold on his body and streamed out the window, running down the side of the building. The dustup with Wallace already behind him, he got busy thinking about his next move, and where he was going to get the money he needed.

Wherever it was, he was certain to find it. He was going to save Penny. Find her a cure.

A cure that had waited far too long.

XIV

THROUGH A MIRROR DARKLY

PETER PARKER LOOKED OUT at the night sky through the window of his small apartment. The scratchy voice on his police scanner barked out announcements, except Peter had changed the frequency. No longer was he just attending to the major emergency calls—now any summons, no matter how trivial, was coming through. The almost steady stream of chatter was overwhelming, but he didn't want to take a chance that some seemingly insignificant problem—people experiencing a small sandstorm on a Coney Island beach, for instance—could slip past Peter when it might lead him to his prey.

Come on, Marko. Come on. Turn up. Give me something to go on. Make yourself known so I can find you and give you what's coming to you.

"L20 Parkway, abandoned vehicle," the scanner announced. *"Elderly man in center of Wabash, sorry, Parkway Avenue . . ."*

Still nothing. He turned and glared at the scanner, as if mentally commanding it to give him something useful.

There was a knock at the door. "Who is it?" he called, not really interested.

"It's me."

Mary Jane. He heaved a sigh. Only the day before, he would have sprung across the apartment and thrown the door open, overjoyed to see her. Now, somehow, Mary Jane's presence seemed irrelevant. He had matters of far greater concern on his mind. It was as if she belonged to a part of his life that—if he hadn't left it behind—had at least become inconsequential.

Still, he couldn't just leave her standing out in the hallway. He crossed to the door, opened it, and turned back to the police scanner.

"I'm not here about what happened in the restaurant. I'm sorry that happened," she said, her hands fluttering slightly in agitation. Whether she was or not was of no great concern—the restaurant incident was a lifetime ago. "But Aunt May called me, told me about this convict and what he did and Uncle Ben. She's worried about you."

"She worries too much," Peter said curtly.

Mary Jane was about to reply, but the chatter of the scanner cut in. "Could you turn that down?" she asked. He petulantly considered turning it up instead. The anger within him burned like fire, over Uncle Ben's death, over the police department's ineptness. He wanted to take it all out on someone, preferably Flint Marko.

But Marko wasn't here, and Mary Jane was, and there was no reason to misplace his aggression on her just because she was trying to help . . . even though he didn't need it. So he turned the police scanner down to a low murmur. Enough so that he could still pick out what was being said, but not so much that it drowned out what she was saying to him.

"Your aunt hopes you won't do something foolish," she said.

"Like try to find my uncle's killer? Why wouldn't I?" He could understand that Aunt May was concerned about him. But why was Mary Jane telling him this? She, unlike May, knew Peter's secret. She knew what he could do, and how he was more than capable of taking care of himself. Why was she coming here, relaying May's worries? Why wasn't she with Aunt May, assuring her that Peter was a grown man who could make intelligent and informed decisions, and she could rest easy?

Mary Jane's hand hovered above his forearm as if she wanted to rest it upon it affectionately, but she withheld it. Instead her voice dropped to an understanding tone. "I know how that night has always been on your mind. You hunted down the wrong man, but you couldn't have known when you pushed him that he wasn't—"

He wasn't the wrong man. He was a criminal and a thief, and if he didn't kill Uncle Ben, there's no saying that he wouldn't have if given the opportunity, and there's no telling whom else the creep did kill in his career that we'll never even know about, and you weren't there, you don't know what happened, you don't know what you're talking about.

His jaw tight, he said, "He had a gun on me. I made a move. He fell. I didn't push him."

"I'm not accusing you of anything. I understand how you must feel."

Do you? At least you have a living mother and father. It may be dysfunctional as hell, but you have them. As long as they're alive, there's hope that things can be straightened out, matters settled, closure made. How could you possibly understand?

"I'm here," Mary Jane went on, "because I loved your uncle Ben too. And if I can help you in some way, I'm here to . . . to be here . . ." Flustered, she said, "I just want—"

Okay, enough. This was way too little, way too late. Peter was currently seeing the world through a blinding wall of pain and anger, and Mary Jane was simply throwing meaningless words to him from the other side of it. "I don't need your help," he said brusquely. "Thank you for coming."

If she was put off by his tone, she didn't show it. Perhaps she expected it and had decided ahead of time that she wasn't going to let it bother her. "We all need help sometimes, Peter. Even Spider-Man. This pride of *his,*" she emphasized, as if speaking about a different person altogether, "maybe even he's not perfect."

She waited a moment for him to respond. He didn't.

The last thing Peter wanted to do was prolong her stay. She nodded once, a silent acknowledgment of his wishes, then walked out the door, closing it softly behind her. Peter returned to the police scanner and turned it up louder than before, hoping that it would drown out the frustration that was roiling within him. Hoping that it would drown out her voice that was still echoing in his head.

He glanced at the clock: 8:45 P.M. What had Mary Jane been doing here when she should have been onstage?

He brushed the thought from his mind and went back to listening to the reports.

Eventually tiring of doing nothing other than hunkering down next to the police radio, Peter pulled on his Spider-Man costume, ready to leap into action at a moment's notice. With the mask in his hand, he looked out the window for what seemed the hundredth time that evening and muttered, "Where are you, Marko?"

He no longer gave any thought to Mary Jane's visit, never even considered picking up the phone and calling Aunt May to assuage her fears.

The rest of the world seemed to fall away until there was only him and, somewhere out there, Flint Marko.

He considered randomly swinging around the city, searching for Sandman, hoping to stumble over him, but that was likely a waste of time. Waiting for a police summons to at least steer him in the right direction was clearly the more logical way to go. But logic didn't do a damn thing to satisfy his desire for action. He felt like a racehorse trapped behind a gate that refused to open.

More time passed, and Peter—tired of ineffectual pacing—lay down on the bed, continuing to listen to the scanner. With everything that was on his mind, one thing was for certain: no way he was going to fall asleep this night.

Naturally, within the hour, he was dead to the world.

The scanner crackled at him, *"Car 604, domestic disturbance at 3415 Belmont . . . apartment B . . . woman caller is at knifepoint, hysterical . . ."*

Deep in slumber, Peter was unaware of the thick black

ooze that was separating itself from the shadows of his closet . . . and now slowly creeping toward him.

Instead he was in the grip of a nightmare, twitching in bed, groaning in mental pain. Twisting in his dream, he saw the criminal Dennis Caradine tripping over a pipe and falling to his death—except now Peter was there shoving him hard, grinning dementedly, just as Mary Jane had said . . . but that wasn't how it really went down . . . was it?

Uncle Ben's murder scene flared up. Ben lying there, dead, eyes closed . . . Ben's head snapping around, eyes opened . . . except there were no eyes, nothing but worms crawling out . . . Flint Marko walking past the macabre scene, whistling casually, innocent of suspicion.

It isn't right, it isn't fair, this shouldn't have happened, I should be able to do something about it, you can, you can do whatever you want now, nothing can—

Peter's mind recoiled against itself, bewildered and uncertain of what was happening. He was talking to himself, as if his mind had somehow split right down the middle. Even in his dream state, he wondered if he was somehow losing control of his entire Spider-Man persona. Ben was gone, the murder site was gone, Marko was gone, and instead the city spun dizzily beneath him, skyscrapers whipping past, the chill air permeating him, and he felt giddy, reveling in his power, enjoying it in a way not before experienced since it all began. It was all new and liberating, and he couldn't understand why. He heard the distant sound of car horns honking, and sirens yowling, and suddenly he realized that the wind was all too real.

Caught in that twilight area between sleep and wakefulness, he fought his way back to consciousness. He should close the window since it was obviously getting way too drafty . . .

Peter opened his eyes, waking to see the world through the filter of his eye pieces, which meant that he had put on his mask. Odd. He didn't remember doing that.

And he was rocking slowly back and forth.

And he was upside down.

What am I, sleep web slinging now?

Am I still asleep? No. Definitely not.

That thought lingered right up to the moment that he caught a glimpse of his reflection in the mirrored glass of a skyscraper.

Wrong. Still dreaming.

It was like watching an image on TV, since it seemed to bear no resemblance to Spider-Man at all.

Oh, there was Spider-Man all right, or the image of Spider-Man, hanging upside down on a webline—except his costume was no longer blue and red.

It was solid black.

The eyepieces—no longer white, but silvery—leaped out at him, a stark contrast against the ebony mask that he was now wearing.

He could see the outlines of the web pattern against the black, also with that same silvery hue to them, along with his chest emblem.

It was an alien Spider-Man, a bizarre version.

Peter's still fatigued mind processed that he wasn't just watching a separate image. It was his own reflection.

"Whoa!" he shouted, and almost lost his grip on the webstrand before clutching it tightly and maintaining his place. "What the . . . what *is* this?!"

He'd always known the right way to catapult yourself out of a dream was to pinch yourself. He attempted that now, pinching his arm through the suit. He felt the pain; *that* torpedoed the entire dream theory. Even stranger, though, was that the suit seemed to pull away from his skin, like elastic. When he released it, it snapped back. *"Ow! Sticks!"*

Whatever this tarry stuff was, it hadn't simply covered the suit. It had actually permeated it, been absorbed through, adhering to his skin.

The Goblin? Harry? This must be his doing. He must have regained his memory and . . .

Even as the thought crossed his mind, he dismissed it. Harry had been focused on one thing: the death of Peter Parker. If he'd regressed to his villainous mental state, had come to Peter's apartment and found him asleep, he would simply have killed him. The Sandman? Didn't seem likely. So where the hell had this thing come from? A lab experiment gone wrong? A trap by an enemy he hadn't even encountered?

Panic welled within him . . . but faded just as quickly. He felt an almost soothing sense of peace and well-being, so much so that it never occurred to him to question it. He stopped to study, really *study,* the way his reflection appeared in the building. Not satisfied with the distance, he vaulted free of the webline and landed on the building's side. He flexed one arm, then the other; amazingly, his muscles were larger. He felt stronger too, nearly bursting with power.

It was as if he were reborn . . . no. More than that. He was truly alive for the first time in his life.

It wasn't just the strength he sensed burgeoning within him. He was more attuned not only to his own body, but to the entirety of the city as well. The full potential of his spider-sense pulsed in his brain—as if invisible weblines radiated in every direction, and he was at their center. Just as with a real spider, any small vibration in any of the lines instantly caught his attention.

He wanted to do more.

He *could* do more.

Whether that was coming from a deep-seated need or from somewhere else within that had only now manifested, he couldn't say.

Peter was oblivious to the concept that whatever had bonded with him might have its own mind, its own agenda. That while he was busy testing the limits of his own abilities, the creature was doing the exact same thing.

The black-suited Spider-Man ran. Moving at breakneck speed, he sprinted down the face of the building and then leaped powerfully. He somersaulted in midair, bounded off a lower rooftop, and landed with perfect precision upon a narrow ledge. Not something that would have been beyond his abilities to accomplish before . . . but not this effortlessly. He would have been looking ahead, calculating distances, making sure that he could pull it off. Instead, as if his body no longer needed his conscious mind to function, he simply leaped into action, moving with far greater sureness and facility than ever before.

"No problem," he said, confirming it for himself. "How'd I do that?" He caught his reflection in the mirrored glass, turned this way and that, said, "Gotta be this suit. But how did . . . ?"

As a scientist, his first impulse was to go home, remove the suit (presuming he could), and find some way to study it. It was the height of recklessness to be throwing himself around hundreds of feet in the air without the slightest true comprehension of what this . . . this thing . . . could and could not do.

But the impulse was quickly smothered, again by some part of his mind that wasn't his.

This time, though, Peter started to fight it. Although he didn't consciously experience it, part of his core personality started to rise through the "static" that the suit was creating within his mind, like a deep-sea diver in distress, struggling back toward the surface.

The alien symbiote—for that was what had attached itself to him—fought for its own survival. It reached deep within Peter, found that which was most distressing him, then plucked the single strand on Peter's newly heightened spider-sense that would lead him straight to his quarry.

Peter, not realizing that the symbiote had triggered the response, suddenly knew, just *knew,* exactly where Flint Marko was. Something in his head did a fast "zoom in," a movie unspooling in his brain just for him, and his concerns about the creature bore no further thought. Instinct kicked into overdrive as Peter bounded away from the building, webbing down toward the street, moving dangerously fast.

Peter Parker wasn't the only individual in the city with a police band.

Eddie Brock had arrived at the First American Savings Bank barely minutes after the alarm had been called in. He was hoping, praying, that it would be Sandman, because Jameson had put a bounty out on pictures of "the new freak in town."

The good news was that he had gotten his wish. The bad news was that, because of traffic and some horrendously crappy luck, Eddie had gotten there after the real action.

Two cop cars lay on their backs, flipped over like a child's toys. Steam rose from them, the cops all unconscious within—Sandman had tossed them the moment they'd arrived, not giving them even half a chance. The bank windows were shattered, and since there was almost no glass on the outside, it meant that Sandman had smashed them in. Obviously he wasn't making any attempts at stealth these days. The unconscious bodies of several bank guards littered the street.

Looks like it was a hell of a show, thought Brock, then a hissing sound guided his camera lens toward a subway grating on the sidewalk. Sure enough, a large, steady stream of sand was heading right toward it and into it. Brock immediately started snapping pictures. "Hey! Sandy! Look over here! Smile for the birdie!" he desperately shouted, knowing that pictures of a partly formed Sandman were going to nab a far higher dollar—more than that crappy fifty bucks from his first picture—than just a bunch of sand slipping through the grating.

Sandman didn't, unfortunately, seem predisposed to cooperate.

Suddenly Brock saw a form that was both familiar and yet unfamiliar drop down near the grating just as the last of the sand filtered through. Was it . . . ? Yeah. Had to be him. But what was with the new tights?

"Hey, Spidey!" he shouted. Whereas Sandman had ignored him, Spider-Man actually stopped and looked in his direction. Focusing the camera on him, Brock remarked, "Going formal these days? Hey, gimme some attitude!"

"How's this?" replied the black-suited Spider-Man. He reached in Brock's direction, and suddenly a webline shot out, snagging Brock's camera. Brock let out an alarmed shriek of protest as Spider-Man sent the camera flying from Brock's hand and slung it against the side of a building. The camera exploded into metal and glass fragments on impact.

Brock was paralyzed with shock as Spider-Man said cavalierly, "New suit, new attitude."

Finally recapturing the ability to speak, Brock squealed, *"Hey! You no good—!"*

At which point Spider-Man paid him as much mind as Sandman had. He yanked up the grating and dropped down to the subway below, allowing the grating to slam shut behind him.

Brimming with indignation, Brock had never felt

more helpless. But in short order, he decided there was no need for him to feel that way at all. Spider-Man had screwed him over? Fine, the least he could do was return the favor.

Pulling out a small digital camera from his breast pocket, Brock thought, *You wanna dance, Mr. Spider-Man-in-Black? Fine. Then we're gonna dance.* And he started taking pictures of the robbery scene with an eye toward what would most suit his purposes.

Marko was pleased to see that it took his "eyes" no time at all to adapt to the darkness of the subway. Considering his night vision had been for crap before, it was good to discover yet another useful aspect of his transformation.

Bags of money were secured in either hand. The merge trick came with ease this time, barely any effort at all. Once he'd poured his way through the grating, he'd re-formed and pulled the two bags of money from his chest like a magician.

He started down the subway tunnel, moving as quickly as he could. No sight or sound of an oncoming train, so that much was good. It was late now, and there was no chance that Wallace was still at the research center.

Marko was basically homeless, but that didn't matter to him; as Sandman, he needed no creature comforts. He'd probably make his way over toward a convenient sandpit, spread himself out there, wait until—

He didn't need his eyes to see.

That his eyes were in the front of his head was an arbitrary decision on his part. His body was aware of everything around him, in all directions; he was just the most accustomed to looking forward. But now he suddenly "saw" the shadows moving on the ceiling behind him . . . one shadow in particular.

Him. It had to be him.

With a roar of pure fury over Spider-Man once again mixing into his problems, Sandman spun and glared up at the ceiling.

Nothing.

How could that be?

The anger in Sandman's face was replaced by bewilderment as he leaned forward, looking for some indication that Spider-Man was still there—or had ever been there in the first place.

Spider-Man came out of nowhere, slamming his fist into Marko's jaw with such force that it actually rocked him back on his heels. Sandman gaped at his opponent, who now appeared to be wearing some sort of stealth costume that would enable him to blend in with the darkness. Cute. Stupid if he thought it gave him the edge to win this fight, but cute nevertheless.

"You again?" Sandman demanded. "I guess you didn't learn your lesson."

"This time *I'm* gonna school *you.*"

Sandman saw little point in continuing—Spider-Man meant as much to him as an actual spider would. Why bother wasting time? What point was there in Spider-Man's engaging in a battle that he couldn't possibly win? "What do you want?" Sandman demanded in exasperation. At this point he was so fed up that he might actually consider tossing the web slinger a couple hundred grand if it would just make him go away.

"Remember Ben Parker? The old man you shot down in cold blood?"

The question came so completely out of left field that it caught Sandman off guard. What did *that* have to do with anything? "I . . . it was . . . ," Marko stammered, unsure of how to respond. He shook off the momentary confusion and snapped, "What's it to you, anyway?"

"Everything."

To his utter shock, Spider-Man yanked off his mask. Marko hadn't given the slightest thought as to what the web slinger really looked like, but he was surprised to see just how young he was.

Then Marko looked, really looked closely, and even though the young man's face was twisted in rage, Sandman nevertheless recognized just who was facing him.

My God, this is personal.

"He was an old man," snapped Peter Parker. "Why not just force him out of the car? He couldn't have been a problem for a big guy like you. Why? Why'd you have to kill him?" Parker pressed forward and Sandman actually backed up, not in the face of his power, but because of his foe's anger, battering at him as if it had weight and substance. "You're a coward, like you were that night. Well"—Parker's voice dropped into a tough-guy cadence that was a reasonable facsimile of Marko's own—"I'm gonna beat you up real bad. And then I'm gonna do it again. And then I'm takin' what's left of you back to that cell where you can rot for the rest of your life."

Sandman shook his head. "That ain't gonna happen. I've got an important thing to take care of . . . something I swore I'd see to." He briefly considered telling Spider-Man exactly what was going on with his daughter, but decided against it. He didn't need this guy's sympathy or his understanding. He just needed him to get the hell out of the way, and if he wasn't going to do it willingly, then he'd make it happen against Spider-Man's will. "And you ain't standing in my way again. Now step aside."

"I will *never* step aside for you."

"Then I'll just have to take you apart, here and now."

With a deft motion, Spider-Man pulled his mask back on and made a little inviting wave of his fingers. "Bring it."

Marko took a step forward, his fists cocked, and actually felt sorry for the poor idiot. Not only was Spider-Man a glutton for punishment, but he was still carrying all kinds of grief over the death of the old man.

Screw him anyway. He's the enemy. He's the bad guy. He's trying to stand in the way of my helping Penny.

Nevertheless, Marko was reluctant to launch a full-out assault on Spider-Man . . . and, admittedly, was also a bit stung over the charges of cowardice. Because of that, rather than simply blasting him with a full-on sand assault, Marko came straight at him. *He thinks I'm afraid to take him on? Think again.*

Spider-Man swung a fast double-punch combination, and this time Sandman didn't allow the blows to pass through his body. Instead he willed his form into rock-hard consistency, and both punches slammed into him—one to the face, the other to the chest—with no measurable damage. In fact, Spider-Man stepped back, shaking out the pain in his hands from the impact, and Sandman brought his fist around and up. He caught Spider-Man just under the chin, sending the wallcrawler smashing upward into the ceiling with such force that loose bits of debris and rubble clattered to the tunnel floor.

Spider-Man bounded backward, skittering along the ceiling. Grabbing the bags of money lest he lose them in the dark, Marko pursued Spider-Man back down the tunnel. He snagged various bits of debris, pieces of railroad ties, and kept chucking them at Spider-Man, trying to knock him off the ceiling.

With a quick move, Spider-Man leaped down, grabbing Sandman as he passed. Bracing his feet, he hauled Sandman into the air despite his much greater weight and threw him as hard as he could. The Sandman crashed into a support girder, bending it but thankfully not breaking it. In retaliation, Sandman slammed his fist into the brick tunnel wall, yanked out huge pieces from it, and started throwing them one by one at Spider-Man. He dodged right and left, barely avoiding them, as the sounds of the large pieces of debris hitting the wall echoed up and down the tunnel.

Eddie Brock heard the sounds of struggle echoing up from below. He got down on his knees, peering into the empty space that yawned beneath the grating.

From his vantage point, he could barely see the tracks

far below. Suddenly he saw, or rather was barely able to make out, the black-clad image of Spider-Man being slammed down onto the track. Then his view of Spider-Man was cut off by Sandman, who landed atop Spider-Man, knocking the wind out of him. Sandman grabbed the web slinger and started shoving him back, back toward the third rail. If Spider-Man came into contact with it, he'd be fried.

Without hesitation, Brock pulled out his digital camera and aimed it downward, praying that there'd be enough range on the flash to pick it up. Maybe Spider-Man would visibly sizzle, as if encompassed by lightning. What a picture *that* would make.

Displaying frightening brute strength, the Sandman pushed Spider-Man farther back, until Spider-Man's head was barely inches away from the deadly rail. Just when Brock thought he was going to have the picture of a lifetime, Spider-Man brought his foot up, planted it squarely against Sandman's chest, and shoved as hard as he could. Sandman flew in one direction, Spider-Man in the other, and Spider-Man twisted in midair, landing on the wall just above the third rail.

A massive rush of air blasted down the tunnel, along with blinding light. Brock fell back, barely keeping his grip on his digital camera, as a subway train hurtled past. *With my luck, they're both dead, and I didn't get a picture of it at all!*

Sandman didn't realize that they had reached an intersection in the subway tunnels until the light from an oncoming train illuminated it for him. He literally flattened himself against the wall, his body morphing from its normal thickness to an eighth of an inch deep. He had no idea where Spider-Man had got to. With any luck, the meddling wallcrawler had wound up squashed on the front of the train.

Sandman restored himself to his normal depth as he stepped off the wall . . . and Spider-Man moved forward in a flash, slamming into Marko and staggering him with the surprising force of his charge. Sandman went down, Spider-Man atop him, slugging away as hard as he could. Bits of granitelike sand flew from Marko's face and chin, only to be reabsorbed into his arms.

The ground rumbled beneath them. As one, they looked up and saw another train bearing down on them. They rolled out of the way onto another track, only to find themselves directly in the path of yet another train. They kept going onto another track, and this time Sandman knocked Spider-Man back, sending him skidding down the depression in the tracks.

Spider-Man scrambled to his feet. Sandman stood in the middle of the tracks, and he made the same mocking "bring it" gesture that Spider-Man had earlier made. The distant rumbling of a fourth train headed in their direction, but Sandman didn't care. He still had plenty of time to get out of its way.

Quickly Spider-Man fired a web strand at him. Marko barely had to act to get out of its way and smiled grimly. Clearly Spider-Man was getting rattled if he couldn't even hit a target from such a close distance.

Only when he saw Spider-Man yank hard on the

webline and heard a loud *ca-chunk* did he realize Spider-Man had hit exactly the target he was aiming at: a railroad track switch. When Spider-Man pulled on it, it threw the switch and caused the track beneath Marko's feet to shift.

Sandman fell onto his back, his arms splayed to either side. To his horror, he was out of time as the light from the oncoming train bathed him in its glow. He had a quick glimpse of the stunned engineer, and then the train pounded directly over him.

Had he been thinking quickly, he'd have been able to simply transform himself into sand and avoid it. But enough vestiges of human reactions were still in him that he'd frozen upon seeing the train bearing down on him. The train, unable to even come close to stopping in time, mowed him over, blocking him from view.

Seconds later, the train was gone.

So were Marko's hands.

He stared befuddled at his outstretched arms. They were truncated at the wrists, sand pouring out from the stumps . . . his severed hands lying on either side of the railings.

With a shriek of rage, Marko leaped up from the tracks, transforming into sand in midair. No more screwing around. The tactic of going fairly easy on Spider-Man had lost whatever charm it might have had. Spider-Man backed up and tried to vault out of the way, but was too late as Sandman encased him in sand. He piled on, more and more, until Spider-Man was completely buried.

Time was on Sandman's side. All he had to do now was wait.

He felt Spider-Man struggling beneath him. Every time it seemed that the wallcrawler was going to fight his way to the surface, Sandman pressed him down once more. For one brief moment, Spider-Man managed to get his head above the surface, and he gasped in lungfuls of air. But Sandman quickly hauled him back under again, and this time he made sure not to ease up until he felt Spider-Man's struggling, after long moments, cease.

That's that, he thought.

Spider-Man's hand punched up and out. It startled Marko—Spider-Man should have been down for good, but it didn't concern him. So he had a few seconds' fight left in him. So what? Sandman still had him cold.

A webline flew out of Spider-Man's hand, heading straight up. Sandman's first impulse was not to care—it was obviously the desperate move of a desperate man. But then he remembered how casually he'd assumed that Spider-Man's previous web shot was harmless, and he'd wound up getting his hands cut off.

So Sandman looked up . . .

. . . just in time to see that the webbing had snagged a water pipe directly overhead, and then Spider-Man yanked as hard as he could. The water pipe tore loose from its moorings with a tremendous gush of water. It poured down upon them, flooding the tunnel.

Marko had just enough time to picture what happened to a sand castle when a wave washed over it . . . and then he felt himself starting to dissolve. He tried to pull himself together, to prevent it, and then ultimately to scream in protest. The bags of cash were right nearby, and he reached for them. But his rapidly melting hand didn't permit it, liquefying along with the rest of him. He grabbed one of the handles and tore a bag open . . . and then felt himself swirling down the drain in the middle of the tracks.

Consciousness slid away from Marko as he slithered down the drain, his thought before dissipating being: *Penny, I'm sorry, I'm so sorry, damn that Spider-Man, let me live so she can live and he can die . . .*

And then he was gone.

Minutes later, when the remains of his body dribbled from a drainage pipe into the East River, there was no indication that the dark brown substance was anything other than dirt mixed with water and had ever been anything other than lifeless mud.

XV

PATHS BOTH LOST AND FOUND

"Rent!"

Peter felt as if he'd just gone ten rounds with a cement mixer. He was worn out physically, emotionally . . . every way possible.

Earlier, when he had emerged from the subway tunnel squinting against the daylight, dark clouds had started gathering ominously, suggesting an imminent weather change. The day went from pleasant to stormy in minutes, and rain was pouring down as he slogged to his apartment building. The clothes he was wearing ill-fit him, which made sense since he'd grabbed them out of a Goodwill deposit box. It was the only choice he had: there was no way he was going to be able to sneak in and out of his apartment in broad daylight, dressed in a skintight, black Spider-Man outfit.

Now, as he staggered down the hallway toward his apartment, his landlord, Mr. Ditkovitch, stepped out of his own residence and blocked Peter's path. Peter could see Ursula inside, washing a dish.

"Rent!" snarled Ditkovitch.

Peter slowly turned toward him. "Rent?" he echoed.

"R-E-N-T!"

Every time in the past when Ditkovitch had harassed him for rent—which was admittedly perpetually overdue—Peter had stammeringly promised to make good on the debt. Ditkovitch and his power over Peter had always loomed large. Now, however, Peter stared at Ditkovitch, and instead of quaking in fear or being consumed with regret that he was behind, all he could think was *Who the hell does this guy think he is?*

He suddenly envisioned Ditkovitch dangling twenty stories . . . no, make it fifty stories . . . high above the ground, a single gossamer thread his only link from death. There was the acerbic landlord, screeching like a howler monkey, begging for his life, and right above him, dancing about like a loon, was the deliriously happy, black-suited Spider-Man.

Peter had never realized just how angry Ditkovitch's rants made him until that very moment. Doing nothing to restrain it, Peter stepped toward him. The motion was so decisive and unexpected that Ditkovitch automatically took a step backward, looking confused, as if they were doing a waltz and Peter had abruptly decided to lead.

"Rent?" Peter said, and his voice grew progressively louder with each passing second. "Rent, when you fix the showerhead. Rent! When you stop painting over the mold. Rent! When the hot water's hot and the heater gets repaired and you fix my windows and patch my ceiling and the smell of your sardines doesn't creep under my door!"

Ditkovitch's eyes were popping. Ursula, witness to Peter's unexpected explosion, looked as if she didn't know whether to be frightened or thrilled. Peter turned and went to his door, only to discover that it stuck worse than when it had frustrated Mary Jane. He whirled and bellowed at Ditkovitch, his fury reaching fever pitch.

"You want rent? Fix this damn door!"

He shoved so hard that he actually ripped the door off its top hinge. He glanced back, and Ditkovitch looked terrified. As for Ursula, whatever entertainment she'd found in Peter upbraiding the surly landlord had given over to pure fear at Peter's outburst.

Even Peter was stunned at his ferocity. Without another word, he entered his apartment. He rebalanced the door so that, although it was still free of its hinge, it was at least securely closed. Then he threw the bolt for good measure and stood in the middle of his room.

He looked down at his hands. They were shaking. His entire body was trembling. He had no idea how to feel. Part of him was giddy, riding some sort of bizarre emotional high. But another part was intimidated by the intensity of the feelings he'd unleashed. Particularly so since he had no idea just how far they could lead. Would he possibly have completely blown his stack at Ditkovitch? Lost his temper? Punched him? Ditkovitch wasn't a supercriminal with a sandy body that he could make rock hard with a thought. He was a normal human whose head could literally be shattered by the force of a single blow.

Lightning blasted the sky outside, and Peter jumped at his reflection in the mirror. For a split second he thought he saw something else in it—the black spider-suit, but even larger than it was at the moment, with bristling teeth and an impossibly long, frightening tongue lashing out like a serpent's. Then it was gone . . . except the image of it had been seared into Peter's brain, and now he was beginning to experience the same sense of intimidation that he'd inflicted on Ditkovitch.

He stepped back, studying his image in the mirror. On impulse, he rearranged his hair, bangs now hanging over his forehead, giving it a looser, more aggressive look, and there was steel in his eyes. Then he looked at the busted hinge. Pulling open the top of his shirt, he looked down at the black and silver costume. *Is it making me feel this way? Is that even possible? Of course it is. Anything's possible because I don't know what the hell this thing is. But I've got to find out.*

Shucking the outer clothing, he started pulling off the suit. The gloves and mask he'd easily been able to remove earlier and tuck away in his pockets. Perhaps that had resulted from a meeting of the minds between himself and the costume: after all, he couldn't very well walk around in street clothes with his mask on, and with his mask off, he couldn't have his gloved hands protruding from his shirtsleeves. But now the rest of the outfit didn't appear to want to go anywhere. Somewhere in the back of his head, he was having second thoughts, telling himself that he should leave it on, that he had never felt so free before, so powerful. *Is that me telling me that? Or is it . . . this . . . ?*

That terrifying thought was all he needed to spur him on. Unfortunately it did not come without a price.

The suit was indeed sticking to his skin, and it was like peeling off a coating of glue. He fought not to cry out as the costume resisted his efforts before finally giving way.

When he did manage to pull it off over his head, it made loud popping sounds, as if he were pulling an octopus's tentacles clear but the suckers were trying to hold on.

It took long minutes before he was finally divested of the costume. Part of that came from its incredible adhesion to his skin, and part from that Peter was fighting not only the costume but also *himself* every step of the way. Toward the end it went faster; it seemed the less of the costume he was wearing, the more diminished its influence upon him. . . . *Is that really true? Is it influencing me? My God . . . what if it decided to turn me into a mass murderer? Except it would never do that . . . except . . . how do I know that?*

He threw open the trunk that sat at the foot of his bed where he habitually tossed all random stuff scattered around the apartment whenever somebody (i.e., Mary Jane) came to visit and he needed to clean up fast. Wadding up the black suit, he tossed it into the trunk. He stared at the crumpled ebony heap, waiting for it to move. To do something. To spring back out at him and wrestle him to the ground. Instead it simply sat there as if to say, *What's your problem? I'm just an article of clothing, for crying out loud. It's all in your head, boy. All in your head.*

I got enough stuff going on in my head without you there, Peter thought frantically, and yet he felt an impulse to reach down, put the suit back on, let the world know that the power of Spider-Man was to be feared and—

Shaking it off, he slammed the trunk lid shut, then locked it for good measure. He sank into a chair, unable to take his eyes off it, still trembling from the intensity of his emotions.

When the phone jangled sometime later, Peter was still in the chair.

He jumped a few feet, startled by the noise, and when he grabbed up the phone, he was relieved to hear Aunt May's voice. He wasn't sure he could handle Mary Jane right then.

"Peter," she said, getting right to it, "I'm worried about you. I told Mary Jane, and maybe I shouldn't have, but this business with this Marcus person—"

"Marko. Flint Marko. And you don't have to be worried about anything, Aunt May."

"I don't?"

"No." He was about to tell her more, but after taking another glance at the trunk, he suddenly felt the need to get out of the apartment as fast as he could. "I'll be right over, and I'll tell you all about it."

He'd had to be judicious in the retelling. Several times he almost stumbled over a pronoun, nearly saying *I* rather than *he* in describing Spider-Man's confrontation with Flint Marko. He helped himself by sticking as closely to the truth as he could. He explained that Spider-Man apparently listened in on police band radios; that Marko's being sought in connection with the death of Ben Parker had been broadcast; that Spider-Man had confronted Marko, a battle had ensued, and . . .

Peter wondered if he'd be able to go into the specifics of what had happened, as "told to him by Spider-Man." He didn't hesitate, as it turned out. Indeed, he went into nearly excruciating detail, including Sandman's agonizing last moments and his being reduced to nothing but a small river of mud.

A fitting end for someone who was little more than creeping slime.

Aunt May's eyes widened as the narrative progressed. When Peter finished, he leaned back in his chair and let out a long breath, feeling exhausted just in the recounting. He waited for May to say, "Thank God Ben can finally rest easy" or "Heaven bless Spider-Man for ridding the world of such a monster." In short, he wanted her to react with the same sort of adulation and praise that the rest of the city had heaped upon him during the "We Love Spider-Man" ceremony.

Instead, to his surprise, May said nothing at first. After some seconds had passed, she finally remarked, "Oh. I see."

That was it.

Not exactly the reaction that Peter had expected or hoped for.

He was about to ask her if she fully understood everything—that Marko was gone, Uncle Ben avenged, the city safe. Before he could:

"Spider-Man?" she asked, as if she thought Peter might be misinformed. "I don't understand. Spider-Man doesn't kill people."

Peter was stunned at the response. Until that moment, he hadn't even registered the full ramifications of what he'd done. He didn't regret for an instant how Marko went out. How could Aunt May even begin to understand? When you're in a fight for your life, you don't hold back. If you have an opportunity for a killing blow, you take it, and especially when someone deserves it as much as Flint Marko did . . .

Except . . .

When did "deserves" have anything to do with it? Did Norman Osborn deserve to die for all he'd done? Yes. Dr. Octopus? Unquestionably. Yet given the opportunities in both instances, Peter had never even come close to taking them out. Both had perished, but not by his doing. The Goblin had impaled himself on his own glider in a failed attempt to kill Spider-Man, and Octopus had nobly sacrificed himself to save the city. In the case of Sandman, though, it had been no quarter asked nor given.

And it had never occurred to Peter that it should be otherwise. Was that wrong? A bad thing?

"I thought you'd be . . ." he began, and then, as much to convince himself as her, he asserted, "He deserved it, didn't he?" hoping that Aunt May would respond in the affirmative, settling the question for him.

May Parker did him no favors in that regard. "I don't think it's our place to decide who deserves to live or die," she said, sounding a bit surprised and even disappointed that Peter would have to ask such a thing.

"Aunt May, he *killed Uncle Ben.*"

She nodded. "Ben meant everything to us, but he wouldn't want us living one second of our lives with revenge in our hearts. It's like a poison. A venom. It can take us over. Before you know it, turn us into something ugly."

Peter was stupefied by her reaction and said, "I'm sorry, I guess I . . ."

In his mind, he saw once again that brief glimpse of a ravening beast reflected in the mirror. Had it been real? In his mind? A glimpse of things to come?

It's like a poison. A venom. It can take us over.

Peter took a deep breath, exhaled. How should he feel? Confused? Ashamed? Grief-stricken? Would he have done things differently if he'd had it to do all over again?

Who knew? That frightened him more than anything else.

He nodded, apparently in agreement and understanding of what she was saying, but his thoughts were in turmoil, harboring the same brooding fury from earlier. Had the suit placed it there, or exacerbated what was already present, or . . . ?

Peter had no idea, but he knew he had to find out.

Returning to his apartment (and mercifully not encountering Ditkovitch while doing so), Peter again stared at the trunk for a long while, trying to decide the best way to get a sample of this . . . this whatever it was . . . off his costume. He couldn't bring himself to do it. He was afraid that, if he opened the trunk, he'd be wearing the costume inside of five minutes. He simply didn't trust himself. *It couldn't have come out of nowhere. It had to be hiding here somewhere.* That thought was daunting, because it ascribed some sentience to whatever had bonded itself to his costume. At the very least an animal-level intelligence, or perhaps even more. He didn't like to consider that possibility, but he had no other options.

Peter crawled on the floor and checked under the bed.

Nothing there but dust bunnies the size of his head. He continued to look around . . . and then his gaze lit on the closet. Of course. It made perfect sense. He'd even had a strange feeling that the shadows in there had been shifting. It must have been the suit, or the thing on the suit, that had been residing in there, waiting for its opportunity. The more Peter thought of the aspects of intelligence the thing possessed, the more concerned he became.

He went to the closet and opened the door, not sure what he was looking for. If it was some sort of living thing, maybe there would be some sort of secretion or excretion . . . something that he could gather as a sample. He moved his clothes around, pulled out the shoes that were piled on the floor, and nearly missed what he was looking for. But he noticed it just before he tossed one of his shoes aside. Slowly he turned it over and looked at the sole.

Some sort of black splotch of goo was on it.

If he had given it a casual glance, he would just have thought he'd stepped in some street tar. Because of everything that had happened to him with the suit, he knew better. He tried to remember the last time he had worn the shoes, and it came to him immediately: the opening night of MJ's play.

As he got a scraper and a specimen jar to transfer the goo into, he ran through in his mind everything that had transpired that night. The play, the ride out to the Palisades, hanging in the web hammock with MJ, riding back, Harry's assault . . .

Once again his concerns returned to Harry. Was it some sort of weapon that Harry had thrown at him?

Something he'd developed in a lab and . . . ? No. No, it made no sense. Harry was many things, but he simply didn't possess the scientific genius or invention of his father. Still, it could have been something that OsCorp had developed and he'd incorporated into his arsenal. But it didn't seem right. Maybe . . .

That shooting star?

Could it have . . . ?

"Aw, c'mon," he muttered as he transferred the inert goo into the jar. He couldn't believe he was entertaining the notion that something from outer space—a meteor or asteroid—had made landfall near him and discharged some sort of alien life-form. And that alien-life form had attached itself to Peter's shoe, come home with him . . .

Still . . . he was reminded of Sherlock Holmes's great precept: *Whenever you eliminated the impossible, whatever remains—however improbable—must be the truth.*

Harry had inflicted some sort of self-replicating virus on him during their battle. Impossible.

A creature had hitched a ride on a meteor, fallen to earth, and seized Peter Parker as its host. Impossible.

Peter didn't foresee a shortage of impossible theories; just improbable ones. Holding up the jar and staring at the black goo within, Peter hoped that the man to whom he was bringing this sample would be able to point him toward the right impossibility.

Dr. Curtis Connors stared with fascination at the specimen jar, shaking it slightly and watching the goo move around within. Peter stood several feet away, glancing around Connors's office/laboratory, fascinated as always to see what his favorite professor was working on. He noticed a chart on the wall of different types of lizards, and an anatomical model for a lizard nearby. He considered that rather curious, since to the best of his knowledge, Connors wasn't a herpetologist. So what was the sudden interest in lizards?

Connors was careful as he examined the bottle since he had to do it one-handed. Peter glanced at the flapping sleeve where Connors's right arm wasn't and wondered if Connors had taken such an interest in lizards because he was planning to try to regrow his missing arm, just as some types of lizards were capable of doing when losing a limb. Then Peter shook his head and smiled. Creatures from outer space, and now a teacher embarking on a scheme out of a 1950s B movie. That was the problem when one lived a life where one used spider powers to fight guys made out of sand: it was impossible to distinguish between likelihood and absurdity.

"Where'd this come from?" Connors finally asked.

"I don't know." That was certainly true enough. Peter had thoughts, but nothing definite. "It was on my shoe. Would you check it out? I'm curious what it is."

"Yeah. I am too. I'll let you know." Connors's gaze shifted to Peter. "By the way, I saw your lab partner in the news the other day. Quite the sensation, our Miss Stacy in a romantic entanglement with Spider-Man."

"I . . ." Peter shifted uncomfortably from one foot to the other. "I wouldn't call it an entanglement. It was just a kiss . . ."

"Well, when you do something that publicly, you're asking people to draw their own conclusions."

"Yeah, I . . . I guess you are," Peter admitted. Certainly Mary Jane had done so, and none of them were to his favor. He wondered, for the first time since his entire world had gone dark, how she was doing.

The Jazz Room was a long-standing establishment down in the Lower East Side. During its heyday, top jazz musicians would stop in unexpectedly and start jamming with whoever was onstage. But that was many years ago, and the Jazz Room wasn't what it used to be.

Then again, I'm not what I used to be either, thought Mary Jane.

Stepping out into a crisp, bright Manhattan afternoon, Mary Jane squinted and waited for her eyes to adapt. She'd only been in there for fifteen minutes. She wondered what it was going to be like when she was there for a full eight-hour shift. Glancing behind, she saw the sign WAITRESS/SINGER WANTED that had been hanging in the window being removed by the manager. People were going on about their business, hurrying to jobs or appointments or to spend time with friends or family. Mary Jane watched them go and once again had that orphan-outside-a-banquet feeling. She was, as the Bible said, in the world but not of it. She felt a desperate need to be a part of not only the world, but of something that would take her outside her own worries and frustrations. She walked through the city, seeing couples holding hands, exchanging a kiss or two, making even the simple act of crossing the street seem romantic. Feeling masochistic, she walked past the Broadhurst Theater. It was as if she'd never performed there. She was even beginning to wonder if it had ever happened, or if it had all been some sort of dream that had disappeared all too quickly upon waking.

MJ heard sirens and what she was reasonably sure was a fire truck in the distance. Police cars hurtled past. People watched them go by, talked to each other, speculated about what was happening. She even heard, "Spider-Man?" as couples queried each other as to whether the famed web slinger would be involving himself.

Mary Jane had no idea.

But thinking about him, about the life that had deserted her, prompted Mary Jane to step into a doorway, removing herself from the crowded street. She pulled out her cell phone from her bag and started scrolling down the directory of names. She stopped on Peter's, naturally. Her impulse was to try to reconnect with him, to heal the fractures in their relationship. But in the past days, he had become almost unrecognizable . . . and now there was this new business with his uncle Ben. How was she supposed to be there for him when he had made it clear he wanted no part of her?

She needed to be with someone she felt needed her in return, and from whom she could find mutual support.

She continued to scroll down, then back, looking for a name to leap out at her. Finally, one did.

Why hadn't she thought of him sooner?

She hesitated only a moment before clicking the dial button, then waited for the connection to be made. It rang twice, three times, four, and she prepared herself to be connected to voice mail . . . when she was startled by a sudden pickup.

"Hello, Harry? It's Mary Jane. Would you . . . like some company?"

Harry Osborn tucked the tail end of his shirt into his pants, having sprinted from the bathroom to grab the phone. Nearby in the great room, a small easel had been set up. On it was a reasonably professional looking depiction of the view of Manhattan through Harry's window. It had been ages since Harry had painted; he'd forgotten how much it relaxed him. Of course, his father had never thought much of it.

"You and Peter?" he asked, cheered at the prospect.

"Just me," came Mary Jane's voice over the phone.

Harry paused, taking in that little fact and its implications, then said, "You kidding? Sure. C'mon over."

"You sure I wouldn't be intruding?"

"No, you're not intruding." He laughed, considering the thought absurd. "I'm just hanging out. Come over."

"Okay then. See ya."

He hung up the phone, then called, "Bernard!" He moved toward the door and shouted, louder this time, *"Berrnaaaard!"*

As if he'd materialized out of nowhere, Bernard appeared at the doorway. "Yes, Harry?" Upon the passing of Norman Osborn, Bernard's inclination had been to address him as "Mr. Osborn," but Harry had quickly put a stop to that. As far as Harry was concerned, Mr. Osborn was his father . . . and the associations that implied were more than he cared to consider.

"We're having a guest. We need . . ." Harry thought fast and seized upon the obvious. "Food."

"Right away, sir."

Harry nodded in approval, confident that Bernard had everything in hand, and stepped back into the great room. As Harry moved back to his cityscape, his gaze rested upon his father's portrait looming above.

Then, for some reason, he glanced toward the chaise lounge in the corner of the room.

Norman Osborn was lying on it.

Harry gasped.

His father was there on the chaise, and he was clearly dead, a vicious wound evident on his chest through the huge red splotch discoloring his shirt. And Spider-Man was there, laying him out, neatly arranging the corpse. . . .

Harry staggered back, holding his head. He slammed shut his eyes, and when he dared to open them again, the chaise was vacant. Terrified that some other vision would reoccupy it, he turned away and found himself staring at the large mirror hanging on the wall.

Something was drawing him to it. Something that was there but not there, something that he felt he should know, but didn't.

"You've taken your eye off the ball."

The voice, soft and disturbing, was spoken from just behind his ear. It was his father's voice, and a disoriented Harry stumbled forward toward the mirror. Unable to stop himself, he fell against it, putting his hands against the glass at the last second.

A circuit connected . . . a dizzying array of images flashed through Harry's mind. He cried out, remembering, not wanting to, needing the information, fearing it, and there was Spider-Man lying bound and helpless, his unmasked face gazing up plaintively at Harry, and it was Peter's face, and his father's body, and Harry standing in a large capsule, wallowing in green gas, and in combat with Peter, hurtling through dizzying heights, trying to kill him, and being slammed backward off his Sky Stick, and Peter looking down at him with all manner of mock sympathy, and Harry heard his own voice asking, "My dad. He died, didn't he?" and Peter was just nodding sympathetically, the bastard, he knew, *he knew, he had done it, he—*

Harry sank to his knees, sobbing, except the sobs were intermingled with choked laughter, and once again his father's voice came to him: *"Where've you been?"* With tremendous effort, Harry raised his head and saw Norman Osborn, likewise on his knees, staring back at him from the mirror.

"Remember me?" his father purred.

"Yes, Father," Harry said with the voice of the damned. "I remember everything."

"You haven't killed Peter Parker."

Never in his life had Harry stood up to his father. Never. But Norman was no longer in his life, and Harry defiantly told him, "Things are different now. Peter and Mary Jane are my friends."

His father's face twisted in contempt. "You have no friends. She's Peter's girl. He's always taken everything away from you. He took me from you."

At that, something within Harry Osborn snapped. It was the part of him that had spent a lifetime trying to make his father happy, to live up to his demands, to maybe, somehow, win his approval. But it was never going to happen. His father was insatiable, and if Harry killed Peter, Norman would want Mary Jane dead, and once she was gone, his former business rivals, and then more and more, and it was enough, dammit, enough. Like a drunk who had hit rock bottom, Harry Osborn had a moment of clarity, bellowing, *"I won't listen to you anymore!"* Doubled over, he pounded the floor in frustration, like a child having a tantrum, and demanded, "I have a chance for my own life! *Let me be!*"

He hit the floor until his knuckles were bleeding . . . and when he looked up into the mirror, he saw his own reflection. Norman Osborn was gone.

"I'm free," Harry whispered, his voice choked with emotion. "I'm free."

He could not have been more grateful.

Or more wrong.

XVI

FAMILY REUNION

MARY JANE WAS SO happy to see a smiling face that she nearly cried with joy. She warned herself that would be something of an overreaction, though, and so nodded gratefully as Bernard opened the elevator door that led to the entrance hall of Harry's penthouse.

Perhaps it was her imagination, but Bernard looked far more relaxed than in the days when Norman Osborn was holding court here. She summoned the image of Norman to her mind, thought of things he had said, and decided she was very likely not imagining things.

Harry walked up, a wide grin on his face and a lightness in his step that she hadn't seen for many a month. "Hi! Hungry?"

"Starving," she replied.

He bowed and gestured for her to precede him. She fully expected that they were going to head straight to a dining table decked with some sort of impressive feast. To her surprise, Harry guided her into the kitchen. It was immaculate, stainless steel. She could see her reflections in the countertops and cabinets.

She turned to Harry, nervousness in her voice. "If

you're expecting me to cook dinner, this isn't going to end well, unless you're really hungry for boiled water."

He laughed at that. "If you want to pitch in, feel free, but I"—he affected an amazingly ghastly French accent—"am zee chef for zis evening."

"Really," she replied skeptically, one eyebrow arched almost to the top of her forehead.

"Mais, oui."

"May we what?"

Harry sighed as if greatly put upon. "Yes. Really."

"Okay, well . . . sure, I'll be happy to help, if you can come up with something that I can't possibly burn."

"You can help with the salad. No one can burn a salad."

"Spoken like someone who's never seen me make a salad."

A small table was already set in the center. Harry pulled out the ingredients for the salad, steered a nervous Mary Jane over to them, then pulled an impressive array of ingredients from the refrigerator. Deftly he cracked several eggs into a mixing bowl. That alone caused Mary Jane to marvel at his culinary prowess; every time she tried to break an egg, there were yolk and whites all over the place and shell in the mix.

Harry finished beating the eggs. While he did so, a pan was heating up on the stove top. Putting down the egg mixture, he sliced off a pat of butter and tossed it onto the pan. "I hope you like garlic," he said as the butter started to sizzle.

"Love it."

"How about some music?"

He pushed a button on a nearby wall unit. Chubby Checker singing "The Twist" filtered through the kitchen.

Mary Jane started singing along, doing the Twist in the middle of the kitchen. Harry promptly joined in. Each of them had a long wooden spoon in hand, and they started "fencing" with them as if they were swords, never missing a step or a word in the song. They continued doing so until Mary Jane suddenly saw smoke rising from the pan. *"The butter!"* she shouted in alarm.

Harry never missed a beat. He slid gracefully over to the stove and slowly poured the eggs in. While Chubby Checker was singing about his little sis, Harry gestured toward the array of ingredients and looked at her questioningly. "All of 'em. Go for it," she urged him. With an approving nod, Harry expertly mixed in mushrooms, ham bits, tomato, chopped onion, and garlic. The pan was wide enough that he was actually making two omelets at the same time. Mary Jane was amazed at his confidence; in fact, she couldn't recall having ever seen Harry Osborn really confident at anything. This was a wonderful change in him.

It's because his father is gone. I'm probably going to go to hell for thinking this, but if that's what it took for Harry to become the man he's capable of being, then it's for the best.

He flipped one omelet and then the other high in the air. She let out a delighted squeal of alarm, certain an omelet was going to wind up on the floor. Harry caught them on the pan with such dexterity that she would have thought him a chef trained at Le Cordon Bleu.

The meal was a blur of laughter, music, and reminiscing about things that were pleasant while blissfully ignoring things that weren't.

Eventually discussion turned to Harry's having mentioned that he had written a play for Mary Jane, and she insisted on seeing it. Harry demurred, trying to convince her that it wasn't worth the time it would take to dig it up, but she persisted and wheedled, and eventually Harry was seated next to her with an old composition book balanced between them. The song "It Had to Be You" was playing in the background.

"Well, I'm embarrassed," said Harry, sounding chagrined that he'd given in to Mary Jane's pleas. "It's kind of corny. I was in the eleventh grade. You say to this guy, Richard"—he adjusted his voice to a feminine pitch—" 'I've been everywhere, Richard.' " Realizing that it would be better if Mary Jane did the speech, he slid the composition book more over toward her. "Here, you read it. I wrote it for you."

She read slowly, trying to make out the handwriting. As she progressed, it became easier for her to understand, and she spoke with more confidence. " 'I've been everywhere, Richard. The mountains of India, the open plains of Africa, the isles of ancient Greece. What's wrong with dreaming? Nothing like a little self-deception to get you through the night.' "

"Oh, God," moaned Harry, slumping back in the couch and covering his face in mortification. "Did I write that?"

"Harry, it's beautiful," she insisted.

He looked at her in surprise. "Would you like the part?"

"Thank you. I'd love to be in your play."

They warmly regarded each other, and then Mary Jane leaned toward him. "You know," she said, gently touching the top of his head where the bandage had been, "there's not even a scar, barely."

Her hand rested there a moment, then she moved in closer. Harry responded immediately.

Their lips together. Warm. Pleasant.

She kissed him again, trying to project everything she wanted and needed onto him, and she was transported, and she was back to that night in the alley, the rain coming down . . .

She was back with Peter . . .

And ashamed.

She pulled away, knowing that what she was doing was wrong. Not out of a sense of loyalty to Peter, but because she was trying to force herself to feel something for Harry that—dammit—just wasn't there. It had never been, not even when they had been dating. Hell, it had been one of the reasons they'd stopped seeing each other. It wasn't just the ruthless unpleasantness of Norman Osborn. It was that, then and now, she was making the huge mistake of trying to make love happen. It didn't work that way. And using Harry in a pointless attempt to make it happen was cruel and unfair, as if the poor guy hadn't been through enough already.

"Oh . . . sorry," she said.

"Don't be."

"I didn't mean . . ."

"It's okay. Please," he insisted, and moved toward her again.

"I should go."

He gently put a hand on her shoulder. "Please don't leave."

As delicately as she could, she removed the hand from her shoulder. She held it firmly away, although there was compassion on her face. "Harry, it's been lovely. I didn't mean for you to think . . ."

Harry was trembling with . . . what? Passion? Rage? Confusion? All of those and more. "What am I supposed to think?" he demanded, his voice rising. "What am I supposed to feel?" His eyes narrowed, his tone was accusatory. "You're thinking about Peter, aren't you." Not a question.

Mary Jane could have lied, but Harry deserved so much better than that. "I . . . guess I am."

Harry's head snapped around. Then he shook it as if something painful were rattling around in his skull. Desperately, like a man lurching after a life preserver, he cried out, "No! Don't go! Mary Jane, please!"

She was on her feet, grabbing her coat. "I'm sorry."

"Don't leave me alone!"

Mary Jane was never more torn. Harry's desperation was painful, but she couldn't stay. Things were spiraling out of control; it was her fault, not his, and if she didn't leave, she'd just be leading him along. As bad as this moment was, remaining would be far, far worse.

His voice echoing behind her, she made it to the

elevator. Harry was still crying out behind her, but the door closed, cutting off all sound. Mary Jane sagged against the elevator wall and piteously sobbed.

She was surprising herself with her capacity for feeling terrible. Every time she thought she hit bottom, she found new lows.

They say that misery loves company, but Mary Jane realized at that point that it simply wasn't true—misery liked to be alone in a small dark room where no one could see it.

As it turned out, Mary Jane was not alone in her misery. It was being shared by Harry Osborn, and it would not have cheered her to know that Harry's situation—as unlikely as it might have seemed—was far worse than her own.

"You're thinking about Peter, aren't you." Harry Osborn snapped at her.

"I . . . guess I am."

She looked ashamed, confused, and then before Harry could speak again, the voice was back. His father's voice, echoing mockingly in his head. *So much for friendship,* chuckled Norman Osborn. *Time for old friends to meet again.* Suddenly the prospect of Mary Jane leaving him paled in comparison to the prospect of being alone with his father's voice in his ear. "No! Don't go! Mary Jane, please!"

But he was helpless to stop her. Norman's voice thundered in his head, *"Let her go!"* and Harry, desperate, frantic, begged for her to stay. She ignored him. She fled from him.

Harry trembled in the middle of the great room, and when he turned and faced the mirror—

There he was.

Norman Osborn, the man who despised him. Norman Osborn, who scorned him as a weakling and as useless.

Norman Osborn, the only one who was always there for him.

Always.

Not Mary Jane. Not Peter. None of them.

Just him.

"There, there," said Norman in what he probably fancied was a consoling manner. He put his arms out. "Come to me, son. Come to me."

And Harry did.

Feeling like a dish towel just put through the wringer, Mary Jane stumbled into her apartment later that night. Shell-shocked, listless, at her wit's end as to which way to turn, she noticed that her answering machine was blinking. She reached over and pushed the button.

"Hi, MJ. It's Peter," came his voice. Tears started to roll down her face. She had never been so happy to hear it before. *"Listen, I just want to talk to you about us. I know I've—"*

The message suddenly stopped. Huh? Peering more closely at the answering machine—

The phone line was no longer jacked into the wall. It must have come out during Peter's call, cutting off the message. But why would that be?

The only possible answer: someone had broken into

her apartment to pull the jack out . . . and might well still be there. She turned to leave and let out an alarmed shriek.

The Goblin was standing right behind her.

At least it looked like the Goblin, although his costume and mask were different . . . the top of his head, hair and everything, was exposed and . . .

Harry?! But how . . . ?

He clapped a hand over her mouth. Her eyes widened in horror, and he spoke in a low, soothing voice that was terrifying just because it sounded so friendly. "Since you love him," he told her with an easy familiarity that almost made her ill, "I think you should call him back . . . and do just as I say . . . or Peter Parker will die."

XVII

ENGAGEMENT ON THE ROCKS (TAKE TWO)

PETER STARED AT HIS various science texts and then tiredly rubbed the bridge of his nose. He leaned back from his desk and stared at the ceiling. His thoughts in turmoil, it was little wonder that he couldn't concentrate on his studies. He wondered if Dr. Connors was any closer to finding out what was up with that weird bit of black goo. Almost against his will, he found his gaze straying toward the trunk. *That way lies madness,* he thought, and even toyed with the idea of just finding a furnace somewhere, tossing the thing in, and being done with it.

There was a knock at the door. He was certain for the first time in a while that it wasn't going to be Ditkovitch. Granted, he hadn't fixed anything in the apartment yet, but neither had he been hassling Peter for rent, so that was a wash.

Opening the door, he saw Ursula standing there. He noticed immediately that she was looking at him differently. Typically she had that sort of puppy-dog-crush air about her that Peter had always found sweetly amusing. Now she was looking at him guardedly, apparently afraid that he was going to take her head off with another outburst. He felt bad about that. She must have known deep down that Peter would never unleash on her the way he had with Ditkovitch.

Or . . . maybe she didn't. But certainly that was her problem, not his.

"Call for you," she said, pointing to the pay phone in the hallway. The receiver was dangling off the hook, swaying back and forth slightly. "It's Mary Jane."

Feeling energetic for the first time that day, Peter moved quickly to the pay phone and grabbed the receiver. "Hi! How are you!"

"Fine." She sounded far away, much farther than simply calling from her apartment would suggest. Obviously she was still concerned about things, but that didn't bother him. The important thing was that they were talking. Everything else could be sorted out if there was at least communication.

"I'm so glad you called. I've been trying to—"

"Can we meet?"

He was surprised by her directness. "You bet! Where?"

"You know that place in Central Park? Near the statue of that dog? I was thinking in an hour, maybe . . ."

"Sure! I'll be there! Love ya!"

There was no answer. Again, more hopefully and more aggressively, Peter said, "Hello? Love ya!" The silence extended and then clicked over into a dial tone, and he realized that she'd hung up. Why should that bother him? That she had called at all was enough to make him giddy with anticipation. He was going to be seeing her again.

He was going to be able to make things right. He ran back into his room, picked up the engagement ring from the sock drawer where he'd hidden it, and tucked it into his pocket. Remembering the last time he'd carried the ring on his person, he certainly hoped that things would work out better this go-around. Then again, anything short of being attacked by the Goblin was going to be an improvement.

Peter grabbed a subway over to Central Park, although truthfully he felt as if he could have run the entire way. When entering the park, he passed a makeshift flower stand. The roses were tempting but pricey, so he settled for a bouquet of peonies. Clutching them tightly to his chest, he made his way through a grove of trees and then spotted Mary Jane in the distance. She was achingly beautiful, the wind blowing her hair ever so gently, looking like something off the cover of a romance novel.

He approached her and drew within a few feet. Concerned somehow that he would shatter "the spell," he didn't want to touch her, as much as he ached to take her in his arms. "Wow. You look so beautiful," he whispered. .

No reply—she just stared at him, and he couldn't get any sense of what was going through her mind. He held out the flowers. "Peonies," he said, then added a bit unnecessarily, "for you."

Still no answer. No movement or taking the flowers from him. He might have been talking to a photograph for all the interaction he was getting.

"You okay?" he asked, his concern starting to grow.

"No. There's . . . something I have to tell you, Peter."

Her voice was clipped and formal, as if she were acting, only badly.

"Okay," he said cautiously.

"It's not working, you and me."

He stared at her. "What?"

"I don't want to see you anymore."

Peter actually laughed, although it was nervous, confused. This had to be some sort of joke. If she didn't want to see him, all she had to do was continue not to return his calls. Why would she go out of her way to contact him and bring him here to make a point of saying that they were through? It smacked of a cruelty that he wouldn't have thought her capable of. "What are you *talking* about?"

"I don't know," she said, flustered. He couldn't tell if she was admitting that she didn't know what she was talking about, or if she was trying to toss out grievances and see if one would stick. "You aren't there for me."

I'm here, now! What the hell more do you want?! But he bit back the more aggressive, angry response and said with labored patience, "I know that. But let's talk about it. Maybe I was selfish. I can do better. I can change."

"It's not that simple."

"But we love each other!" he said with mounting desperation. "We have problems, we work it out. We talk—"

"There's someone else!" The words seemed to surprise her, as if they'd flown out of her mouth of their own accord. "I've . . . fallen in love with someone else."

She turned her back and started walking quickly away. Without thinking, Peter sped around her so rapidly that to an observer, it appeared as if Peter had disappeared from one spot and rematerialized at another. He stood in front of Mary Jane, his face a question, pleading, demanding some sort of explanation.

Either she had none to give . . . or she had no desire to do so. Either way it made no difference. She strode past him, and this time he made no effort to stop her. He simply stood there, holding the peonies, and the ring in the pocket of his trousers now felt as if it were burning against his thigh.

He thought of pursuing her, of running after her down the wooded path that she was taking to leave the area . . .

Oh . . . the hell with it. He had his pride. There was no way he was going to go sprinting after Mary Jane like some pathetic schoolboy.

Which, as it turned out, was a tragic decision on his part. For if he had done so, he might well have spotted Harry Osborn step out of hiding in the shadows, quietly applauding, falling into step next to Mary Jane and remarking, "Bravo," in a soft, triumphant voice. He would have seen Mary Jane looking at Harry with a mix of fear and loathing.

But he saw and heard none of that.

Instead he returned to his apartment, and only after he slumped down onto his bed, lonely and empty, did he realize he was still holding the bouquet. He must have looked like an idiot, coming all this distance carrying a batch of flowers. Disgusted, he threw the peonies toward the foot of his bed and heard them bounce off something.

Well . . . he knew what they were bouncing off, didn't he?

He slid off the bed, stepped around to the foot of it, and stared down at the trunk. The flowers were lying in a heap next to it. He kicked them away, scattering stems and petals to a far corner of the room, and continued to regard the trunk with apprehension . . .

. . . and anticipation.

Other men in the precarious situation that Peter was in would have headed out to a local bar and drowned their sorrows in drink. They would have enjoyed the peaceful oblivion that booze offered. But that wasn't Peter's style.

When he had first become Spider-Man, he had seen his costumed persona as a means of making restitution for his great sin of omission. Theoretically, having recently learned that he wasn't directly responsible for Ben's death, and having wreaked vengeance upon the man who was, he should have had no qualm about retiring the entire double-identity existence. But he was starting to understand that Spider-Man represented far more to him than that. Spider-Man was an escape from the mundane, from the earthbound problems that afflicted Peter. When he was swinging high above the city, what possible problems from below could touch him?

That was what he needed now: the airborne escape. And the suit in its current state provided him even more than that. When he put it on, he was flooded with a sense of . . . of *rightness.* The doubts that followed him, even when he was masked, tended to melt away in the face of the confidence he drew from the suit.

But you don't know what it is. You don't know how it does it.

You don't know what it could be doing to you beyond that. You don't . . .

. . . care.

Even as that immutable truth went through his head, he was reaching down for the trunk, unlatching it, opening the lid, and looking inside. The rationalizations came fast and furious as he reached down for the black suit. He was a scientist, after all—this was a scientific curiosity. What better way to understand it and discover more about it than to become one with it again and see what happened as a result? Granted, using himself as a test subject was a risky venture, but really, what sort of scientist was he if he didn't believe in taking a few risks in the interest of discovery?

Merely holding the black costume caused the sadness and pain to drain from him. At once, Mary Jane seemed small and irrelevant, certainly not worthy of causing him anguish.

Any doubts he might have harbored were erased as he quickly donned the suit. He immediately felt stronger, more self-assured. He considered heading out as Spider-Man, but no. Not yet. For some reason he felt like facing the world as the newly confident Peter Parker.

He pulled clothes on over the black costume, buttoning his long-sleeved shirt over it.

He looked in the mirror to make sure that no part of the costume was visible and liked what he saw.

Peter Parker was someone who couldn't be hurt, couldn't be messed with, couldn't be stepped on as if his feelings meant nothing.

He headed out into the street, walking with his arms swaying loosely, his shoulders straighter. He'd never realized before how tentatively he moved through the world when he wasn't webswinging.

Picturing John Travolta in *Saturday Night Fever,* he started to strut.

Men sidestepped to get out of his way without even realizing they were doing it . . . and women were giving him a second look as he passed by. He shot off smiles to them, even an occasional humorous two-fingered salute.

Things were feeling pretty damned good for the first time in a while. Here he had thought that he needed Mary Jane for the world to be in focus for him—instead Mary Jane's presence had blurred things, like an additional lens on a telescope. She shifted the attention away from what was really important: Peter Parker, the man, the myth, the legend.

As he crossed Broadway, he saw a group of people chatting at a newsstand. Normally he would have ignored it. But then "Spider-Man" was mentioned, leaping out at him and catching his attention. Praising him, no doubt. Perhaps word had gotten out about how he had disposed of Sandman, an action that he had previously felt conflicted about but now wasn't bothering him in the least.

He sidled toward them and was stunned to hear anything but praise. Comments flew fast and furious, and none of them were flattering.

"I think it's awful."

"He's supposed to be a role model."

"Spider-Man was my son's hero before today, but now . . ."

"Edna always said he was a schlemiel, didn't ya, Edna?"

"Schlemiel."

Overcome with curiosity and not a little concern, Peter drew close to the newsstand to see what the commotion was all about.

He stared at the front page of the *Daily Bugle,* at first thinking it had to be some sort of joke. Then he grabbed it up, and his hands tightened on it in cold fury.

SPIDER-MAN, THIEF! the headline blared in what looked like seventy-two point type. Below it a subheading read: SPIDEY SHOWS HIS TRUE COLORS. Splashed across the front page was a photograph so convincing, Peter's first thought was *Did I do that? I don't remember doing that.*

There he was in the black costume, leaping away from the bank with bags of money in either hand.

Peter started to wander away, and the news vendor shouted, "Hey! Where do you think you're going with that? You have to pay for it. Who do you think you are, stealing stuff: Spider-Man?"

The snide comment drew laughter from the others standing around, and Peter's first thought was that if they all had one neck, he'd break it. Then he considered bringing the whole newsstand down around the vendor's ears. Forget it—that would only exacerbate the problem. He fished out a quarter from his pocket and flipped it to the vendor. Then he went back to the paper.

He turned to the story, which went into detail about how Spider-Man had been caught in the act by the aggressive and fearless reportage of the *Daily Bugle.* Sources in the police department asserted that, upon being shown the irrefutable evidence, police captain George Stacy had declared to his men, "We just gave this guy the key to the city, and now he's made a fool out of all of us. Go find him!"

Fearless reportage? What kind of—?

Quickly he flipped back to the cover photo, and there it was, big as life: a photo credit to Eddie Brock.

"I should have known," Peter snarled. He stared at the picture long and hard. It still had that disconcerting feel of familiarity to it, as if he had really committed the crime. He started to second-guess himself, wondering if the suit had somehow compelled him to steal the money and—

Then the anger left Peter as it struck him exactly why the picture looked familiar. "Waaaaiiit a minute," he said, staring at it longer, and then he started to laugh. It drew strange looks from the people nearby, but he didn't care. He was flooded with relief upon discovering the truth.

And now that he knew it, he was going to take it and shove it down J. Jonah Jameson's throat and up Eddie Brock's backside, all at the same time.

XVIII

THE RISE AND FALL OF EDWARD BROCK JR.

EDDIE BROCK'S BRAND-NEW CUBICLE in the *Daily Bugle* city room wasn't much to write home about. It was, however, a start, and he had every confidence that the corner office he coveted would be his sooner or later . . . probably sooner.

The sparsely decorated cubicle held only the three photos that he'd taken of Gwen at the key-to-the-city ceremony. Until recently, his memories of that event were far too painful, considering the shameless display of lip-smacking that Spider-Man had foisted upon the public. That was no longer a concern. *Who had the last laugh, Bug Man? Not you, that's for damned sure.*

A bottle of champagne was on his desk, courtesy of J. Jonah Jameson . . . a remarkably cheap brand, but what else would one expect? Well-wishers and coworkers had gathered in Eddie's cubicle for an impromptu party, and one of them was busily pouring the champagne into plastic cups. They were all toasting him and his continued success at the *Bugle*. Eddie had no delusions that any of them especially liked him. But they could sense an up-and-comer when they saw one, so nobody wanted to be on his bad side. Instead they preferred to bask in reflected glory or, even better, attach themselves to his forward career movement like remora to a shark.

"Right place, right time," he said to an attractive young woman who had been congratulating him on his success. Displaying a modesty he didn't really feel, he added, "I was just lucky."

The champagne had run out, and as typically happened in such instances, the party was starting to break up. The young woman touched his hand and said in a low voice, "This is so wonderful for you."

Brock grinned, and seeing Betty Brant walking past—disdaining to have joined the party, of course—he called to her, "Tell JJ to clear some more wall space!" Betty rolled her eyes and kept going.

Jameson had dropped off a little "Welcome to the *Bugle*" gift earlier: a framed front page of that day's paper. Brock looked around the cubicle, trying to figure out where he could hang it. As he did so, he heard footsteps behind him and turned to see who the latest well-wisher was.

He was both surprised and not surprised to see Peter Parker standing there, leaning against the entrance, his arms folded. "Good morning," Brock said chipperly. "Beautiful day." He tilted his head as if trying to remember some obscure fact. "What was it you said? I'll never get that picture?" With a satisfied chortle he tapped the framed front page. "There's your hero."

Brock stood, trying to figure out what wall area would

properly display the picture as Peter shook his head, his voice laced with disappointment. "Huh. I never thought he'd really do that."

"See, right there, you've made a judgment call," Brock replied. "You've got to see it like it is."

"Funny you should say that, 'cause I was looking at an old photo of mine, and it sure did look similar."

Brock froze.

He tried to laugh it off and didn't succeed. In a slightly strangled voice he said, "Okay, well . . . gotta get back to work."

"You're trash, Brock."

Parker's voice was deep, challenging. It almost cried out for Brock to take a swing at him. There was none of the quavering protest or traces of uncertainty to which Brock had become accustomed. "*Excuse* me?"

Peter casually tossed a large yellow envelope onto Brock's desk. Eddie's eyes went wide when he saw the address printed on the envelope's upper corner: Empire State University Department of Photography.

"Your picture's a fake," Peter said with quiet conviction.

Brock felt as if he were shrinking while Peter was growing in stature. "You grafted two images together. Digital shots you took at the scene of the crime, and a picture from two years ago that I took, where Spider-Man was picking up bags of money that he'd just gotten back from a bank robber. Except in my picture you could see he was handing them back to the bank president, who was smiling. You lifted out the Spider-Man image, Photoshopped the black costume, and presto: instant incrimination."

Brock had walked into this knowing that Parker might figure it out. He'd gambled that Peter might not remember; it was one of Parker's oldest photos and hadn't even been used. It was just sitting around in the *Bugle*'s morgue with hundreds of other old pictures. Still, it wasn't as if Brock were unprepared. He'd run through what he might say a number of times, and now he affected the demeanor of an old pal and confidant. "Look, we could all use a little extra spending money every once in a while," he said in a conspiratorial tone. "I could help you out there." When Peter didn't immediately reply, Brock urged him, "You're such a Boy Scout. Give a guy a break."

Eddie Brock then got the shock of his life.

The normally mild-mannered Peter Parker grabbed Eddie by his necktie and shoved him hard against the wall. Brock slammed up against it with such force that it dislodged a framed photo of Gwen and sent it clattering to the floor, shattering the glass.

Parker's face was almost unrecognizable, distorted in cold fury as he seethed, "You want forgiveness? Get religion."

"What's going on?"

Betty Brant had heard the ruckus and had walked over to see what was happening. She looked in astonishment at Peter, who had never displayed this sort of violent behavior before. "Peter, are you guys okay?"

Feeling his world slipping away from him, Eddie said

with a forced chuckle, "We're fine. Just horsing around." He tried to push Peter away but couldn't budge him. Parker may have looked slight, but he had muscles of iron. "Please, please, I'm begging you," Eddie said in a desperate whisper. "If this gets out, there's not a paper in town that'll hire me. I'll lose everything."

"You should've thought of that earlier."

Drawn over by Betty's concerned inquiry, Robbie Robertson was now standing directly behind her. If Betty was surprised at Peter's display of aggression, Robbie was positively incredulous. "What are you *doing,* Peter?"

Peter stepped back, releasing his hold on Eddie. Brock sagged, gasping, and Parker picked up the envelope that he'd tossed onto Brock's desk. Turning away from Brock, he walked past Robertson, slowing only to shove the envelope at him with such force that Robbie was actually staggered half a step. Parker didn't even bother facing Robertson, but called back to him as he walked away, "Show this to your editor. Tell him to check out his sources."

Peter disappeared down the hallway. Robbie and Betty watched him go and then, in unison, shifted their gaze back to Eddie. Robertson held up the envelope and said quietly, "You want to tell me what this is about, Eddie?"

"Hey, how should I know?" said Brock, trying to bluff it through. He shrugged. "Dude's crazy."

"Is he."

Without another word, Robertson headed to Jameson's office. Betty lingered a moment more, barely veiled contempt in her eyes. Then she too walked away, and Eddie

Brock glanced at his watch, wondering how long it would take to receive The Summons.

Nine minutes.

Nine minutes before he was standing in Jameson's office, all the strength drained out of his legs.

Betty Brant had not been thrilled when Eddie Brock had shown up at the *Bugle* with that incriminating photograph of Spider-Man, for any number of reasons. She hadn't believed that Spider-Man was a crook; she had hated to see Eddie Brock take the photography job away from Peter; Jonah Jameson was never more insufferable than when he felt vindicated about something.

But when she saw Eddie Brock shoved around . . . something was seriously wrong for Peter Parker to be driven to such violence. This wasn't simply anger at being outdone by another photographer. Peter was morally outraged, and she didn't doubt for a second that his anger was righteous.

So when she was told to summon Eddie Brock to Jonah's office, she made certain to leave the door open so she could see as well as hear everything.

Jonah was on the other side of the desk, holding up the documents that had been in the envelope. There were copies of what looked to be several photos, and what appeared to be a detailed written analysis of the two. Robertson was just putting the phone down, ending a call, and he said to Jameson, "Empire State photographic department confirms it."

Fixing a gaze of pure disgust upon Brock, Jameson said, "Pack your things. Get out of my building."

"I was just trying to—"

"You're fired!" Jameson thundered.

For a split second, Betty thought that Brock was going to burst into tears. Instead he squared his shoulders and hurried out of the office as quickly as he could. He cast a glance at Betty, as if looking for sympathy. He found none in her eyes and kept going.

He'd faked the photo. That had to be it. He'd faked the photo, probably using one of Peter's old shots, and Peter had caught him. No wonder he'd been so angry. If it had been Betty, she'd probably have kneed Brock where it hurt. All things considered, she thought Peter Parker had been remarkably restrained. Good riddance.

"You know we're going to have to print a retraction," a grim Robertson said.

"I haven't printed a retraction in twenty years!" snarled Jameson, which wasn't technically true. The *Bugle* printed minor corrections all the time. But that was a far cry from having to admit that a front-page headline was based on a fabrication. "Now on account of this little pip-squeak—!"

Betty saw Jameson's face going purple and was instantly on her feet and in his office. She carried a small sculpture that looked like a miniature gazebo. Four narrow, tinkling chimes were hanging from it, bumped up against each other as she moved. Their pleasant sound was intended to be soothing. "Boss, boss, remember what your wife said. Don't get angry." She placed the sculpture in front of Jameson like an offering before a wrathful god. "Ring the Chimes of Serenity."

Jameson glared at her balefully, then tipped the sculpture slightly. The chimes sang out their cheerful tune. Jameson switched his burning gaze from Betty to the chimes. He didn't look any calmer, but before Betty could say anything, Hoffman entered, displaying his customary air of agitation. "You know that campaign you told me not to run? I ran it."

Jameson made a strangled noise, and Hoffman quickly held up the chimes, ringing them with intense desperation. "Ah, ah, ah . . . remember—the Chimes of Serenity."

Slowly, carefully, Jameson took the chimes from Hoffman and made a halfhearted attempt to concentrate on their ringing. Betty actually thought they were starting to have a calming effect on him. Then Hoffman made the mistake of saying, "And . . . we lost money."

Jameson's hand came to a full stop. The chimes ceased their tinkling. "How much?" he said softly, dangerously.

Hoffman licked his dry lips and leaned forward, whispering an amount in Jameson's ear. Jameson remained immobilized with fury for a moment, then suddenly he upended the chimes and smashed the entire thing onto the desk. The statue shattered, bits of gazebo going one way, little chimes skidding in the other. Hoffman bolted out of the office, nearly running over Betty in his desire to escape.

Consequently he didn't see the surprised expression on Jameson's face as he surveyed the busted sculpture and declared, "Oh! I *do* feel better!"

• • •

Gwen Stacy was feeling better.

The previous day had been a living hell. Although her father had never come out and said he blamed her for the tremendous humiliation of honoring a felon, she couldn't shake the silent accusation in his eyes. And, boy, did she hear about it at school from students, who were saying things like, "So . . . what's it like lip-locking a criminal?" She would have sought solace from Peter Parker, but he hadn't been in class that day.

So when the *Daily Bugle* had hit their front porch in its regular morning delivery and they had seen the bold headline—BUGLE ISSUES APOLOGY, EXPOSES FRAUD PHOTOGRAPHER—relief had swept over her like a wave at the beach. At first her father had been furious that no one from the *Bugle* had bothered to call and tell him ahead of time. But his wife, Helen, had reminded him that their failure to do so paled next to the fact that Gwen—and by extension, he—was off the hook for the key-to-the-city ceremony. Clearly they had nothing to be ashamed of; all of the fault lay with the *Daily Bugle,* and wasn't that the important thing? George Stacy had reluctantly agreed that she was right.

Gwen, up in her room, was finishing brushing her hair when she heard her mother down in the kitchen call, "George! There's someone in the driveway."

Casually dressed in sweats and a T-shirt, she trotted down the stairs. Her father, peering out the kitchen window, turned to her and said, "Gwen, come here." He pointed out the window. "It's that photographer friend of yours."

"What?" *Why did Peter come out here to see me?* She went to the window, and there was Eddie Brock, slowly walking up the driveway. His camera was slung over his shoulder, and he was carrying a small, ribboned candy box. *"Oh, no!"*

"I can summon a unit," her father said, looking more than happy to do so. "Or I can just go out and shoot him if you'd like. I have a gun, and I haven't used it for a while."

He was just kidding . . . maybe. Gwen shook her head. "Stay here. I'll take care of it."

Quickly she headed for the front door, fully aware that her father and mother were going to be watching through the window the entire time. She approached Eddie, who had taken up station near her parked car. "What are you doing here?" she demanded.

"I know you're having family time, but, what a beautiful day," he said with such chipperness that she thought maybe he'd had a psychotic break or something. How could he act as if nothing were wrong? "Could we talk? Gosh, you look swell. Going running?"

"No. Why are you here?"

"Could I come in for a minute?" He gestured toward the house.

Gwen had a feeling that if she let him in, he'd never leave short of her father forcing him out at gunpoint. "I've told you, Eddie. I don't want to see you."

"Maybe you could use a little break." He proffered the box. "I brought you some candy. You said you like the cherry centers."

"Stop trying to take over my life!"

Their next-door neighbor was busy putting his sprinkler out on his lawn, but he stopped to listen in. *Great. That's all I need.*

"I'm not trying to take over your life. You're important to me! Don't act as if we've never met. We stood on that porch"—he pointed, his finger trembling—"you let me kiss you there. You said you cared for me. That you loved me!"

What? "I never said I loved you!" she protested. Becoming increasingly angry, Gwen railed, "How could anybody love you after you tried to disgrace someone who is as noble and principled as Spider-Man by deceiving the public with that phony picture you made up?!"

Eddie couldn't have looked more grief-stricken if he'd been standing at his mother's funeral. "Don't you understand there's a reason for everything? I know you talk to Parker about me. Why can't you talk to me, get my side of the story? Things aren't always what they seem to be, y'know." He reached out, took hold of her arm. "I need a friend right now."

Gwen tried to pull free, but he wasn't releasing her. "Let go of me, Eddie!"

She was certain that she still was in control of the situation, but clearly her parents didn't share that opinion. She heard the hurried sound of running feet and turned to see her father and mother approaching. "Take your hand off her, boy!" Captain Stacy warned him.

"Let her go!" said Helen.

Brock instantly let Gwen loose. His entire body looked shaky, as if his joints were being held together by little more than rubber bands. "How are you, Captain Stacy?" he said with false joviality. He actually had the nerve to put out a hand for a handshake. "Edward Brock, sir. *Daily Bugle.*"

George Stacy looked at the outstretched hand as if it belonged to a leper. Worse: he'd probably have been more inclined to shake a leper's hand. "I know who you are. I want you to leave here."

Eddie lifted up his camera, trying to keep it steady as he peered through the viewfinder. He was so wobbly that Gwen was starting to wonder if he was either drunk or hungover. And he kept up with the random and bizarre attempts at flattery: "For my album, sir. If I could get the family? You have a beautiful house. Is this plastic siding?"

Captain Stacy took a step forward. "Mr. Brock, get off this property or I will arrest you. Is that clear?"

That silenced Eddie. He stared hopelessly, helplessly at the Stacy family, and something in the pure despair of his look made even George Stacy take a measure of pity on him. "Go on, son," he said as gently as he could. "Go home."

Brock looked at Gwen like a man who had just been strapped into the electric chair and was gazing at the life he would never have. Then he forced a smile that was all the more unsettling for its inappropriateness. He turned away from her, walked sadly to the sidewalk, then bizarrely did a little hop/skip/heel-kick motion that looked like something out of a music video.

The Stacys watched in silence as Brock went, and then

Gwen's father said to her in a low voice, "Sometimes, Gwen, you can go too far encouraging these young men."

Gwen turned and looked at him incredulously. "What did *I* do? People like me. That isn't my fault. I didn't ask him here."

"All I'm saying," her father told her with great patience, "is maybe in a way you did. Maybe you made him think somehow that you cared. He's a man. And you're . . . a very attractive young woman."

She bristled at the idea. She understood what her dad was saying, but she had to believe that it was more along the lines of what her grandmother always used to say: when you get near pigs, sooner or later you're going to wind up with some mud on you.

The mud down by the East River stirred.

A copy of that day's *Daily Bugle* floated past a dark, muddy stain that was bobbing in the moonlit water. The floating pile of mud was carried along by the current and then, surprisingly, started to move against it. Anyone observing it would have thought that perhaps it was not mud at all, but a strange type of jellyfish or other sea life that had wandered into the river.

As that was happening, Peter Parker was back in his apartment, having removed the black suit. He had settled Eddie Brock's hash, and it was a beautiful thing. But he'd seen the concern in Betty Brant's eyes, the surprise in Robbie Robertson's. His anger toward Brock was completely justified, and yet it made him feel extremely uncomfortable. He decided it would probably be best to divest himself of the outfit as soon as possible. This he managed to do with minimal effort, for this time around the suit wasn't adhering to his skin with quite such an air of desperation. In Peter's imaginings, he fancied that the suit didn't feel the need to be quite so "clingy"—because it knew it had him. If he'd voluntarily put it back on once, he would do so again and again, done deal. So Peter decided to put it back in the trunk and lock it up, just to show it who was boss.

Yet, curiously, that wasn't where the suit wound up. Instead it lay draped over a chair, looking partly like cloth and partly like a dark puddle.

Meantime a genuine dark puddle over on the river had nearly reached the shore. A tendril slowly stretched up from the puddle, groping along the riverbank as it pulled itself to ground and safety. The puddle began to grow as more and more mud oozed up behind it out of the river, and slowly, slowly, the pile of mud and dirt stood upright and began to gain the mass and form of a human being.

All this while Eddie Brock sat in a bar and drank himself into a stupor, alternating between muttering Gwen Stacy's name miserably and Peter Parker's name with hatred and venom.

XIX

REFLECTIONS

PETER REMEMBERED THE DAYS when the Malibu diner was the best that he and Harry could afford. All right, he admitted to himself, the best that *he* could afford. Harry could probably have bought the whole place with no trouble. But Peter would never have stood for Harry picking up the tab—as Harry could have well afforded—and Harry would never have tolerated Peter spending more money than was good for him. So the Malibu it had been whenever the two of them felt like going out to eat.

Come to think of it, Peter realized, it wasn't as if he were all that much better off financially these days either.

Sitting across from Harry, trying to express the frustration and confusion he was feeling, he brought his friend up to speed about the latest turnaround with MJ. Peter was only having a cup of coffee, while Harry was also having a piece of blueberry pie with his. "Things were fine," Peter insisted. "Then, suddenly, she says there's another guy. Gets this thing in her head, says I'm not there for her."

"She's been having a tough time," Harry said, sounding more sympathetic to Mary Jane than he was to

Peter . . . which, Peter had to admit, annoyed him slightly. "Her career, singing waitress at a jazz club. Not exactly what she had in mind for herself."

Peter blinked in confusion, feeling as if he had just missed a section of the conversation. "A singing waitress . . . ? What about the show?"

"Well, she was fired," Harry said matter-of-factly. "Didn't she tell you?"

Slumping back in the chair, Peter was totally blind-sided. *My God, that explains so much . . . almost everything . . . but how could I have known . . . how could . . .*

"She got fired?" Peter was unable to grasp it. "She told *you,* but she didn't tell *me?* What's going on? I don't get it!" Trying to recapture the high ground of being the victimized half of the couple, Peter said, "You didn't hear me, Harry! There's another guy!"

Harry paused, drumming his fingers on the table. Then, calmly, he said, "That's why I asked you to have coffee with me."

"What are you talking about?"

"The other guy, Pete . . ." He waggled his head slightly, then shrugged in a "What can you do?" manner.

Peter wondered just how many shocks to the system he was supposed to endure in just one outing. "What? Wait a minute. *You're . . .*"

"She came to me one afternoon." Harry tried to sound saddened, but a small smile on his face belied whatever his tone might have implied. "Lost. And she was troubled. She needed someone, and *I was there for her.*" He made certain to emphasize the words Peter had used. "I've always loved her, you know that. It just . . . started."

Peter laughed in incredulity. It was as if he were watching some sort of play unfold in which everyone was a stupendously bad actor. "I don't believe this! I don't believe you!"

"I'm sure you don't," said Harry, sounding sympathetic but not looking it. "I'm sorry, pal. I'm not here to convince you. I just want you to know."

They stared at each other for a few moments, then Peter got up to leave, tossing a few dollars on the table to cover his side of the check. As he did so, the waitress appeared with a pot of coffee. "Can I warm you up?" she asked Harry. At Harry's nod, she refilled his cup. "How was the pie?"

"Soooo good." Harry grinned as Peter walked out.

Peter was in turmoil. His anger was getting in the way of his making sense of it all. How could Mary Jane do this to him? How could Harry? What sort of friends were they? The notion that Harry would move in, take advantage of Mary Jane if she was in that kind of state . . . and Mary Jane! That she would rebound from him to Harry . . . and why? It wasn't as if they had even officially broken up. It was completely insane. . . .

The two words lodged in his head, coming to the forefront of his musings.

Completely. Insane.

Peter had far too much experience with someone like that.

Standing in the street outside the coffee shop, Peter slowly turned to face Harry, who was watching him through the window. Harry met his gaze, saw the suspicion in Peter's eyes, and seemed to welcome it.

Harry's mouth twisted in a fierce and cruel smile. His expression no longer bore the slightest resemblance to any that Peter's friend might have worn. But the question was moot: this wasn't his friend, by any stretch of the imagination, who was looking at him now.

This was the face of insanity. This was the Goblin.

Before Peter could make a move, the waitress leaned in to clear the dishes from the table, blocking Harry from Peter's view. When she moved aside, Harry was gone.

He had to have gone out the back. Peter considered vaulting over the top of the restaurant, but far too many people were around. Plus who knew what resources Harry might have lying in wait, or who might get hurt if another struggle broke out.

There was no way Peter was going to allow Harry to choose the time and place of their next battle . . . a battle that Peter was now eagerly anticipating. As he ran toward home and his costume, he pondered that he shouldn't really be looking forward to such a conflict. But that concern was promptly shouted down by the part of him that wanted to knock that leering grin off Harry's face once and for all.

Harry Osborn, feeling more self-assured than he had in ages, sat in the great room of his town house, calmly stirring a martini with a long spoon. Suddenly he stopped, sensing a change in the atmosphere of the room. He turned and saw a figure standing in the doorway behind him.

He exhaled a relaxed sigh, as if an old friend had come to call and have a pleasant chat. "What took you so long?"

"That was quite a performance," came the taut voice of Peter Parker.

"It wasn't all show. She *did* come to me." Harry gingerly put the martini down on the table next to him, taking care not to spill it.

He expected Peter to continue with the back-and-forth. To try to appeal to his better nature. To insist in mewling tones that Harry wasn't in his right mind, that this could all be avoided.

Instead, to his surprise, Peter advanced on him and announced, "I'm really going to enjoy this."

Remaining cool in the face of the unexpected, Harry replied, "Not as much as I enjoyed it when Mary Jane kissed me. It was the same way she always kissed me. And that taste . . ." He sighed again, recalling. "Strawberries."

He was utterly shocked as Peter hurtled through the air straight at him. Harry had about a split second to react, which wasn't remotely enough time. Peter slammed into him, sending the table and martini crashing to the floor. The combatants fell over the chair, upending it, as both Peter and Harry tumbled across the room.

Harry twisted, sending Peter flying overhead. Peter slammed into a set of shelves upon which various curios had been placed. The top shelf was jolted loose, fell onto the one below it, which fell onto the one below that, and so on until they all hit bottom, crushing all the curios into dust.

Staggering to his feet, Harry raggedly said, "You'll be hearing from my attorney about that. I hope you've got good liability insurance."

Peter wasn't listening. Instead he covered the distance between himself and Harry in one leap, sending the two of them flying backward and crashing into the mirror hanging on the wall.

Into it . . . and through.

They landed inside the Goblin's secret lair, and Peter looked around in confusion, startled over what he was seeing. With superhuman strength, Harry took the opportunity to grab a Sky Stick and swing it around like a baseball bat. It struck Peter in the side of the head, staggering him. Harry brought it sweeping back in the other direction . . . but Peter grabbed the flying device, yanked it from Harry's grasp, and tossed it aside.

He swung a punch at Harry, who ducked under it and came in fast with several quick blows to Peter's gut. Peter faltered, recovered, and fired a blot of webbing at Harry's feet. Harry tried to get out of the way, but the webbing affixed itself to him, holding fast. He tried to yank his feet free, but there was no time as Peter swung a vicious roundhouse that damned near took Harry's head off. As it was, Peter solved Harry's immobility problem, the blow so fierce that it knocked Harry right out of his webbed-up shoes. Harry was flat on his back, and Peter gave him no time to get up. He landed heavily atop Harry and, with an unbelievable ferocity, started hammering him in the face.

Harry's mind was swimming. This wasn't the Peter Parker that he'd encountered last time. To some degree, he'd counted on the notion that, in a head-to-head battle, Peter would always hold back. It was a weakness in Spider-Man's character—a reluctance to be up-front about the murdering cretin that he truly was—that Harry had come to expect. Not this time, though—Peter was cutting loose with the sort of murderous intensity that he had no doubt unleashed upon Norman Osborn.

Harry was on the receiving end of as brutal a pounding as anyone had ever endured. If it weren't for the heightened strength that the green gas had given him, he'd have been long dead. As it was, the room was spinning around him, and Peter wasn't letting up for even a second. The blows came fast and furious; Harry couldn't even begin to mount a defense. His head slumped back, and Peter cocked a fist, looking ready to punch it straight through Harry's head and into the floor below.

Through lips that were thick and swollen, Harry managed to say, "You gonna kill me like you killed my father?"

"Your father was a monster!" Peter shouted. "And you know it! He tried to stab me in the back! I jumped out of the way. He got what he meant for me." He brought his face close to Harry's, and Harry saw a terrifying grin. "He never loved you. Who could love you? No one. Not your father. Not Mary Jane."

Peter was just trying to give back some of the same mind games that Harry had dished out, but he was infuriated nevertheless. "My father loved me!"

"He despised you! *You were an embarrassment!*"

Reveling in tormenting Harry, Peter let down his guard for a second, and Harry seized the opportunity. He brought a fist around and slugged Peter in the side of the head, then hit him again, and a third time. Peter fell sideways off him, and Harry crab-walked backward, scuttling quickly toward a rack that was lined with pumpkin bombs. In a crouch, he grabbed one off the shelf. Harry was having trouble seeing, his right eye having swollen closed, the left not far behind, so he hurled the bomb as best he could.

Through the slit of vision he had left, he saw Peter snag the bomb with a web strand. Harry reached for a second one, then he froze as Peter snapped the bomb around like a yo-yo and sent it hurtling right back at Harry. He threw up his hands to try to ward it off. Too slow. The bomb exploded in Harry's face, blasting him backward, the room immediately filling with acrid smoke.

Harry hit the floor, the nerve endings in his face screaming as if they were on fire. *He's going to kill me. This is it. I'm helpless. He's going to snap my neck or stab me in the chest. I'm sorry, Dad. I tried. I tried so hard . . .*

But the death blow never came. Only silence. Deciding that he had nothing to lose in trying to get out of here, Harry started hauling himself across the floor. He was having no trouble gripping the surface, as his hands were sticky with blood. He registered this fact distantly, as if it were relevant to someone else.

Every movement agonizing, he managed to make his way out of the Goblin's lair. He squinted through his one working eye and saw no sign of Peter. So typical. He had Harry at his mercy, and instead of killing him, he'd decided to leave him alive so that Harry could worry about the next time he'd attack.

Well, that was going to be a mistake, oh, yes. Because next time . . .

With smoke billowing past him, Harry looked down and saw a large shard of the shattered mirror door on the floor in front of him. He glanced into it and gasped, wondering who the hell that poor, grotesque devil was looking back at him. It took Harry a few moments to realize that it was himself.

His horrified, sustained scream resounded through the penthouse.

Some distance away, the black-suited Spider-Man landed on a rooftop, but it was Peter Parker who reacted to the far-off howling that he knew, beyond question, was his friend.

He pulled off the mask and forced himself to remain there, motionless, until the scream finally faded.

At first he felt guilty over what had transpired, but his heart hardened. He'd left Harry alive after Harry had tried, on more than one occasion, to kill him. Harry Osborn was the single greatest threat in Peter's life—knowing his identity, capable of coming at him at any moment. Yet Peter had chosen to be merciful. What reason did he have to feel guilty over the fate that Harry had brought upon himself, just as Harry's father had likewise done?

"He deserved worse," Peter said tightly.

And so did Mary Jane. As demented as Harry had been, Peter was now convinced that he was telling the truth about Mary Jane's coming to him. And she had told him about what was going on in her life without mentioning one word to Peter. She wasn't blameless in any of this.

He wasn't about to go find Mary Jane and pound on her, obviously. But other means of revenge could be just as satisfying and—most important—wouldn't risk getting blood on his nice black suit.

But he had other priorities to attend to. First and foremost . . .

. . . hunting season was now open.

XX

ALL THAT JAZZ

Curtis Connors, working late in his lab, held the phone close to his ear while he waited for the young woman who had answered the phone to summon Mr. Parker from wherever the devil he was. Some half-eaten Chinese food sat in its cartons on the lab table behind him. "Mr. Parker!" he said when he finally heard Peter's voice on the other end. "Dr. Connors here."

"Yes, sir." Peter's voice sounded a little deeper than usual, and Connors almost wondered whether he was speaking to the right person.

Glancing at a small sample of the black goo that was currently sitting on a microscope slide, Connors said, "Quite a specimen you left me, Parker. Its chemistry is not unlike material found in that chondritic meteorite in the seventies. You know it, Parker?" He was reasonably sure that Parker did. Chondritic meteorites were pieces of space rock that had fallen to earth with relatively little differentiation from the stone body from which they'd originated. Connors was referring specifically to the Jilin meteorite shower of 1976, in which—among other things—the largest, single, known chondritic meteorite ever discovered, weighing 1,770 kilograms, had fallen in the People's Republic of China.

But Peter didn't answer immediately. "Parker?" Connors prompted.

"Yeah." Peter sounded almost indifferent, which Connors found disturbing.

"My findings are very preliminary, but this substance seems to be an entire living organism." Parker was acting in an unusually distracted manner, and Connors was hoping he was speaking with enough emphasis to get the boy's attention. He had no idea why Parker sounded so disinterested. Maybe the girl who'd answered the phone was doing a striptease for him. Whatever the reason, Connors didn't care. *"A living organism,"* he emphasized. "Possibly a parasite. It amplifies characteristics of its host . . . especially aggression."

He glanced across the room at the cage that had contained two lab mice. He had put a minuscule amount of the parasite on one of the mice and left the other alone. He had then watched in shock as the treated mouse ripped its companion to shreds. "This could be dangerous," he said, which was possibly an understatement. Suddenly a thought occurred to him. "Peter . . . you didn't keep any, did you? Peter?"

Peter laughed in response. "Doc . . . I'm not stupid. Thanks for the information. Let me know what else you find."

He hung up before Connors could say another word.

The following day was a blur to Peter.

He woke up knowing one thing above all else: life was

simpler with the suit on. Priorities remained in order, and pesky questions of morality simply didn't apply. Matters had become overly complicated, and he was tired of it. Putting on the black suit was like causing the rest of his difficulties to disappear into a pleasant haze of white noise.

His first stop was the *Daily Bugle.* He knew he would always cherish the sight of a sputtering J. Jonah Jameson as Peter strutted into Jonah's office, flopped into a chair, tilted it back, and placed his feet up on Jameson's desk.

"Shoes?" said a stunned Jameson.

Ignoring Jameson's shock, Peter pulled three photos from his portfolio, flicking them across Jameson's desk like cards from a Las Vegas dealer. Each one landed squarely in front of Jameson, one next to the other. His little hunting expedition the previous night had borne fruit, and Jameson was salivating over the trophies: superb shots of a diamond heist in progress, being thwarted by a menacing Spider-Man in his black attire.

The subject of Peter's feet forgotten, Jameson asked, "How much?"

"Well," Peter replied in leisurely fashion, "seeing as how I'm the only photographer you've got . . ."

He lowered his feet, leaned over, and picked up Jameson's personal candy jar. He popped the top before Jonah could say a word, extracted a fancy caramel, unwrapped it, and flipped it into the air.

". . . more." He caught the caramel in his mouth.

"More caramels? Because if that's what you really want—"

Peter half-smiled, knowing that he had the upper hand

and reveling in it. "More money. More than you paid Brock. More than you paid me. More than you paid anybody, ever."

"I can't afford that!"

"Then I walk these over to the *Globe,* and we don't do business anymore. Can you afford *that*?"

Jameson gave Peter a reptilian glare. "Where the hell did *this* come from? I get rid of one punk and another sprouts up, like weeds. You used to be a cream puff."

"Yeah, well . . ." Peter smiled. "Now I have layers."

Beneath his clothing, the black costume approved.

With more money in his pocket than he could remember having in quite a while, Peter strode the streets of New York as if he owned the city.

He winked at passing women and received approving smiles. He passed one particularly sexy young woman and didn't hesitate to reach back and pat her behind. She whirled angrily around, facing him, and he tossed off a flashy finger/thumb wave, as if to say, *The two of us are lookin' good, and we got it goin' on.* She returned the wave, although minus the thumb and with a different finger extended, but Peter was already sauntering away.

He paused outside a men's clothing store with a sign that read: DISCOUNT ITALIAN SUITS. The mannequins in the window had solid black heads, and black arms sticking out from the sleeves. It made it easier for Peter to imagine the suits on him, and he decided that there was no reason to settle for imagining it.

A half hour later, he emerged from the store outfitted

in a flashy new suit with new boots just for a hint of the truly audacious. He rocked back and forth on the boots. Peter once again thought of Travolta and performed a few experimental pelvis thrusts, back and forth, back and forth. Nodding in self-approval, he strutted down the street.

He glanced at his watch and noticed that he had, yet again, missed class. Somehow that didn't bother him at all. It wasn't as if Connors were going to say something that Peter didn't already know. He'd already lost a bit of respect for the old doc after Connors had called the symbiote a "parasite." How could Connors have gotten it so wrong? A parasite was something that simply took from its host without giving anything back. The symbiote, the "organism" as he'd called it, didn't take; it *gave.* It gave him more confidence, enabled him to see just how the world should be treating him . . . and how he should treat it in return.

There was still enough time, though, to get over to ESU and accomplish something really important.

Peter flagged a cab and urged the driver to lay on all possible speed, assuring him he'd cover any tickets the guy might get. Both of them were fortunate that no police cars stopped them, although it might have been that they were moving so fast that the cops thought they couldn't catch up. Peter leaped out of the cab, tossing a twenty to the cabbie while telling him to keep the change, and ran across the campus.

Gwen Stacy had just emerged from the science building when someone seemed to appear out of nowhere directly in front of her. She jumped, so startled that she dropped the books she'd been carrying. Peter deftly plucked them out of the air and restacked them before she'd even registered who the new arrival was.

"Peter!" she exclaimed, taking the books back from him. "You weren't in lab! Where've you been lately?"

"TCB."

She looked confused.

He ticked off the letters on his fingers. "Taking. Care. Of Business." He stretched his arms in either direction and turned in place.

It took Gwen a moment to comprehend that he was waiting for a comment on the suit. "Oh. Very nice. New outfit. And . . ." She stared at him, puzzled. "Are you . . . taller?"

"When a guy's with you, he's always gonna walk a little taller."

Gwen smiled at that and flushed slightly. "Well, now aren't you the smooth talker. So where have you been?"

He waved off the question as if it weren't worth his time. "That's the past. I'm thinking about the future . . . namely this evening."

"What about this evening?"

"You and me. We"—he smiled—"are stepping out."

"Mr. Parker," said Gwen coyly, "are you asking me out on a date?"

"Asking? Who's asking? This," he said suavely, plucking her hand out of the air and kissing her knuckle, "is a fait accompli."

Her instinct was to say no. Her father's warning from

the other day flashed in her head—maybe this was the exact wrong time to start going out on dates.

But Peter Parker was a very different animal from Eddie Brock. It wasn't as if he were a stranger; he was at least a good guy with a lot going on upstairs. She could count on him to spend time with her and be thinking about something else other than what she'd look like with her clothes off.

"Well then"—Gwen smiled—"who am I to fight 'fait'?"

A small jazz combo was in the middle of "One O'Clock Jump," an old Count Basie standard, when Peter guided Gwen into the Jazz Room. The place was packed, with customers tapping their feet to the music. Peter started snapping his fingers to the beat, and Gwen imitated him, grinning.

A hostess escorted them to a table. Gwen, now really getting into the music, moved her hips to the beat and was practically dancing to it by the time the hostess seated them. Peter glanced around the club, looking to spot a familiar face. Gwen, unaware of where Peter's attentions were, said, "Great idea, Pete!" as she sat. "I never put you and jazz together."

"Jazz. Fits in with the natural order of the universe, y'know." He sat opposite her. "Branch of science."

"Now you're talkin'." A small bowl of pretzels was on the table. Gwen picked one up and daintily bit off a piece. Then she started looking around the club, taking in the ambience, leaving Peter free to scope the place out. Finally he found what he was looking for: Mary Jane. She was clear across the way, waiting on another customer.

The band wrapped the Basie number, to strong applause. The pianist stepped away from the piano, heading offstage, perhaps to get a smoke or maybe just hit the bathroom. The trumpet player moved to the microphone and said, "Let's hear from you, Mary Jane."

Mary Jane smiled, starting to head toward the bandstand. The band played some traveling music as she made her way through the cluster of tables to the stage. Gwen saw her and was visibly startled. "Isn't that Mary Jane? Your old girlfriend?"

"Wild, huh?" said Peter, making it sound like a staggering coincidence.

Still not having realized that Peter had deliberately chosen this spot because of Mary Jane's presence, Gwen asked solicitously, concerned that the experience might be too painful for him, "Would you rather go someplace else?"

"I can handle it," he said easily. Then he rose and stepped away from the table.

Mary Jane had just gotten to the microphone and was about to announce the name of the song she was to sing when Peter reached the stage and sat at the piano. MJ was startled to hear the keys sound on the old Steinway, and when she turned and looked to see what was happening, her eyes widened in disbelief. The rest of the musicians were equally taken aback that this stranger from the audience had apparently joined the band. It wasn't unprecedented, but it usually happened much later in the evening when the audience was a lot more inebriated.

"Peter?" Mary Jane gasped.

Peter spoke into the microphone next to the piano. "I'd like to dedicate this to a special lady out there." He looked at Mary Jane, paused for dramatic emphasis, and then shifted his gaze to Gwen. "A *very* special lady." Then, not giving Mary Jane time to register what had just happened, keeping her emotionally off-balance, he turned to the band and said, "Fellas, just straight eights until the turnaround."

He started a fast piano riff, gliding into a free-form jazz composition. Thanks to the black costume, it seemed that the piano lessons his aunt had insisted he take had paid off in the long run. Nice. All he needed to be a virtuoso was some confidence, and he certainly had that in spades these days.

The band started picking up his tempo, and Peter nodded approvingly. "Now that's eighteen karat." He turned to the audience and grinned. "These guys are really in the pocket."

Mary Jane was still standing in the spotlight, clearly not knowing what to do, shifting uncomfortably from one foot to the other like a small child in desperate need of a bathroom. Then the spotlight, much to Peter's secret glee, moved away from Mary Jane and over to him. The crowd naturally shifted their attention with it, some even adjusting their chairs so that their backs were to Mary Jane.

Peter was feeling at home, playing with such expertise one would have thought he'd been part of the band for years. He nodded to the other guys, "Take it on one time, without me now."

Without missing a beat, he sprang from the piano bench and leaped onto the dance floor. He shouted to the crowd, like a 1960s hipster, "Now dig on this!"

Throwing all caution aside, he unleashed a flurry of break-dancing steps with a healthy element of both Elvis thrusts and John Travolta disco tossed in, capped by a series of athletic moves that would have seemed possible only for an Olympic-level gymnast . . . or Spider-Man, of course, but that wouldn't have occurred to any of them.

During a musical break when just the bass and drums were holding down the backbeat, Peter snapped around in an air-guitar move worthy of Chuck Berry and called out, "Now how 'bout a little o' that . . . um-um-*um*!"

The band promptly responded with three similar funky cords. Pushing his luck and his moves beyond all reason, Peter sprang into the air and landed atop the piano bench with a one-handed handstand. As he balanced on the one hand, he reached out with his free hand and worked the keyboard, right on cue.

The musicians looked a little stunned at the gargantuan showboating from their unexpected and, frankly, uninvited new member, but the crowd went nuts. They had never seen anything like it. No one had.

Maintaining his one-handed pose, Peter abruptly switched hands for a low piano part, then changed yet again for a high part. The number built to a crescendo and Peter sprang into the air and landed on the stage in a split, his arms in a *V* formation. The applause was thunderous. He glanced over at Mary Jane and saw her slink away from the microphone. She descended the stairs but didn't move far away from them. Instead she just watched Peter with a look of infinite sadness. Well, if she was feeling sorry for him, then her pity was surely misplaced.

Elated beyond all measure, Peter sprang out onto the dance floor again and swept Gwen out of her chair. Even though there was no longer any music, he dipped her low, his lips moving toward hers. Then, slowly and deliberately, he looked in Mary Jane's direction to ensure that she was watching.

Mary Jane started to sob. Tears were streaming down her face, her mascara running. Peter noticed that the manager had also seen it and was starting to move toward Mary Jane. Good. Maybe he was about to fire her. Wouldn't that just be the perfect end to the perfect—

"That was for her, wasn't it."

Peter looked down at Gwen—she had seen him looking toward Mary Jane. Gwen scowled fiercely, finally catching on. "That's why you brought me here. You son of a bitch!"

She struggled in his grasp, but he didn't care. Gwen had served her purpose. Peter released her, and she stumbled away, almost falling, one hand touching the floor and stabilizing her before she tumbled over. She managed to stand, then backed away from Peter, treating him like a stranger. She grabbed her purse off the table and headed toward the exit. But before Gwen did, she headed to Mary Jane. Peter could make out from where he was standing that she said, "I'm so very sorry," to Mary Jane.

Figures. In the end, the women always stick together.

Suddenly he was annoyed with Gwen. He hadn't given her permission to leave—who the hell did she think she was? Where did she get off, ditching him on their first date? He started moving to intercept her as she went for the exit, and abruptly the manager was in his way. "Hey, you're making trouble," he snapped at Peter. "What're you doing?" He glanced toward Mary Jane and said, "You know this guy?"

Nose to nose with the manager, royally angered that this gnat was trying to shove himself into his affairs, Peter demanded, "You got a problem?"

A large, burly guy with a thick neck and a jacket that barely closed over his chest now stepped into view. *Of course, here comes the bouncer.* "Paul, everything okay here?"

He spoke with a thick Brooklyn accent, so Peter mimicked him. "Yeah, Paul, ever'ting okay heah?"

The bouncer didn't wait for the manager's okay. He grabbed Peter by the arm and said, "Let's go, pal."

"Where are we going? I like it here!"

"Let's just step over—"

Peter grabbed the bouncer's arm, twisted it, and flipped the larger man up and onto the floor. The crowd gasped as one. What had begun as simple entertainment was rapidly devolving into anarchy.

The manager, no slouch himself in the strength and speed department, tried to put a choke hold on Peter while Peter was distracted by the bouncing bouncer. An instant before Peter attended to him, Mary Jane—knowing what the men were up against, and knowing they had no chance—cried out, *"Peter! Stop!"*

"I'm just getting started." Peter laughed. This time he didn't even bother with the pretext of a judo throw. He simply picked the manager up and chucked him across several tables. The customers at those tables tried to intercept the manager in his flight and wound up going down with him in a tumble of arms and legs.

Gwen Stacy was long gone by the point that the melee broke out . . . rather unfortunately since she could have had police there within seconds. But things were now happening so quickly that no one even thought about summoning the authorities.

Total chaos had been unleashed in the Jazz Room, and Peter was in the center of it.

Probably assuming that Peter was high on something, customers came at him from all sides, trying to wrestle him to the floor.

No one even came close to stopping him. Peter was completely out of control, and he didn't care. He had willingly tossed self-control away, surrendered to the sheer joy. And he wasn't just taking joy in the battle; he was wallowing in his superiority. He loved it that no one had a chance against him. It was one lone guy against everybody in the place, and he was mopping up the floor with them.

And it didn't bother him; that was the best thing. Once upon a time, long ago, his annoying conscience would never have allowed him to enjoy what he was doing. He was mopey old Peter Parker, given great power but bending under the weight of the responsibility. No longer. A spine had grown seemingly overnight, and nothing was ever going to drag him down or make him feel guilty again.

Nothing.

The piano player who had taken a break came back onto the stage to discover the rest of the band had deserted him, choosing instead to throw themselves against some demented guy who was apparently kicking everybody's collective asses. He did the only thing that seemed appropriate—he started banging out the *William Tell* overture on the keyboard.

Peter threw two people in either direction and turned just in time to see Mary Jane coming straight at him. She was in no way trying to attack him. Instead she was crying out to him, begging him to stop, to put the people down, what was he trying to prove, had he lost his mind, and on and on . . .

Without hesitation, without even a thought, Peter grabbed Mary Jane and threw her across a table. She skidded across it, kept going, and landed on her back on the floor.

Everything stopped.

Mary Jane approached Peter, completely torn up inside. She knew she had this coming as a result of her unceremoniously dumping him in the park. She'd had no choice: Harry had made her do it. Harry, who had lost his mind. Apparently somehow he'd transformed into something horrifying, and forced her to break it off with Peter.

She was terrified to try to tell Peter the truth, for Harry, as this New Goblin, had warned her that he would be watching her every moment of every day. That wasn't possible, but she wasn't about to test him on it. But now things had gotten out of hand. Peter needed to be dragged somewhere private and talked to, no matter what the risk. He'd understand. He had to.

At no time as she advanced on Peter did she believe that he would hurt her. Not for a second.

The shock barely registered when Peter cavalierly tossed her aside like a sack of wheat.

Fortunately, Mary Jane had taken enough lessons in stagecraft to know how to fall. When she hit the floor, she slapped it with both hands to absorb the impact, so she wasn't really hurt. Nevertheless, she was still stunned by what had just happened. As she lay on the floor, unmoving, silence descended over the club. Until now, Peter had been dispatching burly men without a second thought. But when he started tossing women half his size around, that apparently crossed a line. *Chivalry is not dead? Could have surprised me.*

Peter quickly shoved other people aside to get to her. None of them tried to get in his way, which was probably a wise move. Peter looked down at her, his own expression as incredulous as hers.

"What's happened to you?" she whispered. Her face was covered with dried tears, but she wasn't crying anymore. She was too caught up in trying to comprehend what was going on.

Slowly Peter shook his head. He looked like someone waking from a dream. "I . . . don't know . . ."

The top of his shirt was open and she glimpsed the black costume beneath it.

The black costume.

Mary Jane was no scientific genius, no whiz kid on par with Peter Parker or Curtis Connors. She didn't know about chondritic meteorites, or symbiotes and parasites. She had absolutely no way of knowing the true origins of the black costume that she'd recently seen pictures of Peter sporting around town in.

But she did know two things. One was timing. And the other was Peter Parker.

In a leap of deductive logic that would have impressed Hercule Poirot, she concluded that Peter Parker was acting nothing like himself, and that behavior was traceable almost to the day that he'd started wearing the black costume. She had no idea how it was possible, no clue where it had come from, but with a flash of insight that only she could possibly have had, she realized that Peter wasn't actually wearing the costume.

It was wearing him.

"It's the suit," she whispered.

Peter looked down—yes, she had seen the top of his costume peeping through the dress shirt. He quickly covered it and turned toward the exit. The crowd of people parted like the Red Sea before Moses.

And Mary Jane did something she hadn't done in a long time.

Dear God . . . hear my prayer . . . help him . . . help him and bring him back to me . . . please.

XXI

THE HOST WITH THE MOST

It is said by many that God moves in mysterious ways.

It was also said by Voltaire that God is a comedian playing to an audience too afraid to laugh.

Both explanations, and many more besides, could explain just why, with all the churches in New York City, both Eddie Brock Jr. and Peter Parker wound up at the same one at exactly the same time: just as the sun was beginning to creep up over the horizon. The sky, however, was thick with clouds and rain was coming down, so the sun wasn't having much success in making its presence known.

At that moment, however, they were unaware of each other's presence, for Peter was in the upper bell tower while Eddie was just coming in out of the downpour and walking slowly down the aisle of the empty church.

Having put the pieces of the game into their proper places, God made His moves. The audience remained afraid to laugh.

Still wearing the black costume, Peter sat in the bell tower, looking off toward the horizon. His fancy Italian suit was piled in a heap on the side.

He had no idea what to do. The words of Curtis

Connors were haunting him. When he'd first heard them, he'd laughed them off. But he kept replaying the image of his swatting aside Mary Jane, and it was like having ice-cold water repeatedly dousing him in the face.

A huge church bell hung above him. It was three times his size, but he wasn't really paying attention to it. He was caught up in his inner torment, oblivious not only to its presence, but to the timing mechanism nearby that was ticking down toward the moment when it would set the gears into motion and send the bell ringing.

A part of him was urging him to forget everything that had happened. Find a way to make it up to Mary Jane if he had to, but not to dwell on it.

Even as he thought that, though, he knew it would be impossible. Not only had too much happened, too much more could *still* happen. Just in wearing the costume for a couple of days, he felt as if he was losing touch with his soul. What in God's name would happen a couple of weeks or months from now? Would he even be recognizable as himself? What would he become?

He couldn't chance finding out.

Peter stood and started pulling on the suit, figuring that he would be able to peel it off as easily as he had the last time.

Wrong.

Perhaps sensing that matters had reached a crisis point, the suit refused to yield. Peter pulled at it harder, using the full power of the amazing adhesive abilities that lay in his fingertips. Nothing. The suit stretched like Silly Putty, then snapped right back.

He started digging into it with his nails, pulling as hard as he could.

Oh my God . . . get off me get off me get off me!

The alien symbiote didn't speak back to him, not possessing that power of communication. He sensed a deep-seated feeling permeating him, a feeling originating not from him but from the suit. If he'd had to find words to express the emotions that the costume was projecting, it would have been . . .

Make me.

Sonorous organ music crept through the church as Eddie walked slowly down the aisle. He glanced in the direction of the actual organ, and it sat there, silent. But the music was coming from somewhere. Probably a sexton or someone like that playing recorded music. It was unbearably creepy and added a foreboding Gothic flavor to the chapel.

Feeling sad, lonely, and pathetic, he took a seat and stared at the image of Christ on the cross. A man with good intentions who'd been crucified for his troubles. Eddie Brock could relate.

"Eddie Brock, sir," he introduced himself. "I've been wronged, and the woman I worship will have none of me. I don't qualify as the perfect boyfriend, but . . . who does?"

Jesus didn't answer. That was okay. What could he really have said? Eddie didn't mind its being a one-way conversation. "I ask you, why do I have to suffer for everyone else's imperfections? Why can't I ever have what I want?

What about me?" He thumped his chest. "What about Eddie? I try to do what's right. I follow your rules. I obey the 'thou shalt nots.' I'm a decent person." He raised his voice to get it above the organ music, which seemed to be getting louder. *"I'm a decent person!"*

Eddie frightened himself with his vehemence and the intensity of his emotions. He didn't understand why it had come to this. Why no one else in the world was able to see him the way that he saw himself.

Never for a moment did he consider that he had brought his problems upon himself. Instead they had been forced upon him by a world that judged him and found him wanting without ever truly comprehending him.

"So I come to you today, humbled, humiliated, to ask of you but one thing." He clasped his hands together so hard that he felt them going numb, but he didn't care. Tears were starting to stream down his face, but he didn't care about that either. Nor did he care about the voices of a choir—also recorded—that joined the organ music and got louder and louder, like a chorus of demented angels urging him onward, ever onward. His body trembling, praying harder than he ever had before, he begged for the only thing that would give his life any meaning . . .

"I want you to kill Peter Parker."

The bell thundered to life overhead.

Peter staggered as the bell started to swing. It distracted him for only a moment, as he continued to pull at the costume. It fought back with a life of its own.

Parasite . . . dangerous . . . very dangerous . . . you didn't keep any, did you, Peter? All the words of Curtis Connors flew back at him, and he cursed himself for his stupidity, even as he continued to battle against the costume.

I want my life back! Give me my life back! Peter furiously thought, and the suit redoubled its efforts, seemingly fighting for its own life as well.

The bell clanged above them, deafening, and apparently it seemed to jolt the suit's concentration. He felt it loosening slightly, felt its influence upon him starting to diminish. He was winning the contest of wills. *I've got you now, you bastard,* he thought grimly, not noticing that the black goo was starting to slip through a crack in the flooring.

Eddie Brock, heading out of the church, passed under the bell tower, which was situated above the front doors. The bell was clattering away high above him, and suddenly something fell on his shoulder with a thick splat.

Great. Pigeons are crapping on me. Thanks for answering the prayer, God.

He reached up to brush it off and saw that it wasn't like anything he'd ever seen. At first glance it was akin to tar, but when he reached for it, it seeped into his shirt without a trace. He twisted around, thinking that maybe it had fallen to the floor, but no. Nothing there. Then another drop landed on his other sleeve. This time he never took his eyes off it as, once again, it soaked into his shirt and vanished.

What the hell?

He glanced upward, and there, high above, was the unmistakable form of Spider-Man. He was trying to peel his black costume off, and the damned thing was . . . leaking? No, it was oozing off him as if it was . . . alive . . .

"Sonuvabitch," muttered Eddie Brock.

It was as if Peter were peeling his own skin from his body. This was worse, far worse than that previous time. Both he and the symbiote were struggling for their lives, and no prisoners were being taken.

Between the clanging of the bell and the agony that was ripping through Peter's head, it was all he could do not to pass out. But that wasn't an option; if he did, he knew the symbiote would reassert itself, and next time he might never get it off him. He continued to peel it away, bit by bit, feeling as if he was starting to get some momentum, and so kept at it with growing determination. At one point, when his will started to flag, he mentally pictured Mary Jane being sent tumbling over a table by his hand—by its hand—and he increased his efforts.

Eddie Brock watched in fascination as a drop landed on his hand and then seeped into his skin. He staggered, his mind whirling with thoughts that were simultaneously his own, yet seemed to be coming from somewhere else, as if his own thoughts were magnified and heightened. It was like mainlining a particularly potent narcotic.

He wanted more, much more.

A drop descended from on high, straight toward his face. He opened his mouth and caught it on his tongue, like a snowflake, and swallowed it. It burned pleasantly, like a fine wine.

The shadows around him seemed larger, darker. He kind of liked it.

Spider-Man was screaming overhead. What a wuss. What a little pansy. He clearly wasn't man enough to take what this . . . this whatever it was . . . had to give.

Eddie raised his arms over his head and started screaming in sync with Spider-Man, making fun of him. But where Spider-Man's stemmed from fear and pain, Eddie's was a primal scream of fury against all the raw deals that the world had heaped upon his shoulders. He owed the world for all of that, and this was where he started dealing out the payback.

And Brock's scream was changing as it continued. It was getting deeper with every passing moment, as more of the black goo poured down upon him, until his voice no longer sounded human. Instead it could have been a beast growling: a lion bellowing a challenge, or even a dinosaur from a primeval era unleashing a deafening roar designed to freeze its prey in its tracks.

Peter collapsed, sagging to the floor, his head whirling, the world spinning. It was gone. The creature was gone. He didn't know where it had vanished to and, right now, couldn't bring himself to care. He was more exhausted than he could ever remember, and he knew that if he allowed himself to rest for even a few moments, he would pass out. He didn't dare take the chance, fearing that when he came to, he'd be right back where he started.

He pulled the Italian suit on, every move an exercise in agony. He didn't bother to button the shirt, and he held the shoes rather than wear them. The bell had mercifully stopped ringing, but he could still hear it clanging away between his ears, and he hoped that he hadn't done permanent damage to his hearing.

Climbing to the top of the bell tower, he paused there a moment, waiting for the dizziness to subside, then he fired a webline and swung away from the church. His spider-sense told him that no one was watching him, but he wouldn't have cared if the Mormon Tabernacle Choir was looking on. He had to put as much distance between himself and the church as possible.

He would have to go back. He couldn't leave that . . . that thing just slithering around. But he was going to be prepared. He would return with some sort of containment equipment and be wearing armor if he had to—anything to make sure the creature didn't take him over again.

Through the pelting rain, Peter made his way to his apartment and staggered in through the front door. With bleak amusement, he noted that the hinge had been repaired. He wondered if the shower had also been fixed. No better time to find out. His clothes were soaked from the inclement weather. He pulled them off, dumped them on the floor, and headed for the bathroom. Once there, he turned on the shower and discovered that, yes, the showerhead was now functioning properly.

At least the symbiote did me some good. Then he pictured Mary Jane's stricken face once more and decided that no amount of household repairs was worth the grief that he had brought on.

He allowed the water to wash away his sins.

Thank God it was over.

Eddie Brock headed toward Peter's apartment and spotted his name on the mailbox. Apartment 501.

It was only a confirmation of what he already knew.

The black costume had been a part of Peter. Now it was part of Eddie Brock. What the suit knew, Eddie knew, and the suit knew quite a lot about its previous host.

Brock had initially been stunned to discover that Peter Parker was Spider-Man. The sheer audacity of that creep! Here Eddie had had to bust his ass to take pictures, and obviously all Parker had been doing was setting up a camera, taking pictures of himself in action, and laughing to himself as he collected paycheck after paycheck for self-portraits. To Eddie Brock, it was the final confirmation of the fundamental unfairness of the universe.

But after the shock had worn off, Eddie was pleased about this development. He had begged God to make sure that Peter Parker died, and God had answered his prayer in as efficient and direct a manner as Eddie could possibly have hoped.

He'd granted Eddie power, so much so that killing Peter Parker wouldn't have been any fun if Parker had been a normal human. But because Peter Parker was what he was, Eddie could take genuine pleasure in smashing both Parker and Spider-Man in one shot.

If nothing else, it was a monumental time-saver.

Parker had left the front door of his apartment ajar. Eddie pushed it open gently and entered. He heard the shower running and ignored it. Instead he started going through the drawers. He found assorted clothes in most and a grand total of seven dollars in one. He went to the closet and found a couple of Spider-Man costumes hanging in it. They looked so sad, so useless, that pathetic red and blue.

A picture of a good-looking redhead was on the wall. Brock leaned forward and studied it with curiosity. Quite the looker, she was. He searched the pieces of Peter Parker's thoughts that the symbiote had peeled away when it had departed its previous host and locked into the redhead's identity. *Mary Jane Watson.* He immediately knew all that Peter knew about her.

He thought about when Spider-Man had been kissing Gwen. Knowing now that it had been Peter Parker, he wondered just how many beautiful women Parker felt the need to collect.

Eddie Brock could start collections as well.

He heard the shower go off and silently eased his way out of the apartment. Even if Peter hadn't finished his shower, Brock would have been ready to leave. He had seen enough.

He wasn't quite ready to attack Parker. Not yet. The symbiote wasn't ready. He could sense it within him, still bonding with Eddie on a molecular level. It would take a little while longer, and when it was done . . . when Eddie Brock was ready . . .

All debts would be paid in full.

With interest.

XXII

THE GATHERING WEB

THE SUN EVENTUALLY PUNCHED through the cloud cover, but the day remained cold and dank. Nevertheless, Emma Marko had taken her daughter down to the local playground as she had promised.

Children were playing on the jungle gym and swing set and sandbox, but today Penny wasn't especially energetic. Sure, she'd been excited enough about going over to the playground, but once there, she'd started feeling lethargic. Naturally, Emma didn't force her to run around like a nut. Instead she sat next to her on a bench, reading to Penny from *The Arabian Nights.* Penny was bundled up against the cold, a baseball cap perched jauntily atop her head. Penny leaned against her mother, relaxing, and then Emma felt her stiffen. Then Penny was pointing and saying, "Look! There's Daddy!"

Emma looked where Penny was indicating, praying the child was wrong. No such luck. Sure enough, there was Flint Marko, seated on a bench across the playground. He was watching them like some sort of stalker. He gave a tentative wave at being spotted, and even smiled, but Emma did not return it. Instead, scowling, she drew her daughter tightly to her and said, "I know your father made promises to you, but he's always made promises he couldn't keep. So don't get your hopes up and don't count on him for anything. He'll only break your heart."

"But he came back!" she said plaintively.

Penny looked back at her father, then reacted with surprise and confusion. Emma was likewise surprised to see that Flint was no longer there. Where did he go?

"Mama, my snow globe!"

What? The snow globe was back home, in Penny's bedroom. Why would she be asking for it now? Then she understood what Penny was talking about.

A beautiful, ornate sand castle, similar to the one in Penny's globe, had arisen in the middle of the sandbox. This one, though, was ten feet tall. It hadn't been there seconds ago. Its existence was impossible, and that merely added to the aura of magic that surrounded it.

Penny slid off the bench and approached it before Emma could stop her. The child walked toward it, studying it, then cautiously touched it. She made a small fingerprint in the sand, then lay her palm flat against the surface to make a handprint.

Emma went to Penny and took her firmly by the hand, brushing the stray particles off her palm. Penny offered a token protest, but Emma ignored her, pulling her away from the sand castle . . . never even noticing the larger handprint that had magically appeared next to Penny's.

• • •

As Penny and Emma retreated into the distance, Flint Marko reformed himself from the sand castle and watched them go.

"Ahhh, the family."

Marko spun and faced a figure leaning against a tree, obscured by the shadows. The voice was soft and menacing. "The bulwark. I'll bet money can solve your problems."

"How did you find me?" demanded Marko.

"I sensed you," replied the newcomer. He reached out and plucked invisible strings in the air. "I saw a particular vibration along a particular line that only I could see and followed it right to you."

Marko had no idea what this guy was talking about, but at least he wasn't making any aggressive move. That was probably a good thing. Forming the castle had taken a lot out of him. He was still recovering from having been a creature of mud; for a while he'd thought he would never be able to reconstitute himself. He might be ready for a fight in a while, but not at this very minute. "Do I know you?" he asked suspiciously.

"You should."

"Who are you? What do you want?"

"What you want: Spider-Man. Together he's ours."

Ah. This perked up Marko's ears. Spider-Man had massively inconvenienced him; damn near killed him. He certainly wouldn't mind seizing the opportunity to take that punk down. Whatever sympathy he'd felt for Spider-Man over his personal loss was long gone. Considering the grief that Spider-Man had caused him, returning some aggravation would be a pleasure.

"What's the little girl's name?" asked the stranger.

Marko's eyes narrowed. "Penny."

"Penny. How sweet."

He tried to gauge whether this stranger presented a threat to his daughter and finally decided that he didn't. At least not now. "What's your plan? I'll only go so far. And if you push me more, I'll stomp you into the ground."

"Oooh, I like that," said the man, and he stepped from the shadows . . . and yet seemed to take the shadows with him. "Now you're talking."

Later that night, Peter Parker lingered across the street from Mary Jane's apartment.

He had spent much of the day sleeping off complete exhaustion. Considering all that he had been through, it was understandable. Once he had awakened, he had gathered together containment equipment—large, clear containers that he could seal airtight—screwed up his courage, and returned to the church. He had searched it high and low, but that just simply confirmed what his spider-sense had already told him: the symbiote wasn't there.

He chided himself over waiting so long, but what else could he have done? He checked out the surrounding neighborhood, but there remained no sign of it. Irritated and weary, he went home. He considered calling Gwen and trying to explain what the hell had happened the night before, but really . . . how could he possibly? *Sorry, Gwen, I wasn't myself, I was infested by an evil alien symbiote.* Yeah. That was going to fly.

Gwen would just have to be a problem for another day. What about MJ, though? Everything that he had to say . . . how did one put that in a phone message? He knew he had to see her, and so he went over to her apartment building and prepared to march up to her door and . . .

And . . .

Peter remained where he was for half an hour, wrestling with the best way to approach it. He briefly regretted having parted company with the symbiote—it may have posed a number of problems for him, but leaving him indecisive was certainly not one of them.

Finally Mary Jane emerged from her apartment, ready for work. She adjusted her hair and glanced at her watch. Apparently she was running late, for she started scanning the street for a cab.

A taxi farther down the street started to angle toward her, then another cab—which had been parked curbside with its sign atop reading: OFF DUTY—suddenly roared to life and cut directly across the street toward Mary Jane. She jumped, a little startled, as the cab farther down screeched to a halt to avoid slamming into the one that was now facing Mary Jane.

Taken slightly aback, Mary Jane nevertheless climbed into the back of the overly aggressive cab, pulling the door shut behind her. Moments later the taxi sped away into the night.

The cabbie who had unceremoniously been cut off wasn't taking it lying down. He leaned out of the driver's side window and rattled off a string of invective in a foreign language. Then he turned to Peter and demanded, "Did you see that? Did you see that?!"

Peter had, in fact, although he didn't give it much thought.

What he had not seen was the cabbie in the taxi that had picked up Mary Jane. When Mary Jane had settled into the backseat, a leering Eddie Brock had turned in the seat and said, "Where to, ma'am?"

Nor did Peter see the body of the cab's legitimate owner, since it had been dumped in an alleyway some blocks away.

Nor, worst of all, did his spider-sense tell him that anything was wrong, because the symbiote was now invisible to his spider-sense. If Eddie Brock had come up to Peter on a subway platform and tried to push him in front of an oncoming train, Peter would never have known about it until it was too late. So it was that Peter Parker went home, feeling that he hadn't accomplished anything the entire day, and unaware that his day was only just beginning.

XXIII

CRISIS POINT

HARRY OSBORN SAT IN his apartment in darkness, something he much preferred nowadays. He was facing a wall with assorted television screens on it, each tuned to a different TV station. Typically he used them for various sporting events. Now, though, he was watching a variety of news outlets, and all of them were focusing on the same developing story.

CBS:

"All New York is holding its breath as the hostage situation continues to unfold."

NBC:

A clip of a construction site showed a multidimensional latticework of what could only be described as black webbing, suspended seventy stories above the ground. Several items were snagged in the giant web: construction barrels, a shovel, an industrial Dumpster, and a taxicab. All dotting it like so many flies caught in a spider's web.

ABC:

A SWAT team in riot gear was advancing on the construction site in armored Humvees. The sand beneath them heaved. (Harry loved this part; it was chaotic and destructive. They'd run it twenty times, and each time was better than the last.) The vehicles were sent tumbling. Two Humvees crashed down upon the construction site. Pedestrians in the street scattered as the third vehicle tumbled toward them and crushed an empty taxi.

CNN:

"Every attempt by the police to rescue the hostage has been thwarted by Sandman. Compounding the danger is the appearance of a strange, black-suited figure. Early reports had believed him to be the black-suited Spider-Man, but he has now been identified as something entirely different."

Sure enough, someone in the black spider suit was leering like a jackal as the camera zoomed in on him. He swung down, dispatching members of the SWAT team with disturbing ease. Some tried to get a shot off and didn't even come close. He tossed them aside, juggling them like plates, and showing them to be just as easily breakable.

Harry sighed heavily to the empty room. "So much violence on TV these days."

MSNBC:

They had a helicopter. Good for them. The news camera aboard zoomed in on the taxi that was up in the webbing, and a terrified Mary Jane Watson was in the backseat.

"The hostage has been identified as Mary Jane Watson, an actor recently seen in a brief stint on Broadway. She is currently a singing waitress at a downtown jazz club. We're now going to take you live to the scene, with news action team reporter Jennifer Dugan."

The camera shifted to the site; a miniskirted young woman looked to be in way over her head and knew it. She was game, though, Harry had to credit her that. Running alongside her camera team, she was saying, *"We're only a hundred feet away now, Hal, and . . . wait!"*

The camera view whipped around as the black-suited figure fired black weblines up at the partially completed skyscraper.

Incredibly, the weblines were creating letters.

"It seems to be some kind of message," Jennifer Dugan announced. The camera was only picking up a few letters . . . a *T,* an *O,* some others . . .

"Pull back," said an annoyed Harry to the TV. "Give us a better view."

As if responding to his demand, the cameraman promptly pulled back, and the entire message came into view:

SPIDER-MAN STOP US IF YOU CAN

"If Spider-Man did come, it would be a suicide mission," Dugan declared. *"For what chance would he have against—"*

Harry pushed the mute button. He'd heard enough.

He slumped back in his chair, closed his eyes. He wasn't certain he was capable of feeling anything anymore.

A stiff breeze blew across his apartment from the balcony. He thought he had closed the large glass doors and started to stand up to attend to it. Then he stopped in his tracks.

Peter Parker was standing in the open doorway. He looked . . .

. . . humbled. When he spoke, Harry had to strain to hear him.

"I can't take them both," Peter admitted. "Not by myself."

Harry stood in the shadows for a moment, then stepped forward into the narrow sliver of light cast by the nearby lamp. It was just enough for Peter to see his ruined face. Half of it was now hideous, grotesque, mangled from the bomb that Peter had hurled at him.

Peter was clearly shocked by the sight, taken aback. Here was a stark, irrefutable reminder of the black costume's continuing legacy, and he clearly wanted to look away . . . but could not do so. His shoulders sagged, and he looked stricken with despair, apparently knowing that he had embarked upon a fool's errand but being committed to seeing it through.

"I need your help, Harry."

There were so many things Harry wanted to say at that moment. None of them, though, could surpass the elegant simplicity of "Get out."

Harry turned away and, when he glanced back, saw that Peter had indeed departed. Harry started pacing the room, thinking of Mary Jane trapped, thinking of Peter hurtling toward certain death to save her. Because that was what Peter was going to do; Harry was positive of that. Peter was just that determined, just that "heroic," just that reckless, and just that stupid to go in against overwhelming odds, knowing that he couldn't possibly survive.

You lucky stiff, his father's voice growled in Harry's head. *He's going to die and all you have to do to make that happen is do nothing. And considering you were always good for nothing, this is something that even* you *can't screw up.*

Harry buried his head in his hands, his father's voice overwhelming. He sagged against the wall, choking back a sob . . . then became aware of Bernard standing in the main entranceway of the great room.

"If I may, sir," said Bernard. Harry shrugged. "I've seen things in this house I've never spoken of," the butler continued. "I've watched a darkness come over your father. A madness that cost him his life."

Why was Bernard bringing all this up? "What are you trying to tell me?" Harry said, ghosts screaming in his ears.

Bernard took a deep breath and let it out. "The night your father died, I cleaned his wound. The blade that pierced his body came from his glider, his invention. Only he could have discharged it."

Harry was stunned. Bernard . . . knew? Here he had thought he'd managed to keep his secrets from the faithful servant. Bernard had been out visiting relatives on the night of Peter's attack. Despite the severity of his wounds, Harry had still managed to hide away the more incriminating elements of the Goblin's equipment. When Bernard had returned, Harry had told the appalled retainer that he'd injured himself in a chemical experiment gone terribly wrong, and had refused all pleas to go to the hospital.

But now Bernard was claiming that he'd actually known the truth, going all the way back to his father's "original sins"?

He knew what Norman Osborn had become? Known what he was capable of? Why hadn't he said anything at the time?

The answer was obvious, really. Bernard had been with the family for as long as Harry could remember. The old butler's peculiar code of ethics simply wouldn't have allowed him to tell the world of his master's wrongdoings. Plus, from a practical standpoint, if Bernard did go around and tell people, Norman might well seek him out and kill him. And since Norman had died . . . what point was there in letting people know?

"I know you are defending your father's honor, but there is no question that he died by his own hand," Bernard assured him. "I loved your father as I have loved you, Harry. As your friends love you."

Harry had nothing to say.

So Bernard turned and walked away, leaving Harry in the darkness and to his own miseries.

XXIV

SOMETHING IN THE AIR

IT APPEALED TO MARY Jane's morbid sense of humor that Eddie Brock had left the meter running even as he suspended the cab some seventy-five stories in the air. She currently owed in excess of eighty bucks and couldn't help but think that insult was most definitely being heaped upon injury.

As the cab gently swayed in the wind, she heard what sounded like fingers gently vibrating the strings of a piano. She mulled over her predicament.

"Why do they always come after me?" she wondered aloud. "What, do I have the word BAIT stamped on my forehead? Did somebody stick a CAPTURE ME sign on my back?"

A strand of webbed snapped with a sound like a banjo string coming undone. Her car dropped a few feet, then somersaulted downward. Mary Jane screamed as the taxi tore through several webs and tumbled end over end. Mary Jane was slammed around inside the cab, then it snagged on another level of the massive web and halted seventy stories up.

From far, far below she thought she heard something:

a distant cry of approval. Sick bastards. They were waiting for her to fall. They wanted to see a show. What were things coming to, that—

Suddenly something landed on the hood of the cab. Mary Jane jumped back, startled, assuming that it was her captor.

Instead the masked face of Spider-Man peered in at her.

"Peter!" she gasped with a mixture of both relief and dread. "They're never going to let you out of here alive."

"I . . ." He didn't seem to know what to say. Finally he told her, "I'm sorry I pushed you."

She didn't know whether to laugh or cry and settled for a combination of both. Here she was dangling high above certain death, and Peter was apologizing for what had happened at the Jazz Room. It was really kind of sweet . . . although right now he needed to get his priorities in order.

She spotted her black-clad captor swinging straight toward Spider-Man. Peter wasn't reacting. It was as if he didn't sense the impending danger. Mary Jane let out an alarmed cry and pointed, and Spider-Man turned to see. It wasn't nearly enough time to get out of his attacker's way as a mighty kick knocked Spider-Man headfirst through the windshield. Mary Jane, who had left the plastic partition open between the passenger's and the driver's seat, instantly regretted that as she was showered with glass.

Spider-Man, recovering quickly, vaulted over the rooftop and landed on the trunk, almost sliding off before getting a firm grip. Mary Jane and he looked up as the black-suited creature stood atop the hood, looming over them.

The black goo that constituted its mask receded, revealing the face of the man who'd been driving the cab. His burning eyes stared down at them. Beyond that he had taken her captive, Mary Jane had no clue who he was, but from Spider-Man's reaction she knew that Peter recognized him immediately.

"Hiya, pal, remember me?"

"Oh my God," gasped Spider-Man. "Eddie Brock . . ."

"No. Not Eddie. Not anymore. I'm poison to you now, Spider-Man," he said, flicking his tongue around. "I'm . . . *Venom.* And I just want you to know, I took your advice. You told me if I wanted forgiveness, I should find religion, so I went to church last night and asked for it. I asked for everything that had been taken away from me. Damned if I didn't get it. And more. I was handed power I never dreamed of, Pete. It just . . . poured down on me as if from heaven itself."

"You've got to take off the suit!" Spider-Man told him. "It'll—"

Venom leaped to the rear of the car and kicked Spider-Man across the face, knocking him from the vehicle.

Spider-Man fell, tearing through several strands of web, finally coming to rest about sixty stories up, in a sticky place in the web where the strands were thick enough to obscure the view from the news cameras.

But they had already managed to catch enough.

• • •

When Gwen Stacy had learned that Mary Jane Watson was the one captured in the black webbing at the construction site, nothing that her father had said or done could convince her to stay away from the scene. She knew that she wasn't in any way responsible for Mary Jane's predicament, but after what had happened at the Jazz Room, she felt an odd kinship to her.

She'd even done some research into Mary Jane's past and marveled at the spectacularly bad luck the girl had had. According to police reports, she'd been captured by Dr. Octopus shortly before that madman's all too timely death. And before that, apparently the Green Goblin had dangled her off one of the towers of the Fifty-ninth Street Bridge, then dropped her.

Now, watching the TV monitors while her father organized the rescue efforts, Gwen saw that freakish anti-Spider-Man peel back his face mask through some odd means. She was even more shocked at what it revealed. "Eddie!" she gasped.

Her earlier belief that she had nothing to do with Mary Jane's situation instantly vanished. She ran from the monitor and sought out her father, who was focusing on high above with a pair of binoculars. "That's Eddie up there!" she told him.

"Gwen, step back," Captain Stacy said. "You can't help here."

"I feel responsible."

"You're not responsible for the actions of a madman," her father assured her, but Gwen felt that way nonetheless. Her father, though, was clearly not interested, and she had to admit she couldn't really blame him.

"Excuse me, Captain." Police officer Nauck was hauling a nervous-looking man forward. The man was waving some sort of ID that indicated he was part of a research facility. "This man, he's a doctor. Claims to have some important information."

"What's this about, Dr. . . ." Captain Stacy glanced at the ID. "Dr. Wallace."

"Flint Marko."

Captain Stacy frowned. "What about him?"

"I don't know how to tell you this, but . . ." Dr. Wallace indicated a nearby news monitor that was replaying Sandman's annihilation of the Humvees. "This Sandman creature . . . it's him. Look," he said pleadingly, "I know why he's doing this. It might help you to stop him."

Sixty stories up, Spider-Man struggled in the webbing. As he started to pull free of it, Venom dropped down from overhead and webbed up Peter's wrist, binding it to the giant black web. Before Spider-Man could move, his other wrist was webbed up as well. Pinned, his arms outstretched, Spider-Man was trapped.

Venom came down with a flying knee drop to Spider-Man's ribs, cracking them. Spider-Man yelled in pain, and Venom reached down, yanking Spider-Man's mask clear. Peter gasped for air and hoped that he was still out of range of the TV cameras. The prospect of Aunt May being home, watching this, and seeing Peter's face flashing across the TV screen was unsettling.

Then again, that might turn out to be the least of his problems.

Seventy-three stories above the ground, the industrial steel Dumpster that was hanging in the top portion of the web began to shift position. Strands that held it in place were beginning to break.

Three stories below the Dumpster, Mary Jane watched helplessly as it tilted toward her.

I don't know who Eddie Brock is, or what he wants, but he's really pissing me off, she thought bleakly.

Seeing the imminent threat to Mary Jane, Peter turned toward Venom and said desperately, "What do you want, Eddie?"

"I wanted to see you again, Pete," Venom said with great cheer, as if they were two old buddies hooking up again at a school reunion. "And talk with you and, well, to be honest, I want to kill you."

"We can find a way to settle this."

"You're so right. I was thinking humiliation. Just as you humiliated me. But televised. Live-action coverage." He held his hands up as if envisioning it in a headline or on a marquee. "Spider-Man screws up, and sweet little Mary Jane dies." He lowered his hands and came in close to Peter. Foul breath, like burnt metal, washed over Peter, who wondered if he'd reeked like that when he'd been wearing the thing. "You made me lose my girl. Now I'm going to make you lose yours, with the help of my friend Sandy. I think you've met."

As a terrible groan of metal came from high above, Peter looked up and his heart thudded with alarm.

The Dumpster's steel lid swung open. Cinder blocks, concrete slabs, and heavy metal brackets began to slide out. They rained down onto Mary Jane's taxi, ricocheting off with loud clanging and clanking sounds. Peter could see Mary Jane getting low in the backseat, trying to avoid the deadly impacts. He also saw that they were tearing away the webs that supported the car.

As they rebounded off the cab, they hailed down upon Spider-Man and Venom, tearing through the webs around them. Venom dodged a falling slab of concrete, while a cinder block tore through the web, freeing one of Peter's hands. Peter reached out, grabbed Venom's ankle, and pulled him off-balance. Venom hit the webbing right next to Peter, and the both of them swayed as Peter grappled one-handed with his tormentor while heavy objects fell all around them.

Suddenly a key support of the web was severed by a jagged piece of metal, and the two of them were in free fall. Liberated from the web restraints, Peter struggled at close quarters with Venom as they tumbled end over end.

The ground was coming up incredibly fast, and Peter fired webs at the last instant to break his fall. Out the corner of his eye, he saw Venom doing the same thing, and although the webbing slowed them down, it didn't completely save them from violent landings as they hit the ground hard.

Peter lay there for a moment, unmoving, trying to determine whether he'd broken anything on impact. He moved his limbs and decided that he hadn't, although his chest was still aching from where Venom had been tap-dancing on his ribs. He hauled himself to his feet and discovered that, fortunately, they were blocked from the view of the crowd by a power shovel, a bulldozer, and some other construction equipment.

His Spider-Man mask was lying a couple of feet away. He staggered toward it, picked it up, and pulled it on. As he reeled, the world spinning around him, his spider-sense warned him at the last second as Flint Marko's rock-hard fist came swinging right into his field of vision. But he wasn't fast enough to dodge it. It connected, hard, and Spider-Man stumbled backward, only to meet the fist of Venom, driving him back in the other direction. He fired a web upward to try to get away, but Sandman once again slammed into him. This time the impact sent Spider-Man against one of the steel uprights, knocking the wind out of him.

Penny Marko had initially been unhappy as the news broadcasts had knocked *Jeopardy!* off the air. It was her favorite show, even if her impulse was to pronounce it "GEE-o-party."

But as she'd watched, she found herself fascinated by the images of the person everyone was calling Sandman. They kept showing the same sequences with him over and over, and now she got to her knees and drew close to the screen. She reached up and touched it tentatively as Sandman tossed aside all efforts of the SWAT teams to rescue people. "Mama," she said slowly, "I think that's Daddy."

Emma called back from the kitchen, "What's Daddy?" She emerged to see what Penny was referring to, and Penny pointed wordlessly to the TV. At first Emma laughed and was about to tell Penny that she didn't know what she was talking about. Then she took a closer look, and Penny could see by the change in her mother's expression that Mama likewise thought it was Daddy. She was shaking her head, though, trying to deny it to herself.

"The sand castle," said Penny. Her mother, still appearing shell-shocked, looked wordlessly at the little girl. "I was with him. That's him." She tapped the screen. "He's doing this for me. I can feel it, Mama."

There was a knock at the door so unexpected and intrusive that both Penny and Emma jumped in alarm. Penny headed to the door, ignoring her mother's warnings not to open it for strangers.

A police officer was standing there, and next to him another man.

"Penny?" he said, and when she nodded, he extended a hand and smiled gently. "I'm Dr. Wallace. We need to talk . . . quickly."

Pounded back and forth between Sandman and Venom, Spider-Man's bloodied body slammed to the ground. He lay there, trying to will himself to get to his feet, to grow four extra arms or become ten times as strong. Something, anything that would give him a fighting chance.

High above him he heard the sound of groaning metal and looked skyward through blurred vision. The noise was coming from the Dumpster, shifting in the web and leaning more and more toward Mary Jane's taxi.

Desperately he tried to haul himself to his feet to get there in time, and suddenly the Dumpster tore away and plummeted straight down. Spider-Man, horrified, could only watch as the Dumpster winged the cab, causing it to roll onto its side.

Mary Jane smacked up against the driver's-side door, popping it open. She shrieked as she fell from the car. Grabbing, she snagged the closed door on the driver's side, reached through, and clung to the steering wheel. She dangled there, clutching on for dear life.

"MJ!" screamed Spider-Man.

With effort he willed himself to stand. He swayed in place, tried not to puke inside his mask—

Five hundred tons of sand pulled together, sweeping up tractors and power shovels as it rose to form a gigantic Sandman.

He loomed over Spider-Man, hundreds of feet high, with a roaring sound like that of a tornado brought to life. It—for *he* would simply not have seemed appropriate—came after Spider-Man, smashing the ground with its massive fists and feet as it tried to crush the dodging blue-and-red-clad figure.

Spider-Man had a brief glimmer of hope, because as powerful as Sandman was, Spider-Man had him beat on speed. He was too quick and agile for the lumbering giant to catch. But Sandman apparently came to the same conclusion, for he changed his form again, extending his hands into giant paws that reached down for Spider-Man.

Firing a webline, Spider-Man bounded clear of the terrifying sand hands, but he didn't get far. Venom came leaping forward, intercepting him in midair and landing a powerful kick that knocked Spider-Man into a girder.

Hey, gorgeous, what are you doing here?

Oh, just hanging around.

Mary Jane, clutching the steering wheel like a bat, was busy writing her own jovial dialogue in her head. It was a witty exchange between herself and Peter that would show just how plucky our heroine was and how dashing our hero. It helped take her mind off the fact that her fingers were growing tired.

She tried to haul herself up into the driver's seat. Perhaps she could buckle herself in, last a little longer. But she didn't have the opportunity as her fingers—far more fatigued than she'd thought—gave way, and she plummeted from the car.

Shrieking, tearing through the weaker strands of the gigantic black web, she was finally halted by the bottommost strands of the webbing. She bounced up and down for a few moments, steadying herself, and then looked up to see what new calamity was about to befall her. She was becoming cynical enough to assume that there would certainly be *something.*

Her cynicism paid off. The taxi was ten stories above her and about to tear loose from its precarious perch on the web. When it did, it would crush her, and there was nowhere for her to go.

Dear Lord, please, make it quick. Then she corrected herself. *To hell with that, make it slow, drag it out, give Peter time to get here.*

Spider-Man was running out of time.

He was scampering up one of the girders when a black webline wrapped tightly around his throat, yanking him backward. He dropped two stories, smacking onto a cross-beam. One story below, Venom was pulling on the web-line, strangling him. The world was turning into a red haze around Spider-Man, and in the distance he heard Venom shouting, *"Now! Kill him now!"*

Going on the assumption that Venom wasn't addressing him, Spider-Man figured he was talking to Sand-man. Sure enough, a shadow loomed over the struggling Spider-Man—it was Sandman all right, bigger than King Kong and twice as formidable.

Jennifer Dugan looked out from the TV screen in Harry Osborn's apartment. *"It's hard to believe what's happening . . . I don't know how he could take any more. . . . This . . . this is the end of Spider-Man."*

Harry Osborn wasn't listening.

I'm sorry, MJ . . . I tried . . . no one could have tried more.

Even as he thought that, Spider-Man didn't cease struggling against the webbing that was holding him down, trying to get clear of the massive form of Sandman that was about to annihilate him.

A tiny copper ball sailed out of the clouds and lodged on the back of Sandman's massive head.

Sandman turned, sensing something behind him, and Spider-Man barely had time to see that what had landed on Sandman's head was shaped like a pumpkin before it detonated. Chunks of sandstone exploded from the side of Sandman's head. Stunned by the impact, he crumbled like a massive statue.

Mary Jane didn't know where to look first. She saw the mighty Sandman collapse, she saw Venom on the ground looking up in confusion, and then she twisted around and saw what Venom was already looking at: a man astride what looked like a flying hi-tech snowboard, which was roaring like a jet engine.

She recognized the gadget immediately, the rider a moment later. "Harry!" she cried out in joy.

Though she felt a quick flash of anger over the way Harry had manipulated her to hurt Peter, for whatever reason he was now coming in on the side of the angels. There was still a lot to be explained, a good deal she didn't understand—for one thing, my God, what happened to his face?—but it could wait until they all got out of here alive . . . an optimistic view to have, but at least she suddenly had one.

Harry chortled with self-satisfied glee as he rammed the Sky Stick into Venom, knocking him aside and sending him crashing against a crossbeam like a beanbag. He landed next to Spider-Man, who looked as if he'd just gone twelve rounds with a giant mutant Cuisinart.

Unable to understand what had just happened,

Spider-Man looked up at him tentatively, confused. Instead of bothering to explain, Harry simply extended a hand to his old friend and helped him to his feet.

"I . . . can't believe you're here," Spider-Man said.

Harry nodded. "Apparently just in the nick of time."

Spider-Man rubbed the back of his neck and Harry suspected that, under his mask, Peter was wincing. "Well, five minutes ago would have been good too."

The distant sound of snapping weblines caught their attention. They looked up just in time to see the taxi above Mary Jane tearing loose.

Mary Jane rolled aside, barely avoiding the car as it ripped down through the weakening strands of black web. It continued its death plunge, tumbling end over end several times before crashing to the ground sixty stories below. But in passing, it damaged the web that MJ was clinging to. The entire thing was rapidly shredding.

Clearly she only had seconds left.

Harry revved the Sky Stick. *"Hop on!"* he shouted.

Spider-Man needed no further urging. He leaped aboard, and they raced upward toward Mary Jane.

Too late.

The giant black web gave way. Mary Jane tore loose from the last of its strands into thin air.

No way no way no freaking way, thought Harry desperately as he angled the Sky Stick around, diving after her, and he would have been surprised to learn that Peter was thinking the exact same thing.

"Give it everything!" Spider-Man shouted as the Sky Stick raced to catch up with her.

Harry gunned the engine, zipping after the plummeting Mary Jane. They were heading straight for the ground, Harry now coming to a terrible realization. "We're diving too fast! I won't be able to pull up!"

"Just a little longer—"

"Pete—!"

"Almost . . ."

Harry wanted to be heroic enough that he'd be willing to crash the device into the ground before he'd break off pursuit. With a sinking heart, he knew he wasn't, and he hated himself for that weakness.

"I've got to pull up! Now!"

"Go!" Spider-Man shouted.

He dove from the Sky Stick an instant before Harry pulled up. Spider-Man intercepted Mary Jane in midair and, wrapping his arm around her, fired a web. It snagged an overhead girder and they arced upward, barely missing the ground and soaring mere inches over the head of a boy who was watching in the crowd. "Wicked cool!" crowed the kid.

The crowd went wild as Spider-Man swung along with Mary Jane in his arms. Harry watched it all from a distance—he had just witnessed why exactly Peter Parker was a true hero who, dammit, deserved to get the girl. He resolved right then that his ridiculous crush on Mary Jane was at an end. Peter deserved to have her, and if that was what she wanted—

Harry had made a tactical blunder. Allowing his mind to wander, even for an instant, was a costly mistake.

Venom leaped forward from hiding and latched onto

Harry's Sky Stick. Harry, realizing he'd picked up an unwanted passenger, angled skyward, trying to shake him loose. No luck. Venom bared his vicious teeth and sank them into Harry's ankle. Harry shrieked, yanking his leg away before Venom could get a solid hold.

Venom started to pull himself up, and a stiletto blade clicked out from the back of Harry's bootheel. Harry had only had time to throw together a few pieces of the armor, but what he had chosen had been canny. He jammed the blade down into Venom's shoulder. The creature howled in protest but still didn't let go.

The Sky Stick banked with a whine of its engines. Venom was slammed against a concrete girder high atop the skyscraper. Venom was knocked loose, but the Sky Stick had sustained damage from Venom's assault. The engine was sounding labored, and it was all Harry could do to keep it on course.

Nor was Venom done. Even as he fell, he fired a black webline and reconnected with the craft, swinging below it like a great dark pendulum.

As Harry angled around, he saw Spider-Man landing on an upper portion of the skyscraper, where a small platform had been set up for construction workers. He watched as Spider-Man set Mary Jane down there and breathed a sigh of relief that at least she was safe.

The ground stirred, twisted, grew, and a gigantic Sandman once again rose up before them. The missing portion of his head had reformed.

"Uh-oh," said Harry, which by startling coincidence was exactly what Mary Jane said as Sandman loomed in front of them. Peter Parker said something a bit more colorful, but his mask muffled the words.

On the street below, J. Jonah Jameson fought his way to the front of the crowd, searching the faces of the news photographers. Alerted to the goings-on, he hadn't been able to verify that the *Bugle* had anyone on the scene and decided he couldn't trust anyone but himself to make sure his paper got pictures.

Unfortunately, as the battery of photographers snapped away, capturing incredible action photos, Jameson didn't see a single one of his people. "Parker! Brock!" he called out, momentarily forgetting that he'd fired the latter. "Where's my photographers?!"

He turned and spotted an eight-year-old girl holding a cheap Instamatic camera. "Hey, kid," he barked. "Want a job?"

The girl stared at him incredulously. "No. I'm a kid. Why would I want a job?"

Exasperated, Jonah growled, "How much for that camera?"

Looking at the camera and smelling Jonah's desperation the way that a lion smells weakness, the kid announced, "Forty dollars."

"Forty?!"

The crowd gasped and pointed at some fantastic photo opportunity that Jameson was missing. Muttering, he yanked two twenties from his wallet and forked them over to the kid. "Little crook," he snarled as the girl handed him the camera.

Jameson raised it for a shot, pushed on the shutter release, and couldn't get it to do anything. Then he stared at the back of the camera and popped it open to verify what he'd already figured out: it was empty.

The kid held up a small box. "Film's extra," she said serenely.

Spider-Man grabbed Mary Jane in a tackle hold and leaped with her out of harm's way as a gigantic sand fist pounded into the building. It trembled violently under the impact but remained standing.

Harry saw it all, but was distracted by his own problem. Venom was still climbing quickly up toward him. Tripping a switch, Harry ignited the thrusters on the bottom of the Sky Stick. They roared to life, and the rocket exhausts torched the shrieking Venom. Burning like a Roman candle, the flaming beast tumbled well away from the Sky Stick.

Freed of Venom, Harry shot straight toward Sandman. The towering creature had just taken a swipe at Spider-Man, who swung himself and MJ to safety . . . *safety* being a relative term. Trying desperately to buy Peter some time, Harry buzzed past Sandman's face as a distraction. *I'm worth at least thirty million dollars, and I'm a flying sand mite. What a comedown.*

In trying to get Sandman's attention, Harry was all too successful. Turning away from Spider-Man and Mary Jane, Sandman opened wide his hand and sent it blowing toward Harry at gale force. Harry tried to angle away from the blast but was enveloped in a small tornado of sand. He shielded his eyes with one arm, as the sand flurry worked its way into the innermost recesses of the Sky Stick. Harry cut hard on the engine, dropping down out of the assault, but then the engine started to choke and sputter. He tried to get it under control but to no avail as the vehicle hurtled across the sky, its gyros and servos disabled and its steering mechanism completely shot. Fighting to stay aloft, Harry veered behind a distant building, cut off from the war that now waged without him.

With Mary Jane safely out of the line of fire, Spider-Man was running across a girder when a sandstone arm smacked him hard across the face. It sent him flying downward, and he crashed hard into a half-constructed floor.

Sandman had reduced himself to his normal size, but that didn't make him any less formidable. Having transformed his hand into a sandstone sledgehammer, he raised it above the head of a defenseless Spider-Man and growled, "Got no choice. You're in my way."

"Daddy, stop!"

To Peter's astonishment, Marko froze in place, and he turned his head in the direction from which the plea had come: a slowly rising construction elevator. A little girl was emerging from it, along with her mother.

"Penny?" whispered Marko. He hadn't lowered the sledgehammer, and Spider-Man could have taken that moment to lash out. Instead he made no move at all, waiting to see how this unexpected interruption would play out. "I . . . I have to do this," Marko insisted. "You don't understand."

"I do understand."

"Flint," Emma said, "the doctor came. He told us everything."

Penny sounded as if she was more concerned about her father's and the doctor's feelings than her own welfare as she said, "He tried but he can't help me."

A crestfallen Flint Marko lowered his sledgehammer arm, all the fight gone out of him. The little girl, seeming much older than her years, continued to speak to her father in slow, measured tones as she approached. "But it's okay, Daddy. It means you don't have to keep doing this. You don't have to hurt people anymore. You can come home."

Marko shook his head. "I can't come home. I . . ." He shifted his gaze to his wife. "I killed a man, Emma. I didn't mean to, but I did."

He turned to Spider-Man. Penny held on to her mother, unsure of how to react to what her father was saying. Peter could relate to that; he wasn't sure how to react either.

"I needed money for the medicine," Marko said to him. "I told your uncle . . . all I wanted was the car. I was scared. He said, 'Why don't you put the gun away and go home?' I turned to see my buddy running over with the cash. I was scared, and your uncle stood up, and I don't know, my gun went off . . ."

Spider-Man listened carefully, dumbfounded, scarcely believing it.

"There was a flash, a puff of smoke," Marko continued, "and I was standing there with this stupid expression on my face and the old guy on the ground. My buddy, good ol' Caradine, he jumped in the car and peeled outta there. Left me behind to take the fall. I got on the ground next to . . . to Ben." Marko said the name uncomfortably, as if claiming a familiarity that he wasn't entitled to. "He looked puzzled, like he couldn't understand what had gone wrong. I tried to pull him to his feet, shouted at him to get up. Then I heard the siren. I let his body slide outta my hands and to the pavement, and then I lit outta there just as the crowd was gathering. I . . ." He shook his head, reliving the pain, the suffering made real. "I spent a lotta nights wishin' I could take it back."

Peter was silent. All of this was so different from what he had imagined. It had never occurred to him that a hardened criminal such as Flint Marko could possibly show remorse . . . could possibly care about others. Peter thought of the regret he had endured over his belief that his inaction had resulted in Ben's death, and how he had wished in vain that he too could take back his actions.

And, yes, he had recently done some things because of the symbiote. But they hadn't come out of nowhere. They'd been fueled by his inner demons. The symbiote had simply unleashed the potential for evil that lurked within him . . . that probably lurked in everyone.

And he thought of what Aunt May had said . . . about what Uncle Ben would have really wanted for them.

Marko knelt down next to his daughter. "I still want to be with you more than anything. But I did wrong. Gotta pay for what I did."

With a choked sob, Penny pulled against her mother's hand, and this time—a bit to Spider-Man's surprise—Emma released her. "I don't want you to leave," she wailed, and threw her arms around her father. She looked up at Spider-Man and said, "Won't you forgive him? I know he did a terrible thing to you, but he's a good man."

Peter knew perfectly well that what he said, that his beliefs, weren't going to make a bit of difference in terms of what happened to Flint Marko. But there was more involved than this. There was a little girl who desperately needed to believe that her father stood for something valuable and good. And he wasn't entirely sure that she was wrong to believe that.

"We've all done terrible things," Spider-Man told her. "I . . ." He paused a long moment, then finally managed to get the words out. "I forgive him."

A sudden sound came from above them. They all looked up to see Venom, who had reappeared atop the partially completed building. An earsplitting roar resounded, and Spider-Man shouted to Marko, "Get your family out of here!"

Marko hesitated, looking from Spider-Man to the frightened faces of Penny and Emma. He hugged them fervently as Spider-Man again cried out, *"Go! Save them!"*

Aware of the danger, Marko quickly clambered onto the construction elevator with his family, shielding them with his body should Venom try to attack them.

Venom wasn't the least bit interested in assaulting Flint Marko's family. Instead his full focus was on Spider-Man, and he lunged with a howl of rage.

Spider-Man leaped toward him, prepared to end this one way or the other.

Harry Osborn had impressed the hell out of himself.

He had always given little credibility to his own technological or scientific abilities, but when push came to shove, he was able to get the job done. In this instance, he had landed the Sky Stick, completed the makeshift repairs, and gotten it off the ground again, all in a few minutes. Hurtling toward the construction site, he now saw Venom and Spider-Man slugging it out and gunned the engine so he could get there to help.

Grabbing a steel pike, Venom swung it around and bashed Spider-Man across the chest with it. His ribs already damaged from earlier, Spider-Man felt a new jolt of pain rip across his torso as he was thrown back against a girder. Venom flipped the pike around, revealing its sharp, jagged edge.

Clinging to the girder as much for support as anything else, Spider-Man grated, "Don't give in to the anger, Eddie. It just feeds the suit. It wants you to hate. Give it up!"

Venom hesitated, and just for a moment Spider-Man thought he was getting through. But then Venom's voice grew firm, even challenging. "How can I give this up? Finally, I'm somebody. Look at them down there"—he pointed at the crowds below—"waiting for my next move." He advanced on Spider-Man and said cheerfully, "I like being bad. It makes me happy."

His slow advance turned into a rapid charge as he

thrust the pike forward for the death blow. Spider-Man braced himself, prepared to dodge but not sure if he would make it.

From out of nowhere, Harry flew in, placing himself directly between the pike and Spider-Man.

"Harry!" shouted Peter, and his heart shattered as the pike impaled Harry Osborn. Harry pitched backward as the pike slid out of him . . . losing control of the Sky Stick and crash-landing atop a construction platform.

Giving Harry no further attention, as if he had just stepped on an ant, Venom lunged again with the steel pike. Spider-Man twisted aside, and the pike struck the girder with a loud, almost deafening clang.

The black goo of the Venom suit vibrated, migrating away from the shrillness, moving in ripples across Brock's body. Venom stumbled back, pained.

Peter saw it all and remembered when he himself had been struggling to divest himself of the black suit. The church bell had been thundering overhead, but Peter had simply chalked up his ridding himself of the symbiote as some sort of battle of wills that he'd won. Now, though, he realized the truth.

"Sound," he murmured.

Venom had meantime recovered. He raised the jagged pike and charged yet again. There was only a split second—Spider-Man kicked up into his hands a length of rebar at his feet and, in one fluid motion, struck it against the girder. This time, with Peter's full muscle behind it, it generated a clang so sonorous that Peter could feel the fillings in his teeth vibrating in response. Because the rebar itself was generating the sound, the symbiote would be vulnerable to it . . . at least in theory.

He lowered the rebar to meet the oncoming Venom, and Venom—staggering from the ringing—was unable to control his forward motion. He impaled himself upon the makeshift tuning fork that Spider-Man had fashioned and gasped in surprise. The deadly pike dropped from Venom's hands.

Peter had taken care not to make the wound mortal. Eddie Brock would be in a world of hurt for a long time, but it wasn't intended to be fatal by any means. With any luck, though, it would be fatal for the symbiote because of the tonality.

Peter's eyes widened in shock. Whatever the symbiote had done to him, it didn't compare with what it had done to Brock.

It slithered off him, in response to the sound assault . . . *but it left nothing behind.*

All that remained of Eddie Brock was a smoking skeleton, and Spider-Man couldn't help but wonder in horror if Brock had even been present at all. It might well have been the alien creature all along, talking and acting the way it believed Eddie Brock was supposed to.

The gelatinous black goo reared up, forming a hideous face with gleaming fangs and serpentlike tongue.

It had absorbed the materials of Eddie's form and fashioned it into its own rudimentary body. An arm or tentacle or some sort of appendage emerged from its amorphous structure as it snarled, "Never wound what you can't kill."

It snared Spider-Man by the leg and started to draw him forward. It opened its mouth impossibly wide, ready to swallow Spider-Man whole.

At that moment, a desperate Peter spotted a sling suspended from a crane. The sling was holding what appeared to be hundreds of steel rods. He fired a webline, snagged it, and yanked with all his might.

The sling tilted wildly, dumping out steel rods, which, in turn, struck against the girders as they fell.

A virtual hailstorm of eighty ringing rods pierced the creature in rapid succession, the sonic vibrations ripping it apart, bit by bit.

The symbiote sizzled, evaporated, and Peter was sure he heard the creature screaming in protest as the last of the black goo burned off into an inky smoke.

Immediately he gave the creature no further thought, for his attention was entirely on Harry. He fired a webline and swung over toward the platform where Harry had crash-landed. Mary Jane, whom he had brought to safety a short distance away, had already run to Harry, and now she was kneeling by his side. MJ was shaking her head in disbelief, saying, "Oh, no . . . no, no, no," over and over.

Harry grimaced, weak, clutching his chest where an ugly red splotch was spreading quickly. "He got me pretty good."

"I'll get help."

"No." Harry clutched Mary Jane's hand before she could move. "Stay with me."

She cradled his head in her lap. He smiled sadly up at her and said, "Sorry. About everything."

"But in the end you came. For Pete and me."

"I was kind of brave back there, wasn't I."

She stroked his hair. "I'm so proud of you. I could never be that brave. Like Peter or you."

"No." Harry shook his head, although the movement clearly pained him. "It's there inside you. And Peter's only strong because you're there." He coughed weakly, then said, "Hold my hand."

Mary Jane took his hand and kissed it gently. Harry's eyes fluttered, but he fought to keep them open as Peter showed up and knelt next to him, pulling his mask off so Harry could see his face. "Don't leave us, pal," Peter urged. "We need you. MJ needs you."

"It's you she loves," Harry said. "It's only, ever, been you."

He fought for breath as Peter touched the side of his face that had been terribly mangled. "I . . . should never have hurt you," Peter said. "Said those things."

"I forgive you, Pete."

Peter looked at him in amazement. "How could you forgive me?"

To Harry, the answer was so simple that he was surprised Peter even needed to ask. "You're . . . my friend."

Peter was smiling through his tears as Harry took his hand and grasped it firmly one last time. Harry returned the smile, and with that on his lips, with the rays of a rising sun stretching over the horizon, Harry Osborn passed away.

Peter Parker is now more open to the idea of one's life flashing before one's eyes when death is imminent. But his own death is not imminent, and it is not the entirety of his existence that he is experiencing now. It is simply the most recent days.

He sees himself, Mary Jane, Aunt May, and the Stacy family surrounding Harry's gravesite. His casket is in the ground. Peter and Mary Jane drop in some flowers.

Gwen is standing there, now an austere, more thoughtful, no-nonsense young woman. She stands next to her father, across the lawn from Peter and MJ and Aunt May. Gwen and Peter eye each other. She moves toward him. Peter moves away from Mary Jane, toward Gwen. Mary Jane and Gwen exchange a look and smile. Peter and Gwen, facing one another, speak not a word between them. There is forgiveness and understanding between them. They embrace. Then Gwen looks again toward Mary Jane. She moves to MJ and hugs her as well. As all parties at the cemetery affirm their affection and support to each other, Peter muses to himself.

The air is clear today. The lessons have been learned, but not easily . . . and they will be taught again . . . they are those things we know but often get forgotten along the way. That all we have that truly matters in this world is the love of our friends and our family, and that they are worthy of the highest trait that we can aspire to: our forgiveness. That is the gift my friend Harry gave me.

Peter's world spins forward once more, and he hears a jazz band's playing of a torch song. It grows louder, and Mary Jane is singing, standing in front of the band, bathed in a soft spotlight, wearing a rather simple but divine gown.

A sparse number of patrons are at a few tables, a couple at the bar. Everyone is captured by the song and the soft mood of the room. In the front window of the Jazz Room is a poster showing Mary Jane's attractive, enchanting photograph. Above it, on a small marquee, are the words: FEATURING MARY JANE WATSON, *and beneath it is a clipping from a newspaper review giving her performance three stars, describing her as a "new enchanting songbird who has flown into town."*

Peter sees himself gazing at the picture, reading the review, then moving to the doorway. He enters. Mary Jane keeps singing . . .

As she sings, she smiles, surprised and pleased, upon seeing Peter standing in the doorway.

She stops singing, and the band continues behind her. Peter steps toward the dance floor and mouths the word Dance?

She waits and then moves away from the microphone and onto the dance floor. They meet and slowly come together to dance as the band moves into its rendition of "Falling in Love."

The lounge's manager and bouncer eye Peter warily. MJ had told them, pleaded with them, that Peter's mayhem had been the result of clashing prescription drugs, an aberration that would never recur. Still, they never take their eyes off him. Well, let them stare. The last thing on Peter's mind is causing trouble.

And Peter suddenly understands why his life or at least recent events are flashing before his eyes. It isn't because he is on the edge of death. It is because he is on the edge of finally living.

After a few moments he brings his cheek close to hers and whispers, We have a lot to talk about.

Let's not talk about the relationship. Just shut up and dance.

And so they do. And in his mind's eye, Peter sees Spider-Man swinging across the city, through its cavernous streets, and Mary Jane is in his arms, laughing in delight.

And all is as it should be.

About the Author

PETER DAVID is the *New York Times* best-selling author of numerous *Star Trek* novels, including *Imzadi, A Rock and a Hard Place,* and the incredibly popular *New Frontier* series. He is also the author of the best-selling movie novelizations for *Spider-Man, Spider-Man 2, The Hulk,* and *Fantastic Four* and has written dozens of other books, including his acclaimed original novel *Sir Apropos of Nothing,* and its sequels, *The Woad to Wuin* and *Tong Lashing.*

David is also well-known for his comic-book work, particularly his award-winning run on *The Incredible Hulk,* and has written for just about every famous comic-book super hero.

He lives in New York with his wife and daughters.